SOUL MISTAKES

Also by E.A. Kafkalas
Franke & Petra
The Second Heart

SOUL MISTAKES

by EA Kafkalas

SOUL MISTAKES © 2014 by E.A. Kafkalas. All rights reserved. No part of this book may be used or reproduced in any manner whatsoever without written permission escape the case of brief quotation embodied in critical articles or reviews. For more information

Eakafkalas.com

ISBN: 978-1-631-92217-6

Cover design by EA Kafkalas

For my muse

one

Cremation. The idea filled her mind as the antiseptic odors of Belmont's Funeral Home assaulted her nostrils. Alex had pondered cremation since her mother's death seven years ago. Mindy had told her it was because incinerating her mother's body was the only way to wipe her out completely. Although the statement rang true, Alex knew there was more to it. The whole idea of embalming a body and displaying it for view was totally fucked up. The thought of people saying, "Gee, doesn't she look lovely" or "She's never looked better" made her skin crawl. How lovely could you look when you were dead? Whatever happened after death—and Alex certainly hadn't worked that equation out yet—did it matter what you looked like in the hereafter? Why did they bury you in your Sunday best—were you going to spend eternity at a fancy ball? If your soul was recycled—or if you were about to become worm food—what difference did it make how you were dressed? These questions haunted her every time she set foot in a funeral home.

Even as a child she had wondered why the most beautiful old homes became funeral homes. Were they too large to house love? After a certain amount of square footage did a real estate agent just say, "Oh, too large for a family, must be a place for dead people?" The Belmont's Home was breathtaking; from the moment you stepped through the beveled glass doorway you were met by a craftsmanship which no longer existed.

Easels with signs were propped in front of each doorway.

She stopped to appreciate the crown molding running around the top of each room, then the windows at either end of the lobby with intricate beveled glass designs in the top half of each window. Her breath caught when the simple calligraphy on the sign displayed the two most horrifying words she ever read—Martineli funeral.

When Simon told her Willie had called and Mrs. Martineli was dead, she had been chopping vegetables in the kitchen and almost cut her thumb off. As the warm liquid gushed out covering the onions in crimson goo, she watched helplessly. Her lip quivered, her eyes clouded—then Simon's hand was on her arm steadying her before she passed out. He tended to her wound, all the while talking, but she couldn't hear a word he was saying. All she could think was Mindy must be devastated. To Simon, all she could say was, "I have to go."

Stopping outside the room, she took in the painted cream walls boasting three large windows. The sunlight poured through the beveled glass windows slicing up the space in to tiny streaks of light and shadow. Folding chairs had been placed out in neat little lines, seven across and five rows deep. An elderly gentleman sat on the aisle seat in the back row patting his eyes with a handkerchief. His leathery complexion made her think he must have been a tradesman of some kind who spent numerous hours baking in the hot sun. Surprisingly he had a full head of hair the color of snow. She tried to remember who he was.

The front of the room appeared to be a sea of flowers. In the center of the sea floated a pewter coffin—lid open. She lingered in the back, tempted to sit quietly with the old man. Not having seen Mrs. Martineli for five years, she was in no hurry to see her lying in a coffin.

The room was abuzz. Simon's brother's funeral had been similar. Peter died suddenly when a drunk driver jumped the curb and hit him as he was walking home from school. He was only fifteen and the family had been devastated. The coffin had been open and he lay surrounded by various sports equipment, a gesture she found odd. Did they think he was going to play on God's baseball team? She had no time to ponder any of it with Simon sobbing over his baby brother's death. Her inability to find the right words to comfort Simon made her feel inept. His body shook and he held her hand so tightly the blood stopped flowing to her fingers. Right now she wished her hand was numb in his.

Her mother's funeral, truth be told, was a welcome event. Alex had been an accident, a fact her mother missed no opportunity to remind her of. She never knew her father because her mother had no idea who he was. All she knew was it was some *John* and her birth had put her mother out of work for three months. Evidently no one wanted to screw a pregnant whore. Before she understood what her mother did for a living, she used to dream of her father coming to take her away to live in a wonderful home. Only when she realized the true nature of her mother's work did she know her father would always remain a mystery. How could he be looking for her when he didn't even know she existed?

Moving further in to the room, she recognized the faces of people she had known as a teenager. There was the heavy-set woman in the corner, practically poured in to a black dress, her breasts pushing against the bodice in an attempt to break free. On second glance Alex identified her as Mrs. Goldberg, the town baker. The standing joke among the townspeople was she ate more than she sold. Alex had a soft spot in her heart for Mrs. Goldberg because Mrs. G. would always sneak a donut or a pastry to her whenever she knew her mother had kicked her out of the house.

Standing next to her was a tall skinny young man whose suit hung off his body, suggesting he had lost a considerable amount of weight recently or he was wearing someone else's clothes. His pale blond hair seemed to melt in to his sallow complexion making him look ghostlike. Alex wondered if he had been or still was ill. Either way he was tall enough and alive enough to delight in Mrs. Goldberg's breasts as he was at the perfect angle to see straight down her dress.

Her heart stopped—thinking she had indeed seen Mrs. Martineli—then she remembered the woman standing at the beginning of the receiving line was Mrs. Martineli's sister.

Louisa caught her eye and smiled warmly. Then Louisa tipped her neck in the direction of her niece.

Mindy stood at the end of the receiving line. Five years had passed since they'd last spoken. Five years since Mindy had violently ended what Alex thought would be the longest relationship she would ever have with any human being.

Mindy wore a black chemise dress with a scoop neck. The dress tapered down to a belted waist and flared back out again. There was no evidence she had borne two children, as she still had an hourglass figure. Despite all that had happened, Mindy still took her breath away.

Mindy's dress blended in to the slate-black suit of the tall, sturdy man against whom she leaned for support. Alex thought that under more pleasant circumstances his straw blond hair, Nordic face with the chiseled, dimpled chin would make him look like he'd stepped out of the pages of *Gentleman's Quarterly*.

Regaining the use of her feet Alex moved slowly toward them. She knew Mindy had married and it was her husband Mindy leaned against. What she was unprepared for was the sudden hostility she felt toward him. Mindy had been everything to Alex.

Mindy's skin looked as inviting as the day Alex first touched it. Mindy had let her hair grow but pulled it back in to a conservative bun, hiding the finest black curls.

Moving in front of Mindy, she stared into the tiny oceans of blue she had once spent hours adrift in. Now the seas were murky. She watched Mindy's eyes brighten at the sight of her.

The two women stood staring at each other. After a five-year silence, words did not come easily for either of them.

She wanted water to ease her dry mouth into speaking. Instead she reached out a hand and managed to choke out, "Mindy, I'm sorry."

Mindy ignored the hand being offered and instead drew her close, closing the distance between them, and through her grief she whispered, "You came."

"I had to," Alex said, letting the familiar warmth take her to a time and place she thought no longer existed.

"Thank you." Mindy brushed her lips against Alex cheek.

And then, for the first time in their entire relationship, Alex pulled away first, setting Mindy back against her husband. Reminding her of where they each were in their lives now. And she knew she had to get out of the room as quickly as possible. Mindy introduced Alex to her husband. He enfolded Alex's hand in a warm handshake and expressed delight at finally meeting her. Numbly, she thanked him and turned to make her escape.

She cursed herself for having told Simon not to come, wanting nothing more than to feel his strong arms around her. Having no desire to see Mrs. Martineli painted up and laid out like one of Madame Tussaud's wax figures, she moved though the beveled glass door into the warm sunlight *Wolfe was right. 'You can't go home again,'* Alex thought as she sat on the marble steps of the funeral home and remembered how it all began.

* * *

Alex parked her bike against the battered brick wall of the tenement house, jumped up to reach the bottom rung of the fire escape, hoisted herself up, and begin began her ascent to the third floor window leading to her apartment. Beer permeated the air of the dark room serving as part living room, part kitchen. Until she had visited other homes, she thought empty beer cans strewn about the house was merely a decorating choice. Now she knew her mother was just a slob. She stopped temporarily at the refrigerator encrusted with dirt and food stains. She winced as she touched the door, then pulled it open and took out a can of soda. All of her attempts to keep the place clean did nothing to diminish her mother's ill temper or elicit any words of praise, so she ceased doing it. And her time in the apartment was limited now she had discovered schoolwork, basketball, and Mindy.

She made her way through the debris to her room—the only bastion of clean in the apartment. Voices drifted from her mother's bedroom. Alex stopped suddenly , set the soda can down, and retreated as quickly as possible. A lone beer can tripped her, sending her flat onto her face in to several other beer cans. The crash brought her mother into the room. Looking up she saw her mother, naked from the waist up, followed by her trick, still with his trousers on. His chest had little gray hairs sprouting from it and he practically had a set of breasts of his own. He was, she decided, the ugliest man she had ever seen. Alex scrambled to get to her feet as her mother howled at her, "What the fuck are you doing home from school?"

Knowing the drill, she tried to defuse the time bomb of her mother's temper. In a very even tone, she explained she had come to pick up a notebook she needed for class. Apologizing profusely, she tried to back slowly toward the window through which she'd entered.

But her mother's arm shot out and caught her wrist. "Not so fast. How many times do I have to tell you not to bother me when I have a client?"

Alex apologized again trying to break free from her mother's grip.

But her mother was determined to teach her a lesson. Her mother seized the man's belt, pulled it out of his trousers with one fluid gesture. She cracked it against the floor. The man stepped out of her way but made no attempt to stop her.

Alex protested. She was too old to be bent over someone's knee and was certainly not going to be entertainment for this sad, pathetic man. But Alex was unprepared for what came next. She put her hand out to brace herself as her mother hurled her toward the brick wall. Her hands tingled, but she was closer to the window and escape was in sight. And then she felt it, the first lash of the belt as it whizzed across her back. Her heart stopped. Nothing like this had ever happened before. The second lash tore through her shirt and her skin. She screamed. She felt blood on her back and perspiration on her face and she crammed the collar of her rugby shirt into her mouth to keep from screaming. Alex had learned a long time ago not to react. The more of a reaction she gave, the longer the beating would take. Each lash was more violent than the one before. She felt like her head would explode from the pounding. Everything went blurry and pain radiated up her body as her knees hit the floor. Falling onto her back Alex saw her mother drop the belt. The client had opened his pants and was jerking off. Nausea seized Alex and she choked it back down, as it was too painful to move. She heard the door slam. Dirt from the floor irritated the open wounds. Helpless, unable to move, and then she remembered nothing until ...

A voice traveled through the fog repeating her name. Warm flesh touched her cheek. Reluctantly Alex opened her eyes and found herself adrift in Mindy's tranquil eyes.

"Alex can you hear me? What happened?"

"Nothing. How'd you find me?"

Mindy explained when Alex didn't show up for practice she came looking for her.

Mindy touched Alex's shoulder and gasped. "There's blood on your arm."

Alex continued to assure her everything was all right. But Mindy persisted wanting to know exactly what went on. Alex tried desperately to think of an explanation.

When Mindy finally asked if it was a break-in, Alex nodded her head yes and took a deep breath. But when Mindy suggested they call the police, Alex grabbed her sleeves and screamed, "No!"

"But you're hurt."

"I'll be fine. Just help me up." Alex held out her hand and Mindy took it. Her legs felt weak, but some of the pain in her back had subsided. When Mindy pulled her to her feet it was all Alex could do not to wrap her arms around her for support.

"Let me see your back."

Grabbing Mindy's arms, Alex held her at arm's length and said, "Later."

"But, Alex—" Mindy was becoming agitated.

"It's not bad."

"So, let me see it." It wasn't a request. Mindy was demanding now.

And as much as Alex didn't want to deny Mindy anything, this was something she could not grant her. Not until they were both someplace safe. "Trust me."

"You're hurt. I want to help."

Help. No one ever wanted to help. Before she met Mindy she didn't know people could help each other.

"The best way to help is to get me out of here."

"Okay. Come back to my house."

"No. I don't want your parents involved."

"Involved in what?"

"Mindy, you gotta swear to me you won't tell anyone about this until I say it's okay."

"You haven't told me anything, Alex."

"I will. I promise. Just not right now."

Mindy looked skeptical. "I don't know about this."

"Do you trust me or not?"

Mindy replied without hesitation, "Of course I trust you."

There really was nowhere else to go, so they settled on Mindy's house. She insisted on putting her jacket on and wouldn't take Mindy's help.

"I think you should ride in front of me." Mindy suggested.

"No. Go slow, I'll keep up."

Alex took extra care to make sure Mindy couldn't see her pain as she rode. She just wished Mindy would quit looking back.

When they arrived at the Martineli's her entire body was drenched in perspiration. Alex wished she knew whether her jacket, which now clung to her back, was being held on by sweat or blood. She had the sinking feeling it was an ugly combination of the two.

They parked the bikes in the garage and Mindy made a final attempt. "Alex," Mindy touched her drenched forehead, "I wish you'd let me call the police. You don't look so good."

The warmth of her touch was almost enough to make Alex concede. "There's no need. I feel safe here."

"At least let me tell my Mom," Mindy said.

"You promised."

"I know," Mindy conceded, closing the garage door and leading her in to the house.

Mrs. Martineli was sitting at the kitchen table doing a crossword puzzle when they walked in. She was a short woman with pudgy cheeks, short brown curly hair, and her daughter's brilliant blue eyes. From the first day Alex met her, less than a year before, she fell in love with Mrs. Martineli.

Italian sausage was cooking on the stove and a pot of tomato sauce was simmering. Her kitchen always smelled wonderful—full of aromas as exotic as the countries they came from. The kitchen was the center of the Martineli's world. Not only did they have the most incredible meals around the huge oak table, they spent hours playing cards and games, having tea or ice cream and cookies.

Every time Alex entered the room, she felt a sense of security wash over her.

"Hi, girls." Mrs. Martineli looked up from her puzzle. "Are you joining us for dinner, Alexandra?"

"Can she, Mom?" The question was a formality. They both already knew the answer. But Alex loved hearing the answer every time.

"Of course, darling. You know Alexandra is always welcome here." Mindy kissed her mother on the cheek and ran upstairs.

Alex wanted to kiss Mindy's mother on the cheek. Instead she thanked her and added, "You're very sweet."

"It's all the sugar I use in my tea."

They both laughed.

"Alexandra, did you know you have a tear in your jacket?"

Alex thought her heart would stop, knowing Mrs. Martineli would want to fix the jacket. It was just like her to notice. She always made you feel like you were the center of her universe at that very moment.

"Why don't you take it off and I'll fix it for you."

This was not happening, Alex told herself. She could not let this happen. "That's okay, Mrs. M. I don't want you to go to any trouble on my account."

"It's no trouble at all. Here let me have it." Mrs. Martineli took hold of the lapel, trapping her.

Alex tried to ease the coat off slowly since her back had stiffened and it hurt to move.

"Let me help you," she offered.

"No, I can do it. I'm just a little stiff from basketball practice." Alex managed to pull the coat off and give it to her. "Thank you for doing this," she said and started backing toward the stairs.

Mrs. Martineli's eyes widened and she looked at her. "Do you know your jacket is—"

But her thought was interrupted by Mindy's exclamation of "Jesus Christ!" as she bounded down the stairs and stopped behind Alex.

Mrs. Martineli didn't bother to scold Mindy for taking the Lord's name in vane. Instead she moved to see what Mindy was looking at and gasped in horror.

Alex turned slowly to see them looking at each other. No one spoke for several minutes and then Mrs. Martineli took her face in her hands. "Who did this to you?"

Mrs. Martineli's hands burned against her cheeks. Alex knew she was waiting for an answer, but she couldn't find a way to tell this woman, who she wished with all her soul was her real mother, all the atrocities her birth mother had committed. Her throat constricted and she blinked to fight back the tears. The last thing she wanted to do was cry right now.

Mrs. Martineli said tenderly, "Okay, let's get you cleaned up and then we'll call your mother."

"No!"

On this matter Alex knew Mrs. Martineli would not budge. "She has a right to know, Alexandra."

Alex assured Mrs. Martineli she would tell her.

"I don't think you'll tell her anything, Alex." Mindy blinked back the tears forming in her eyes. "'Cuz she already knows. Doesn't she?"

Mrs. Martineli looked horrified. Alex knew a beating of any kind was beyond her comprehension. Mrs. Martineli's voice lowered to a whisper as she asked, "Your mother did this to you?"

* * *

"Thought I'd find you out here. Mindy said you were here."

She looked up to see Mindy's brother, Willie, standing above her. He looked older than she remembered, but this day was taking its toll on everyone. There was no denying Willie and Mindy were related. They had the same hair, the same skin tone and eye color. His beard and moustache were trimmed now into a fine line. And he had finally cut his hair short. When Alex was in high school his beard was scraggly and his hair long enough to pull back in to a ponytail. His father was always after him to get it cut.

Willie bent to kiss her on the cheek. "I'm glad you came."

Willie had made the call. He had gotten in touch with her a year prior, breaking the silence and reminding her no matter what had happened he always thought of her as a sister.

"Never could stay in a funeral parlor too long."

He held out his hand. "They're about to say the 'family' good-bye."

"I can't, Willie. That's for family."

He knelt beside her. "Alex, you are family."

Knowing in some respect he was correct could not motivate her to see Mrs. Martineli in the casket. She wanted to remember her cooking in her kitchen, caring for her when she was injured, "I can't see her like that."

He touched his forehead to hers.

"I did love her. You know I did, don't you?"

"Yeah." He kissed her lightly on the forehead. "She knew too, Alex." Then he rose to go in. "I won't take long. Wait for me?"

"I will."

* * *

Mindy caught up with Alex after school as she was unlocking her bike chain. When Mindy asked where she was going Alex shrugged and said, "Just for a ride."

Mindy's eyes begged to go with her, but she wouldn't ask, especially not after Alex ran from her that morning. Mindy had said, "God, Alex, I love you." The comment was innocent enough but it made Alex ride off leaving Mindy trailing behind. Alex couldn't seem to pedal fast enough.

Rising to her feet Alex drew a deep breath, knowing she would have to deal with Mindy soon enough. The very thought of having hurt Mindy tugged at her heart all day. She looked Mindy in the eyes and said, "You're welcome to tag along."

They rode in silence, past Mindy's house, past the park, and out of town. Pedaling like mad, taking the back hills at the edge of town leading up into the forest, Alex had no idea where they were going; she just needed to keep pedaling. She needed to feel her muscles tighten, her heart pound, needed to think about something other than the beautiful girl riding next to her. As if there were anything else to think about. Alex fought the urge to look at Mindy as they raced through the woods. She tried not to think about Mindy's dark hair trailing behind her in the wind, those exquisite ringlets Alex wanted to run her fingers through. She tried not to think about Mindy's breasts, which she'd begun to notice. Or about how Mindy's touch excited her, or about what Mindy actually meant when she said she loved her. Loved her like friend? Like a sister? Like—?

They rode for about forty-five minutes until they ended up at the abandoned quarry and could go no further without plunging over the edge of the rock in to the river some hundred feet below. They came to a screeching stop and Alex finally looked at Mindy. Mindy's face was red from exhaustion and she was taking shallow breaths. How could she have been so stupid? Alex should have realized not everyone loses herself by riding for hours. Of course Mindy was tired; she wasn't used to this level of exercise.

"I wasn't trying to kill you. I promise. Let's take a break." Alex parked her bike on one of the rocks and climbed up to overlook the water.

"Good idea." Mindy followed her.

Alex sat down and stretched her legs. Mindy collapsed beside her. She noticed Mindy trying to catch her breath, determined not to complain. That was just one of the things she loved about Mindy. But Alex was trying not to think about that now. She turned her attention to the scenery. From where they sat atop the quarry you could see the running water below and if you turned around you could look back over the town. She tried to pick out Mindy's house, but they all looked the same, like tiny boxes on a grid.

"You know, Alex, I feel kind of stupid. I never noticed how much you got beat up. I mean, sometimes in gym class I'd notice you were black and blue, but I guess I didn't want to think about it."

"Don't worry about it."

"But I do." Mindy reached for Alex hand. "I can't help but worry about you."

Mindy's touch sent a current of warmth through Alex and she wanted nothing more than to hug Mindy. Before Mindy, touching someone never entered her mind. Probably because the only touch she knew was the back of a hand or a closed fist. Here, with this gentle young woman offering her tenderness, Alex was unable to fathom how to respond.

Alex bent her legs so she could wrap her arms around her knees and stretch her back. They needed to talk about something different. "Are you going to help out with the team at away games, too?"

"Of course." Mindy propped herself up on one elbow. Her dark curls cascaded down her shoulder.

Alex hugged her knees tighter. She noticed Mindy's eyes lost some of their brilliance, as they did when she was troubled.

"Can I ask you a question? Why did you run away from me this morning?"

Alex rubbed the surface of the rocks, looking at how smooth they were in places, as she tried desperately to think of an answer. All the while she could feel Mindy's eyes on her. Finally she had to admit, "I don't know."

Mindy lay back on the rocks and closed her eyes. The last thing Alex wanted to do was hurt Mindy. Words raced through her mind but did not find their way to her lips. All she had ever wanted was for someone to say they loved her. But when Mindy did—she ran. Mindy touched something inside. Sensations Alex never thought existed were awakening, and as much as she didn't want to stop them, she was terrified by them. "Did you mean it?" Alex asked.

Mindy's eyes snapped open and she looked at her, "I thought you knew. Of course I meant it."

Then Alex was forced to admit no one had ever said that to her before.

Mindy looked stunned. "No one?"

"You and your Mom are right about my Mom; she's certainly physical. But she hasn't mastered affection. And the guys I've gone out with usually find out about my Mom and just assume...anyway, I don't believe anything they say."

"They just don't know a good thing when they see one."

Alex couldn't help but smile.

"Now that's what I like to see." Mindy took Alex hand again and moved closer. "Alex, you're very special to me." Mindy's hand was under her chin now, so Alex couldn't look away. The sparkle had returned to Mindy's eyes. "I want you to know you don't have to feel the same way, but I do love you."

Knowing Mindy had meant what she said helped Alex find her voice. "I've never felt this way before." She squeezed Mindy's hand and was egged on when Mindy returned the squeeze. "No one's ever made me feel this good about myself. Even when things seem rotten, just seeing you makes me feel like everything will be okay." Alex watched Mindy's mouth bend in to a s mile. "But that's not all; sometimes I just want to hold you...or have you hold me. I like being near you. Is that strange?" Alex said. She let herself look in to Mindy's eyes and saw tears. "Oh shit, I said something wrong didn't I?"

"No." Mindy touched Alex's lips with her finger. "You didn't say anything wrong. I'm just happy you feel the same way."

"Those are happy tears?" Alex had heard about them, but never witnessed them before.

Mindy nodded and touched her forehead to Alex's. She took Alex's other hand and seemed to be studying it. Without looking up, Mindy quietly said, "Sometimes I want to kiss you. Do you ever," Mindy looked directly into her eyes, "want to kiss me?"

Alex marveled at Mindy's bravery giving voice to the one question she had wanted to ask more than anything. She couldn't let it grow stale in the air. Alex leaned in and lightly brushed her lips against Mindy's. Mindy's lips were softer than her skin, as if that could be possible. "Oh, my God, I just—"

"I know." Mindy's delight made the corners of her mouth bend into a perfect smile and then without another word Mindy kissed Alex full on the lips. Where Alex's kiss had been chaste, Mindy's kiss was the complete opposite. Mindy's tongue begged entry and before Alex could think, her mouth opened and they were kissing like she'd seen lovers kiss in the movies. And Alex liked it. It was all she could do to breathe when Mindy pulled away. Was it possible your whole world could change with just one kiss? Because for the first time in her life Alex felt she had truly found her home, and it was in Mindy's arms. Alex knew then passion and desire is what she had been running from, and she knew with total certainty—she wouldn't run again. But all she could manage to say was, "Can we do it again?"

* * *

She jumped at the sound of Willie's voice.

"Sorry, I didn't mean to startle you."

He sat down beside her. "You know, I woke up this morning and went into Mom's room half expecting to see her there."

She turned to look at him. Really look at him. He looked older than she remembered. His eyes were beginning to sink back and there were tiny wisps of gray hair near his temples. Death seemed to age people, she reminded herself. "I'm sorry."

He laid his head on her shoulder. "She missed you these past few years."

"I missed her, too." She said laying her head against his. She missed the warmth of this family. Willie had always been there for her when she needed to talk. He was as wonderful to her as any of the Martinelis.

"Guess neither of us could stay in one place too long."

"There was a time I could have stayed forever."

"Not me. I had to keep moving." He stood up and walked across to the parking lot.

She trailed him. He was fragile and she recognized it. She knew just how much he needed a friend right now—because she needed one, too.

"I just tried to say good-bye for the last time and she couldn't even hear me. But maybe it's better that way." He cried.

She pulled him to her, whispering softly, "It's okay."

His arms wrapped clumsily around her trying to pull her closer and she tightened her embrace.

"I never told her just how much I loved her."

His body shook against her as he cried. She passed her fingers through his curls trying to calm him. "She knew, Willie. I know she did."

Pushing him back, she looked in to his eyes. Tears continued to fall down his cheeks and she dried them with her fingers. "Hey, why don't we get out of here?"

"In a minute." He pulled a handkerchief from his pocket and dried his eyes.

There were ghosts here. Ghosts she had to confront. Perhaps she should have stayed away, but when Willie called, she had to see for herself.

"So, you want to go? Or do you want to wait for Mindy?"

"Maybe you could drop me by my hotel. I can see Mindy tomorrow."

"What hotel?"

She knew he wasn't asking which one, but she ignored the shocked tone in his voice.

"Alex, why would you even think of staying in a hotel?"

"I just thought it would be easier for everyone."

"You mean it would be easier for you." There was a stern look just like the ones Mrs. Martineli would give when she was scolding you. The resemblance took her by surprise.

"Okay, I thought it would be easier for me."

He crossed his arms in defiance. "Well, you can walk if you want to go to a hotel. Or you can come home with me."

It was a silly gesture. Two could play at that game. "I guess I'll walk then."

He seized her hand. "Running away doesn't solve anything."

"I'm not the one that ran away, Willie."

There was a sorrow in his eyes and an understanding, as if he had known all along. "That's not important. What is important is you come home, Alex. It is your home, too."

"But, Willie—"

"I don't know what happened between the two of you. But whatever it was, hasn't it been long enough?" He tugged at her hand. "Come on. I'll get your things. Then we can go shoot some baskets for old times' sake."

All these years and Mindy had said nothing.

"Do it for me. I really could use a friend right now."

This man was the only brother Alex knew. How could she deny him? "All right."

"Thanks."

"But I'm not so sure about the basketball."

"Sure you are," he grinned.

She remembered what a charmer he could be. "We'll see."

two

Willie parked the car in the driveway. Alex looked out the window at the large gray stone house that had been her fortress—her castle. There was no moat to separate her from her real mother and the projects, only about two city miles.

The hedges were neatly trimmed and the Japanese irises in full bloom. Along the paved walkway grew large patches of English lavender. She remembered Mrs. Martineli decked out in her oversized straw hat, bright yellow tee shirt, and faded blue jeans. Mrs. Martineli would be kneeling on the grass humming to herself, unaware of anything else in the world other than the sweet smell of flowers and the warm, wet earth beneath her hands. Mrs. Martineli never wore gloves—she claimed she liked the feel of the earth between her fingers. She loved her garden almost as much as she loved her kitchen.

Willie was already pulling her suitcase from the trunk of his beat up Volvo station wagon when Alex opened the car door. She remembered when the Martineli's gave Willie the car he was upset it would ruin his status with the girls. But he soon found out it was the best way to cart all his photographic equipment around. And she had no doubt Willie had on more than one occasion enjoyed the spaciousness of the large backseat. She reached for her suitcase but he pushed her away and quickly moved around the side of the house to the kitchen.

Rosemary and basil wafted up from the pots on the sink making her throat constrict and Alex closed her eyes hoping when she opened them Mrs. Martineli would be sitting at the kitchen table doing her crossword puzzle. But she wasn't.

Willie threw his coat over the chair and offered her a beer, which she gladly accepted. He held the icy can out to her just as he had the night she won her first championship game. Only then she wasn't old enough to legally drink.

"Brings back memories, doesn't it?" He raised his can and toasted his mother.

"Basketball," he said after they had both taken a sip.

(What would basketball be without Mrs. Martineli bringing them a fresh pitcher of lemonade?) Alex tried to put him off, but he took the beer out of her hand, handed her the overnight bag and told her to change.

"Should I use your room?"

"You mean yours," he corrected her; "I never got it back after you left."

She moved up the back staircase quickly, trying not to think about too much of anything. In the doorway of her old room Alex had to stop and catch her breath. Willie was right. Nothing had changed. Above the bed still hung the black and white photograph of her making a dunk shot Willie had taken and framed for her seventeenth birthday.

Her bag moved as she sat it on the waterbed and she felt her pulse quicken. She hadn't slept in a waterbed for over five years. Once Simon had been excited to book a room with a waterbed for their vacation and she made him call the hotel and change the reservation. She told him waterbeds made her seasick. In reality, Alex knew she could never sleep in a waterbed with anyone but Mindy—not then, not now, not ever. Sitting down on the bed she let the wave roll under her and lift her up. She tried to look around the room, but her eyes were clouding up and all she could think about was Mindy and the first time…

* * *

She had changed in to a flannel nightgown Mindy had given her. Alex contemplated her reflection in the mirror, perplexed by the white ruffle circling her neck and her wrists. On Mindy the ruffles always looked perfect, but Alex just felt silly. The blue in the gown would have accented Mindy's olive complexion and dark curls bringing out the color of her eyes. She picked up the brush to comb her hair when Mindy's reflection joined hers. Mindy took the brush out of Alex's hand and combed through her straight brown hair. The gentle pull of the bristles and warmth of Mindy's free hand on her shoulder excited her. She met Mindy's eyes in the mirror and both of them smiled. Alex rose, turned, took the brush out of Mindy's hand and set it on the dresser. Their lips met in tender kisses that quickly deepened in to a delicate dance of tongue caressing tongue. Pulses quickened and hearts pounded. They had spent the past three nights together, talking, kissing, and cuddling until they gave in to exhaustion. Each night became more glorious than the one before.

Mindy stopped just long enough to turn out the lights and lock the door, and then she pulled Alex down into the gentle waves of the waterbed and sought out her lips again. Shifting so she was on top of Alex, Mindy kissed every contour and crevice of her face, stopping only to ask, "What's this?" as she brushed her finger over a shallow indentation near Alex's temple.

Her finger barely filled the hole, but when it happened Mindy could have put the whole tip of her finger in to it. Alex remembered it taking over an hour to stop the bleeding. She should have had stitches, but she was too young to have known at the time.

Alex paused for a moment, thinking this is what they had done for the past few evenings. They'd bared their souls, their secrets, and their pasts. Alex knew she would tell Mindy whatever she asked.

Mindy's eyes widened in horror as Alex related the incident when she was five. She had been playing with her mother's nail polish and her mother struck her with a coat hanger. Mindy could hear no more. Instead she touched her lips to the scar and kissed it as if her lips would draw out all the pain and erase the horrible memory. And for a moment they did.

Tenderly Mindy kissed each eyelid, her nose, and lips—lingering on Alex's lips before giving voice to the question looming silently between them the past several nights, "Do you want to make love?"

The question had crossed Alex's mind, but she didn't know what they would do. Now the question lay in the air—Mindy's eyes begging for an answer. Alex reached up and touched one of Mindy's curls, "I do, but ..."

"But what?"

Alex stalled for a way to tell her. She stroked Mindy's cheek. Mindy's skin was so soft . Alex wanted to touch Mindy everywhere. Perhaps it was that simple. But she couldn't be sure. "Do you know what to do?"

Mindy chuckled. "Because we're both girls, or because you never?"

Alex closed her eyes, thinking about the horrible incident with Louis. His sweaty hands all over her, tugging, pawing, crushing her breasts in his rough hands ... but, that's not what she wanted with Mindy. This was different. She was already damp from Mindy's kisses. With Louis she hadn't even been wet when he pushed into her, tearing at her with each thrust. She never told Mindy what happened; she had been too ashamed. With all of her physical strength she couldn't stop him. Her pushing and punching only seemed to fuel his actions. Even her verbal protests were silenced with his rough kisses. At the time, she thought if she pushed it far enough into the back of her mind it would just not exist. But now she knew she had to tell her. "Once," she whispered, "and it was awful."

"It's not the same, I know. Derek and I fooled around a couple of times, but I never understood what all the fuss was about. But, with you ... when we touch ... I feel like electricity racing through my body. I feel so alive."

Alex nodded in agreement.

"And I know I want to kiss you and I want to know what my touch does to every inch of your body, and I want to feel what yours does to mine. I don't think we need instructions."

Alex wasn't looking for instructions. "I just want it to be special."

"Just being with you is special, Alex. I love you."

Alex loved Mindy with all her heart. She had since the very first day she met her. Repeating the words "I love you" seemed insignificant. She had to do more. "So, do you know what to do?" She asked again.

They agreed losing the nightgowns would be a good idea and Mindy did so with one fluid gesture, leaving Alex breathless at the sight of the naked woman on top of her. Alex didn't have to turn away like she did in the locker room after gym class, afraid Mindy would catch her looking. She could take her time and study every soft, delicate curve. She could stare at Mindy's breasts and know they were hers to touch. Her throat was tight, words seemed to stick, and all she could whisper was, "Beautiful."

The word seemed to convey everything and Mindy smiled. Her eyes danced with delight. Then Mindy's hands were on her nightgown and Alex was seized with terror at the thought of Mindy seeing the legacy of scars her mother had left. And as Mindy kissed her tears away, comforting her as best she could, Alex finally let her pull her nightgown off.

Mindy whispered, "You're perfect, Alex."

* * *

Willie called to her from the kitchen snapping her back into the present. Alex unzipped her suitcase. She pulled out a pair of jeans. She could walk out of the house in the morning and have to go back to make sure she had locked the door, unable to remember in a matter of seconds a simple task, but the memory of her first time with Mindy was burned into her synapses like a favorite movie you saw so often you could recite the lines by heart.

Any awkwardness was made up for by tenderness and sheer electricity. The incident with Louis was soon forgotten, not only because it was rough and disgusting, but also because Mindy was her first true love. She had wanted so desperately to please her and vice versa.

Alex slipped out of her dress. This house was filled with so many memories. She remembered how they had spent hours that first night discovering what each other liked, listening to the others response to each touch. She was lost in Mindy's softness. Alex wanted to crawl inside her new love, away from all the ugliness in her life, because Mindy was the most beautiful thing she had known.

Taking an old tee shirt from her bag, she pulled it on over her head. Mindy had to remind her to breathe when she lost consciousness. She had actually passed out. At the time she had been embarrassed. It was only later Alex realized what a compliment it was. She finished dressing. There were too many unresolved issues in this house. Simon should have known better than to let her come alone. The safest thing to do was to go to the funeral tomorrow and go home as soon as possible.

She returned to the kitchen where Willie sat waiting. He'd traded his suit for a pair of faded blue jeans beginning to tear at the knees and a faded burgundy tee shirt complete with stains from the dark room. The sight warmed her; this was the Willie she knew.

"Ready?"

She picked up her beer can and opened the back door. "Age before beauty."

"So what are you waiting for?" He took hold of the door.

"Now, just for that, I'm not going to let you win."

"Let me win? Sweetheart, you don't have a chance." He let the door close behind them and went into the garage to retrieve the basketball.

She set the beers on the picnic table and took a deep whiff of Mrs. Martineli's herb garden. She used to pick fresh herbs for her at dinnertime. Mrs. Martineli would be waiting by the door with a scissors in hand when she returned from basketball practice. She would smile and say, "You're just the one I was waiting for, Alex," place the scissors in her hand and tell her what herbs to cut.

"Think quick." Willie hurled the ball at her and she turned instinctively and caught it.

She stopped to examine the orange sphere that made life beyond the Martineli's possible. The orange sphere that led her to Mindy, made college possible, and fit so easily into her hand. She dropped it and dribbled, listening to the high-pitched ping as it hit the pavement and the quiet thud as it met her hand. There was a percussive beauty to it she had always loved and as she settled in to the rhythm of the dribble she felt centered.

"You sure you remember how to play this?"

"Just like riding a bike," she explained and punctuated the sentence by shooting the ball into the basket. "See?"

"Okay, let's play." He snatched the ball up and dribbled toward the basket. She was on him, blocking his every move. He tried to move to the opposite side, but she was his shadow. "Alex, you're not going to believe this, but your shoe is untied."

"You're right," she smiled at him, "I don't believe it."

"Wising up in your old age." He moved back and shot. The ball twirled around the rim and fell off in to her waiting hand.

She dribbled back to the foul line quickly. He followed, trying to block her. She moved gracefully from side to side, dribbling behind her back whenever Willie would try and take the ball.

She knew dribbling behind her back drove him crazy and she could hear how perturbed he was in his voice. "Are you going to shoot or what?"

Basketball had been their game. Willie had taught her a lot and he was a decent player. But this was their area of sibling rivalry. The court was the place she knew beyond a shadow of a doubt Willie thought of her not just as a girl his parents took in, but also as his own flesh and blood. There were no holds barred on the court and the two of them could be reduced at times to behavior befitting a kindergarten playground.

"Don't rush me."

"Rush you? I would never dream of it."

"Good." She pushed past him toward the basket for a jump shot. The ball went in and she retrieved it for him. "Here."

"Thanks." He dribbled to the foul line at breakneck speed. Alex cut him off, snagged the ball, shot and scored.

"Shit!"

"You're taking this too seriously," she cautioned as she guarded him. "You have to loosen up."

She knew her teasing was unappreciated as he tried to elbow past her. But as he lifted the ball to shoot, she knocked it out of his hand and snatched it up. His protests were too late as she shot from behind the foul line and scored.

"God damn it! I taught you how to play this game."

"Did a good job." She tossed him the ball.

"Too good." He set the ball down. "Time for beer." He took a sip of his beer and then flopped down into the grass.

She reached for the can and took a long sip. "You'd think by now," she said sitting beside him, "you'd find a better medicine."

"Never," he said reaching for the ball and clinging to it.

"At sixty you'll still be looking for someone to play with."

"Remind me not to ask you."

She grabbed her heart in jest. "I'm crushed."

"Well, I'd like to play with someone I can beat."

She could feel his eyes on her and she continued to sip her beer quietly.

"That's not going to happen is it?"

She stood up and offered him her hand. "It might."

He took her hand and pulled her back down into the grass. And then looked at her again.

"What?"

"You were as good as they say, weren't you?"

They said a lot of things in those days, she thought. She was the star player on the team, the anomaly—the little white girl that could play. Playing well had kept her scholarship for four years. But thinking about what they said or wrote about her just made her head hurt. Even now when someone brought it up she was always embarrassed. "Maybe; I don't know." She finished her beer.

He put his hand on hers and she looked into his eyes. "What happened with you and Mindy?"

She had to move. This was one conversation she did not want to have with him. "I need another beer."

"I'm serious."

She turned her beer can upside down and a lone drop trickled out. "So am I."

"Okay. Let's go in to the kitchen." He set the ball down and she followed him. He pulled two fresh beers from the fridge and handed her one. "Now tell me."

She tried to avoid the question by opening the refrigerator to search for something to eat. The contents were a clear indication Mrs. Martineli was no longer around. In the past the fridge would be chock-full of fresh fruit and Tupperware containers of leftovers. Now there was a lone container of fried chicken. Just as she reached for it, she heard him say, "I know you two were lovers."

Her appetite was gone; she let the door close but couldn't turn to look at him. Instead she rested her head against the cool plastic of the fridge door trying to think of a response.

His hand was on her shoulder and she felt the warmth between them. "Alex, it's okay." He guided her into a chair.

If Mindy had told him they were lovers, why hadn't she told him the whole story? She looked at him as he sat down across from her. "Why didn't Mindy tell you?"

"Mindy didn't tell me anything."

She felt the muscles in the back of her neck tighten. Pretty soon her head would be in a vise-grip and she would need a bag of ice and four Advil to pull it out of the vise. "We need to change the subject," she told him as she massaged her temples.

"Alex," he reached across the table and took her hand. "I've missed you. When you didn't come back," he squeezed her hand, "I lost a sister."

"That's sweet."

"Jesus, I'm not saying it to be sweet."

She felt his eyes on her, not just looking at her but boring into her skin, as if he were trying to see through her. And she knew what she had always known: they were kindred spirits. They both internalized things; they sought solace in physical activity, in the comfort of the home; and they shared the same taste in almost everything. When she couldn't sleep at night she would find him in the kitchen raiding the refrigerator. They would heat up plates of leftovers and talk about everything. She had spent thirteen years as an only child, struggling to survive her mother's wrath. But the day she entered the Martineli's home she found her family. They embraced her without question as if she had been there from the beginning. "I've missed you, too."

"So?" His eyes pleaded for an answer.

"How did you know? Was it obvious? The way we looked at each other or talked about each other. That's how Simon said he knew."

He looked down at his hands and said almost too quietly to be heard, "It was the way you were making love in my bed."

Suddenly she felt exposed in a way she didn't ever want to feel again. "You saw us?"

"God, no. I would have needed therapy if I had seen my two sisters in bed together."

She knew he thought of her like a sister. To remind him she wasn't would have been cruel. But he had to know, "I never thought of Mindy as my sister."

"I know you didn't." He got up and opened the cupboard, looking for something. "Listen, when Mindy dropped that creepy Derek, I was relieved. I didn't give it a second thought that she didn't see anyone else. After my mistakes, well, I was just happy she was concentrating on her studies and not dating teenage boys. I was so happy not to have to worry about her having sex." He pulled a bottle of whiskey out of the cabinet and poured himself a glass. "Something stronger?" he offered.

"Willie, we don't have to talk about this."

"No. We don't have to." He closed the bottle. "I just think we need to."

She wished she could convince him they didn't, but he seemed adamant about knowing.

"No one ever made Mindy happier than you did. Plus with you, there wasn't the risk of breaking my mother's heart again."

"Finding out Mindy was a lesbian wouldn't have done much for her heart."

"After I fathered a child at sixteen, I think Mindy's way was paved to do anything she wanted."

"Your mother loved you, Willie. Anyone could see that."

"I know, and I broke her heart."

There were tears in his eyes. "You know that's not true." She tried to reassure him. But he persisted until she pulled him in to her arms and held him as he sobbed. She tried to reassure him it was okay, his mother loved him. He was the apple of her eye; it was obvious to everyone, everyone except him. His body shook against her and she ran her hand through his curls, trying to soothe him. He needed to cry and she let him, rocking him gently until he pulled away and dried his eyes.

"I'm sorry."

"There's nothing to be sorry for."

He took another sip of his whiskey, followed by a long sip of beer. "I wasn't expecting to blubber all over you like that."

She reassured him there was nothing to be ashamed of or apologize for.

He smiled feebly at her. "So why do I have a brother-in-law?"

"We went away, Willie. Distance tends to color your perspective. People change …"

"Let's not forget 'we grew apart'."

The anger in his voice couldn't be disguised, but she didn't know what he wanted her to say. She couldn't tell him what she didn't know. The break was quick and painful, but it lacked explanation. It lacked reason, logic… She had spent years trying to forget, but it wasn't something you could just forget. "You can get as angry as you want, Willie. I can't tell you, because I don't know."

He looked confused, but she tried to explain Mindy ended it without a reason. After that, she couldn't come back to the Martineli's. She couldn't face Mindy again.

"Alex this was your home, too."

"Willie, I'm a kid from the streets. My mother was a whore; I never knew a father. The best thing that ever happened to me was your family. But when Mindy said it was over, it didn't matter how much I wanted to see you or your mom. I couldn't face you." She stopped to catch her breath. "You may think what Mindy and I did was okay. But I'm not so sure your mother would have agreed."

"My family loved you, Alex, like their own. Don't you know what that means?"

She put her finger to his lips. "Your sister didn't tell you what happened. Don't ask me to."

There was a long silence, as neither of them knew what to say. She knew Willie could launch into a sermon about unconditional love at any minute. That's what he was driving at and she wasn't in the mood to hear it. "You know," she said standing up, "we've seen each other recently. Why now?"

"It's a funeral. People think about making peace with each other. I guess I just want you two to make peace." He looked up at her. "Why did you come back now?"

"For you," she said, touching his shoulder. "I think we should turn in."

He stood and took her in his arms, hugging her tightly. Then he kissed her forehead tenderly and said, "I'm sorry. I didn't mean to upset you."

She ruffled his hair. "It's forgotten." And when he smiled back at her she turned to go upstairs. "Goodnight." Forgotten, she told herself. Then why did she feel like a scab had just been picked off an old wound?

* * *

Mindy was standing at the foot of her bed staring at the portrait Simon had painted of her. She moved beside Mindy and looked at it. Normally she didn't like pictures of herself, but she really loved this one. It was simple. She had on faded blue jeans and a light green tee shirt that seemed to bring out the hazel tinge in her eyes. He had let her sit in the big oversized chair she had found at a yard sale. Her legs were bent, so her arms wrapped around them and her chin rested on her knees. It was the only pose they had found that would keep her from fidgeting. As a result the portrait was very relaxed and very natural. Mindy turned to look at her. "I've been meaning to ask you all weekend, who painted this?"

"Simon did it."

"Is he in love with you?"

She knew from the tone of Mindy's voice it wasn't a question, but more of an accusation. She had no idea what would give Mindy that impression. And if she was really jealous, she had nothing to be jealous of. "Simon is just a friend."

She sat on the edge of the desk. "Well, he certainly does trust you. I mean, he lent you his car to pick me up." She looked directly at her. "What else does he do for you?"

She tried to reassure her Simon was nothing more than a friend. But Mindy wouldn't hear it.

"Have you seen the way he looks at you? He's in love with you, Alex."

That wasn't true. It couldn't be, and even if it was— "It's you I love." She drew Mindy in to her arms.

Mindy jerked away violently and she took the movement like she would have taken a slap in the face. She watched bewildered as Mindy moved to the opposite side of the room.

"So you're not denying he's in love with you?"

"I don't know if he's in love with me!" she yelled. "And I don't care. I'm not in love with him and I can't believe we're having this conversation."

"It's entirely possible you could be seeing someone else."

She tried again, moving behind Mindy and wrapping her arms around her. "You know that's not true; it's you I'm crazy about." She kissed the back of Mindy's neck and felt Mindy's body stiffen.

"Stop that."

At that moment, she realized that words could knock the wind out of you just like a punch could. "You used to like that."

"I think the key word there is used to."

"Mindy, what's gotten in to you?"

"Nothing." Mindy sat down on the edge of the bed and crossed her arms.

She sat next to her cautiously, afraid to touch her. She had sensed something was wrong, but she thought Mindy would tell her. After all, Mindy always told her everything. But it was clear Mindy was not going to just tell her. "Something is definitely wrong. It's been wrong all weekend. I'm sorry I didn't ask before. I was just so happy you were here. But you've been so cold, except in bed, and then you always cry afterwards. I thought it was because you missed me, but that's not it. Is it?"

"I don't think you really want to hear what I have to say."

She shivered at the iciness of Mindy's voice. But she persisted, "If you have a problem, maybe I can help."

"I doubt that."

"Why?" She was kneeling in front of her now, but Mindy wouldn't look at her.

"Because the problem is you."

"Me?"

"I don't love you anymore, Alex."

No! This was not happening. This could not happen! "I don't understand."

"I think we should end it."

"Just like that?" She snapped her fingers for emphasis.

"Yes, just like that." Mindy repeated the gesture.

"But why?"

"I told you already."

You haven't told me anything. "How the hell does something like this happen?"

"It just does." Mindy was growing increasingly agitated.

No. It doesn't. It doesn't just happen. There has to be a reason, God damn it. There has to be. "Oh, my God. You met someone else."

"No."

"That's why you kept asking me about Simon. You met someone at school."

"Just because you have someone else doesn't mean I do."

"Baby, there's no reason to be jealous of Simon. I'm not in love with Simon."

"I'm not jealous!" she screamed.

"Then what?"

"Why are you so fucking dense? I just don't want to be with you."

"Then look me in the eyes and say it."

"I don't need to look you in the eyes."

"Yes, you do. If you can't look me in the eyes then you don't mean it."

Mindy took a moment and then turned to face her and said quite deliberately, "I don't love you anymore."

Mindy's sweet Mediterranean blue eyes had iced over and the cool blue sent a chill up her spine. She fought hard to swallow the lump forming in her throat. Don't cry. Not now. Not after that. "What did I do wrong?"

"Nothing."

"I had to do something wrong. People just don't fall out of love."

"Yes they do."

"No they don't," she insisted. She told her whatever the problem was they could work it out. They could fix it; she knew they could fix it. But Mindy would hear nothing of the kind.

"Alex, I just don't want to be with you."

"So this is it?"

"That's what I've been trying to tell you."

"But, I'm still in love with you."

"That's your problem."

"Problem? Loving you isn't a problem; it's a joy. Maybe we're not together right now all the time, but it's only a while until we can be together all the time like we planned."

"Plans change." She picked up her bags.

"Mindy, I need to understand why this is happening."

"It just is, Alex." She moved toward the door, "I'll call a cab."

"No. Don't—"

Mindy slammed the door and she was gone.

* * *

She pulled a tissue from the box on the nightstand and blew her nose. There would be no crying. Not now. She took Simon's pajamas out of her overnight bag and carried them into the bathroom. Whenever she went away she took some article of clothing belonging to Simon so she could wear it and feel his presence—a tradition started when she left for college and took Mindy's favorite Mickey Mouse sweatshirt, which she practically lived in. Ironic, she thought, that the person that Mindy accused her of loving is the same person she ultimately fell in love with. But she never would have noticed Simon's unrequited glances if Mindy hadn't left. Mindy left the door open for Simon.

* * *

He had barged in to her room, as he always did, inviting her to a poetry reading. She turned over so he couldn't see she was crying and asked him if he had ever heard of knocking.

"It's an ancient custom, right? Hey, where's Mindy?"

She bit her lip and said quietly, "She's gone."

"I thought she had another day with you."

"Yeah, well, she left, okay? Why don't you follow her example?"

He sat down on the edge of the bed and touched her shoulder. "You've been crying, haven't you?"

She asked him to leave again, but he didn't move. Instead he asked what happened. She wanted to punch him. She had known him for over a year and she had never once mentioned she was a lesbian. He thought Mindy was just her best friend from back home. "Nothing is wrong, Simon."

"Oh, I get it. This is just a test of the national tear duct function. Had there actually been something to cry about …"

"Simon, you wouldn't understand."

"Why?"

She stared at the cinder block wall, realizing for the first time since she'd lived in the dormitory how much like a prison the pasty white walls looked. She felt his hand on the back of her hair and heard him say, "Alex, you can tell me anything."

Anything? I don't think so. She just sighed.

"Like, if you wanted to say, 'Simon, Mindy isn't just my best friend from back home; she's actually my lover.'"

She turned to look at him. How could he know?

Simon touched her cheek with his fingertip, wiping away a tear. "I would say, 'I know, Alex, and it's cool. You're still my friend. It doesn't matter to me.'"

He propped a pillow up against the wall, kicked off his loafers, leaned back, and opened his arms. She moved into them needing to feel the warmth of another human being. She let him put his arms around her and ask, "So what happened here?"

His sweater was soft and warm beneath her cheek and she closed her eyes to stop the tears from soaking it. His fingers were in her hair now, gently stroking. "Okay, we don't have to talk. You'll tell me when you're ready."

"She said that—that—She—" She buried her face in his chest as the tears started again. She wanted to stop, but she couldn't.

"Shh," he whispered, "take your time."

She wanted to tell him, but she couldn't wrap her lips around the words. Giving them voice gave them a power she didn't want them to have. How could she possibly explain to him her life was over?

"Did she break up with you?"

She nodded.

"That bitch!"

"Don't call her that." The reaction was instinctive, but pointless anymore—she knew it.

"Well, if she broke up with you, she is a bitch, Alex. It's that simple."

She looked at him. For a guy, he was beautiful. He had hazel eyes like her own and wavy brown hair. His moustache and goatee were trimmed into a very fine line like the Shakespearean actors. What if Mindy was right, she asked herself. What if he was in love with her? *I can't deal with this right now.*

"Were you ever in love?" she asked.

"Once."

"What happened?"

He went on to explain Michelle was one of the richest girls in school and also the brightest, sweetest, and prettiest. When her father found out Simon was an artist he forbade Michelle to date him. The threat of having her trust fund cut off turned Michelle into the picture of true daughterly devotion. And Simon was left to lick his wounds.

"I feel lost …"

"Ah," he nodded. "She was your compass."

"She was my whole world."

He kissed her tenderly on top of her head. "I know what you mean."

* * *

The bathroom lay between Mindy's room and Willie's. She pushed the door to Mindy's room closed and locked it. Then she undressed and stepped into the shower. As the hot water poured from the showerhead, pulsating over her body, she turned to put her neck directly into the stream and ease some of the tension. She remembered how she would spend hours in the shower after basketball practice. Mindy liked to massage her back after a tough game. She would start by kneading the knots out of her shoulders and move on down her spine working on the places she had learned to be problem spots, using the bar of soap as her massage oil. She would murmur her approval. Once in a while she would let her know if the spots were too tender and her touch was too hard. But for the most part, Mindy knew exactly what she was doing. And when she could feel Alex's body begin to relax and the day's game melt away, Mindy would lather up her hands, set the soap in the dish, and reach around for her breasts. She would feel Mindy's soft breasts crush into her slippery back. Then Mindy would twist her nipples between her fingers, teasing them until they were taut little buds in her hand. She would try and reach behind her for Mindy, but the shower was Mindy's domain and pleasing her while the water pounded over their bodies was something she loved to do. She would remember thinking—as Mindy turned her around and backed her into the wall, kneeling in front of her—the water always washed away the taste of your lover.

The memory was so strong she would have used her hand to bring herself off, not that it would ever be the same as Mindy's lips and tongue or that she could reach as deep as Mindy's slender fingers—but she had to stop doing this. She snatched the shampoo bottle off the corner of the tub and squeezed some into her hand. Rubbing the lather into her hair, she tried to clear her mind. She had to focus on Simon, she told herself. She rinsed her hair, stepped out, and dried herself off.

Simon's pajamas were a welcome sensation. She had sprayed them with his cologne before packing them, so she could close her eyes at night and at least smell him. Pulling the drawstring tight around her waist, she cuffed the trousers twice, and then buttoned the top. Then she ran a brush through her damp hair and returned to Willie's room.

Sitting on the edge of the bed, she tried to ignore the ripple as she reached for the phone. Simon answered it on the third ring. The rich timbre of his voice washed over her and she tried to lose herself in it. He was glad she called. Happy to report the opening went well and he sold two pieces in the first half hour alone. She was glad to hear everything went well. She knew it was awkward for him not to have her there with him, since she had never missed one of his openings.

When she finally told him she was staying at the Martineli's she could hear the change in his voice.

"So, how is it being there?"

"I keep expecting Mrs. M. to walk in at any minute." She admitted, "It's weird."

"I felt that way when Paul died."

"I know." She remembered how she would look over when they were reading or watching TV and he would have tears in his eyes—for months on end.

There was a long silence, and then Simon asked, "How's Mindy?"

"I only saw her briefly at the viewing." She let the water move beneath her as she leaned back on the bed.

Simon went on to ask how Mindy looked. What Simon really wanted to know was if she was still attracted to Mindy. After five years could the woman who ripped her heart out still be beautiful? He wouldn't ask it, though. Not yet, anyway. But she knew him too well not to know what he wanted to hear. So how could she tell him Mindy was even more stunning? Instead she took another route. "I'll be lonely tonight."

"You'll be back soon."

"Not soon enough."

"You sure you're okay? You sound a bit funny."

"I'm fine." A white lie, to spare his feelings.

"Do you think you'll be spending any time with Mindy?"

"Maybe; I don't know." She reached for the photo of the two of them at graduation on the nightstand. "I don't know. I've been spending most of my time trying to keep Willie together."

"You still love her?"

Simon had always felt threatened by Mindy. In his mind she was the only competition he would ever have. If she had been there she would have put her arms around him. She would have drowned out his questions with kisses. There would have been no talk. But he wasn't there. And she had to remind him he was being paranoid.

"I don't think so, Alex."

"You could have come with me."

"We've been through this; I told you I would postpone the opening if I could."

"Well, I guess we all have our priorities." As soon as she said it, she regretted it, but it was too late to take it back.

"I know you're pissed at me, Alex, because if I had gone with you, you wouldn't have to deal with any of your feelings. So, I'm going to ignore that."

She hated that he knew her so well. She was pissed at him for not being there. Not because she was denying her feelings. Because he knew this territory was shaky ground for both of them, so she had to tread lightly. "I'm sorry, Simon. You're right; it would be so much easier if you were here. I didn't call to fight. I called to tell you how much I love you."

He softened. "I love you, too."

"I'll let you know what time my flight is tomorrow after I call the airport."

His tone was warm again, full of the love she wanted to hear. "Sleep well."

"You, too."

She hung up the phone and touched the metal frame of the photograph. Mindy had gotten her car that night and they drove to the beach. It was the end of May. Too cold for swimming, but okay for walking along the beach, which they did.

* * *

She remembered their hands were linked as they walked down the beach in silence, both preoccupied with their own thoughts, their own terror about leaving each other. She had won a basketball scholarship to the University of Pittsburgh. As long as she maintained a 3.0 and played, it was a free ride. She had applied to Boston where Mindy was accepted, but they had already filled their quota for the year. Mindy had chosen it because it was her father's alma mater and because she knew how much he always wanted Willie to go there. Mindy never dreamt she'd be accepted and Alex wouldn't be. So neither of them was happy, but she knew she was going to give Mindy a ring. She had known it all summer. Unfortunately, the one she wanted to get her was too much and she ended up needing money for school. All she had to give her was her high school ring, but it would have to do.

They sat down to rest on a large rock and Mindy laid her head on her lap. "Look how the stars make shapes."

She was too busy looking at Mindy. The moonlight glowed against her skin. She had spent the last two years wondering how the sexual connection between them could be so intense. She could see Mindy across the room and want her. She let her fingers drift through Mindy's curls and listened as Mindy murmured, "That feels good."

"Mindy?"

"Hmm?"

"I want to give you something."

She opened her eyes.

"It's really not much. Sort of a graduation, going away," (*hope you'll be mine forever*) "kind of present."

She hardly had any money and Mindy hated it when she would spend it on her. So she waited for the standard "You know you didn't have to do that."

"I wanted to get you something really nice, but …"

"Alex, I don't need anything." Mindy turned and put one leg on either side of her lap, took her face in her hands, and looked into her eyes. "I have you. That's all I ever want."

She knew exactly what she meant. But she also knew she wished she had money to buy her fancy presents and take her exotic places. "Like I said, it's not much." She pulled the class ring off her finger and put it in Mindy's hand. "It's just something I thought you could wear to remember me by."

Mindy pulled her ring off and handed it to her, "And you'll wear mine."

They both slipped the rings on and then embraced. When they let go it was only enough to let their lips meet in a slow lingering kiss making her insides spin.

"So this means we're official."

"Official what?" She was still trying to catch her breath.

"Official girlfriends ... lovers ... no, soul mates!" Mindy seemed pleased to have found the right word and she celebrated by kissing Alex's neck.

Though she wanted nothing more than to surrender to the sensations, all she could think about was not seeing her every day. She tried to fight the tears back.

Mindy stopped and looked into her eyes. "I know you think the distance is going to be a problem for us. But I'm going to be with you every minute we're apart. I'm always with you, Alex. Don't you know that?"

"If only that were true."

"Alex, you complete me." She kissed the tears away. "I can't stand to think of how it will be without you. But, I will live for the breaks when we can be with each other and the summers. We can get a beach house..."

* * *

She opened the drawer and set the photo in it, then pulled a tissue from the box and blew her nose. Ridiculous to be crying now about something over long ago, she told herself. And then she cursed Willie for not letting her stay at the Marriott. She had a new life now, a good life with a loving husband. She had a career that seemed to be going well. Things were good. There was no reason to shake them up right now.

She pulled the covers back and crawled under them. According to her watch it was only 9:53, but the viewing and the trip had taken something out of her and sleep would be welcome even at this early hour. She switched off the light and closed her eyes trying to clear her mind of all thoughts.

A car pulled into the driveway. The engine stopped and a car door slammed, followed by the echo of the other door.

"What did I do?"

The voice that replied belonged to Mindy and there was an icy edge to it. "Nothing."

"Don't pull that 'nothing' shit with me. It's getting old."

They were right below the window now at the front door and he persisted. "Just tell me what the fuck I did, okay? I can't fix it if you won't talk to me."

The ice was melting, but into anger. "Look, Mark, it's over."

"Only when you want it to be, Mindy."

"Could you please keep your voice down? Willie is probably asleep. Now where did I put those keys?"

He softened, trying to cajole her, "Mindy, honey, I'm sorry if I yelled. I don't know what you want from me. Can't you just talk to me? Tell me what's wrong. I want to know."

"My mother died. Isn't that enough for you?"

"I'm sorry, baby. If I could bring her back for you, I would. I loved your mother, too. But this has been going on for weeks. Please just talk to me."

"Here they are." The door creaked opened. "There's nothing you can do, Mark. Good night."

"I'll be up in a minute."

"No hurry. I'd prefer to be alone."

She heard the footsteps on the stairs, and then Mindy's bedroom door opened and closed. She heard the springs creek as Mindy fell onto her bed, and then she heard the sobbing.

Mindy's tears used to rip her heart apart, but she couldn't go to her. And she couldn't risk having Mindy race in to be comforted. She found Willie's old bathrobe in the closet, pulled it on and went downstairs to the den. Mark was sitting in Mr. Martineli's leather wing back chair, drink clutched tightly in his hand. In the dim light his features seemed much softer. Mindy married the all-American boy.

"Mind if I join you? As tired as I am, I can't seem to sleep."

He seemed to warm at the idea of company. "Please, help yourself."

She opened the cabinet serving as the Martineli's bar. "I think death isn't anything I'll ever get used to no matter how I old I get," she explained as she poured the amber liquor in to the brandy snifter and sat down across from him.

"Especially when it's someone so wonderful."

The sadness in his voice was genuine and she was forced to agree. She watched as he blinked back the tears and she lifted the glass to her lips. The warm liquid burned as it slid down her throat warming her from her mouth to her stomach.

"You grew up here, didn't you?"

She thought about it for a moment. "Yes, any growing up I did back then, I did in this house."

"It must have been a wonderful place to grow up."

She nodded, "It was."

He went on to tell her Mindy talked about her all the time and seemed surprised at her shock. "You two were like sisters from what I gather."

He didn't know. She traced the rim of her glass with her finger listening to the soft squeak. "That's what people thought."

"I hope you don't think I'm too forward for asking this, but I've often wondered why you didn't keep in touch."

She swallowed the last sip of brandy. *Mindy never told you anything. All these years and she couldn't even be honest with you.* "I guess we grew apart."

He filled his glass again. "I'll drink to that."

There was sadness in his tone, as if he understood loving Mindy would eventually lead to separation. But she couldn't go down that road with him. Whatever his problems were with Mindy, they were his. "What do you do for a living?"

"Interested in knowing about the man who stole your friend's heart, are you?"

From the sound of the argument under the window, she wondered if that was the case. But they did have a family to think about. "I guess you could put it that way."

"I'm an accountant."

"You don't look like an accountant." And how stupid did that sound?

"Not nerdy enough, huh?"

She laughed, "Well, I confess I do subscribe to a certain stereotype. Only because the thought of working with numbers all day makes my head want to explode."

He laughed now. He had a very pleasant laugh, she thought, very rich and deep from the core of his being. The laugh was something you could get used to very easily, she told herself.

"It's really not bad," he assured her.

"You don't know me and numbers." She held out her glass and he filled it.

"I feel the same way about words. But you seem to have a real mastery when it comes to words."

"Just because I'm a writer doesn't mean …"

"Oh, I've read your books."

"You have?"

"Accountants can read, you know."

"That's not what I meant."

He smiled, "I know what you meant. But, I do have children and they do like to be read to at bedtime. I find it best to read them books written especially for them."

"So you read my books to lull your children to sleep."

"Which is precisely why we chose them?"

Touché! At least he could hold his own. And he would need to with Mindy. "I deserved that, didn't I?"

"Yes, you did." He smiled at her. "I'm beginning to see why Mindy liked you so much."

"Which books have you read?"

"Mindy's bought every one."

"And your children—do they like them?"

"What's not to like? Knights, dragons, and damsels… It's the stuff fairy tales are made of. Though I must confess, Mindy is your biggest fan. Followed by Alex."

Did he say Alex?

"Although Alex may be more a fan of your husband's. Alex is quite a little artist himself. We're very proud of him."

He did say Alex.

Mark continued to talk about how Alex admired painters and how they wanted to encourage him.

"What's your other son's name?"

"Jordan. After my grandfather. They're both with my brother now. I didn't want to bring them. I think at their age it's pointless."

"How old are they?"

"Alex just turned four and Jordan will be two and a half next month." Mark glowed with pride as he spoke of his children. He told her Jordan was the linguist in the family learning Spanish from the cleaning woman and watching *Sesame Street*. Then he pulled his wallet from his back pocket and extracted two photos.

Both boys had his blond hair and Mindy's blue eyes. His eyes were blue, too, but an icier blue. While Mindy's were the color of the Mediterranean Sea, his were the color of the Arctic Sea. Alex had blond ringlets of curls cascading around his face and he had Mindy's bee-stung lips. Jordan had straight blond hair and his father's dimple.

"They're lovely," she handed the photographs back to him.

He asked if she and Simon had children and she told him they had been trying and lately toying with the idea of adoption. He reminded her adoption could be a lengthy process.

"Well, it's like Mrs. Martineli used to say: Good things come to those who wait."

"Hopefully she was right."

"She generally was." She set the glass down, knowing full well he was referring to s omething else. "Well, I really should get some rest now. I think the brandy did the trick."

He stood up. "You don't have to leave on my account."

"I'm not, Mark. It's been a pleasure speaking with you. But I think we should probably both get some sleep. Don't you think?"

"I guess you're right." There was sadness in his voice indicating Mark might be spending his night on the couch.

"I'm sure Mindy is waiting for you, Mark. Don't stay up too late."

"I won't."

She went through the kitchen up the back stairs careful not to pass Mindy's room. As she crawled back under the covers, she wondered how Mindy explained the name Alex to Mark. How Mark didn't question naming the first-born son after a friend. Or was someone in his family named Alex? Must be. It was a coincidence. No one would name their child after a lover they dumped. It was downright absurd. When she and Simon had discussed names they looked through the baby books she kept on hand as a source for names for her stories. They read the meanings of the names, said them out loud. They discussed the repercussions of naming your child something old fashioned like Prudence or Opa. They talked about nicknames and agreed the name Richard was out, because it eventually would become Dick. Never had they mentioned naming their daughter Mindy. They did however talk about naming a little girl Angela after Mrs. Martineli. She thought now more than ever if they did have a little girl Angela is what they would name her. She drifted off to sleep dreaming of a daughter.

three

The first light of morning burst into her room stirring her from what little sleep she had. She was never a morning person, but years of basketball training and running always made her rise earlier than she wanted. While she debated whether or not to get up and run, she covered her eyes with her arm. If nothing else she would get up and lower the damn blind. But before she gathered the energy to get out of bed, someone else pulled the blind down. Opening her eyes slowly to allow them time to adjust, she noticed a figure standing there.

"Don't be afraid," Mindy said, softly. "It's just me. Mark told me you were here."

"I was going to stay at the Marriott, but Willie wouldn't hear of it."

She leaned back against the windowsill. "It would have been silly to waste your money."

"How long have you been there?"

"A little while." She smiled. "The years have been good to you. You're even more beautiful."

She wasn't sure how to respond. She looked at Mindy, still in her red satin bathrobe and nightgown, curls in place, face wrinkle free, eyes sparkling. "You haven't aged at all."

"Must be the kids keeping me young." She took a deep breath. "Jesus, Alex, I've missed you."

She was full of surprises this morning. She knew Mindy wanted her to say she missed her too. Mindy was waiting, but she couldn't say it. Even if it was true. She couldn't let her guard down.

"Why didn't your husband come?"

She explained about his latest gallery opening last evening. She had never missed an opening before. She loved seeing Simon dressed in his gallery attire, a pale gray, double-breasted silk suit, with a cranberry turtleneck. She looked at her watch, thinking right about now he would be getting up for his morning run.

"He's very talented." Mindy sat on the edge of the waterbed and the tiny ripple moved her leg.

"Thank you. But how do you—" She stopped herself, remembering the books. "Mark told me you've read all my books. He also told me your son, Alex is quite talented."

She smiled. "He's good. But you're amazing."

"What?"

"I never knew you could write."

"Neither did I—until I did it," she confessed. She would never have thought of writing if she hadn't needed an English credit and taken the creative writing class in her junior year. Professor Stiles was the best professor she had in her entire career at Pitt. Not just because she believed in her so much so she took her final project to a friend that was an agent in New York, but because she helped her find her voice. She had two stories published before she graduated and a nice little contract with the publishing firm. The stories originated from the pain of the break up, but now they had moved so much further.

"My mother was very proud, especially when *The Forgotten Dragon* was picked as one of the best for Christmas in *Time*. She read all of your books, too."

She was glad to hear that. Every time a new one was published she wanted to send her one. But she knew she couldn't open that door again. Still, she had to know if she liked them.

"She loved them. She really missed you, Alex, when you didn't come home."

Mindy said it so naturally as if she had been the one who had chosen not to return, when Mindy was the one who shut her out. "Well, I didn't think I had a home after you and I..." She stopped herself; this was not the time. "I'm sorry. I never meant to hurt her."

"I know you didn't." She cried, softly at first.

"Hey."

"Alex, what am I going to do without her?"

She sounded lost, like Simon after Paul's death. So, she had plenty of practice at what to say. Not that it was what they wanted to hear. "You'll do what she would have wanted you to do. Go on living."

"But, I feel like this huge part of me...died."

"You were close. I'm sure a part of you did. It's hard to let go, Mindy, but we all have to do it at one time or another."

"I feel so empty."

"I know." She placed her hand on Mindy's shoulder and Mindy leaned her head to the side and kissed it. Before she could move it away, Mindy took it in her hand, and then looked up at her and asked if she could hold her.

"Mindy, it's been..."

"A long time. I know." Mindy didn't turn away. "Please."

She didn't move. She didn't know what to do. After all that had happened it seemed like a very large request.

"Do you hate me that much?"

"Hate you?" After all they shared she could never hate Mindy. Hate had never been an option. She was angry with her for a very long time.

"Then what?" Tears were streaming down her cheeks. She didn't move from the bed. Instead she tried to wipe the tears away with her hands.

I don't trust you, she wanted to say. How could she? She had given Mindy her love without any reservations and then Mindy just tossed it back in her face without an explanation. But this wasn't about them. It was about losing her mother. And Mindy had been there when she lost her mother. She had tried to comfort her then and help her make some sense of the situation. The time was not easy—knowing your own mother didn't love you was a hard pill to swallow. But she knew without a doubt Mrs. Martineli loved her, loved her like one of her own. Without question she had opened her home and her heart.

For Mrs. Martineli's sake, she reached out and pulled Mindy into her arms. Mindy's body trembled and she pulled her closer trying to stop the shaking. Before she knew it her fingers were passing through Mindy's curls, stroking her, trying to soothe her pain. The satin pajamas felt warm against her hand. She remembered how Mindy's body was always so warm and she was always so cold.

"I'm getting your pajamas all wet," she sniffled, but didn't let go.

"They're wash and wear."

She looked at her. "Thank you."

Letting go, she suggested she might want to wash her face and get dressed.

"Probably." Mindy stood and moved toward the bathroom door. "When are you leaving?"

"After the funeral."

"So soon?"

"There's a lot on my plate, and I missed Simon's opening."

"But we haven't seen each other in years."

"I know. Maybe we can talk later."

"I'd like that." She closed the door behind her.

She fell back onto the bed. How can she act like nothing happened? She was ready to kick herself for holding Mindy. She should have let her sit there and cry. Instead she let herself remember just how good she felt. Simon was all muscle and angles, while Mindy was all soft curves. She had forgotten how their bodies molded to each other's. Enough! She reached for the phone and quickly punched in her phone number. She needed to hear Simon's voice.

"Christopher-Russell incorporated. May I help you?"

"You do that so well."

"I try. And how are we this morning?"

"Missing you."

"Today is the day, isn't it?"

"Twelve o'clock."

"Are you going to be okay?"

There was a genuine concern in his voice.

"You know me."

"Yes, that's why I'm asking."

"I guess I deserved that after last night."

"Forgotten. Not to change the subject, b ut I forgot to tell you yesterday Roz called. Lunch Friday, big deal. No details."

Roz was her agent and if she wasn't home when Roz called it never seemed to faze her. She adored Simon and would talk to him for hours. She knew better than to think she called and told Simon nothing. When pressed he confessed there had been some offers to turn two of the books into cartoons. She asked if Simon would be interested and he told her they would probably use a different artist. She couldn't fathom her books with someone else's illustrations. They had worked so painstakingly together over them.

"This could be a big deal, baby. Let's not go biting our nose off."

"Simon, everyone loves your illustrations. They help make the books."

"I know, you tell me that all the time. But it's your stories they like, Alex. You're a fine writer."

"I'm telling you everyone here that's read the books has commented on your illustrations."

"I'm your husband, honey; they're trying to be nice."

"I don't know about that. I mean they told me Alex wants to be an artist like you." As soon as she said it she knew it was a mistake. When would she learn to think before she spoke?

"There's another Alex?"

"Mindy's son."

"Mindy named her son after you?"

The worry in his voice wasn't even disguised. She tried to downplay it. "I know, it's weird."

"Weird. Baby, it's downright fucked up. She broke up with you, didn't she?"

"You know she did. Simon you're getting excited over nothing."

"Alex, it's clear she still loves you. Don't you think I have a right to be a little edgy?"

He was right and she knew he was. After all she had put him though because of Mindy, he had a right to be more than edgy. But the conversation had taken a turn for the worse and she was getting agitated. "It's good to know you trust me."

Concern turned to anger in a flash. "Oh, don't twist this around on me. You know I trust you."

"It's just her you're worried about, right?"

"Why is it you can never see what's right in front of your face?"

She tried to explain he wasn't there; he didn't know what was in front of her. He should stop jumping to conclusions. Someone in Mark's family could be named Alex. And then she asked him not to lose sight of the reason she was there.

"Which is?"

"Simon, my mother died. You know as well as I do Mrs. Martineli was the closest thing to a mother I had. I'm sorry you never knew her. She would have liked you."

He apologized immediately and reminded her how crazy he was about her. And she assured him she would be home in his arms later that day.

"I can't wait."

"Until tonight, then." She hung up the phone. Then she gathered her things together and went into the bathroom to shower. Turning on the water, she undressed and stepped in, letting the warm water rush all over her body.

* * *

"I don't understand," Mrs. Martineli was mumbling as she applied ice to her eye, which was beginning to swell shut. "How can she call herself a mother and do these things to you?"

"I was an accident." She held the ice pack against her rib. It was cold, and her rib was tender, but not broken, as the x-rays had shown. Just bruised, the doctor had said.

"She told you that?"

"All the time."

Mrs. Martineli touched her free hand and she reveled in the warmth of it. She loved Mrs. Martineli.

"Not everyone is as special as you are."

Mrs. Martineli touched her cheek. "There's nothing special about me, Alexandra."

Mystified by her modesty all she could say was what she felt. "To me there is."

Mrs. Martineli's hand was under her chin and she lifted it gently until their eyes met. "You are the remarkable one, Alexandra. Now, I have discussed this with Mr. Martineli and we are both in agreement you should not return to your apartment. If that woman is going to continue to brutalize you, we will not be able to sit by and watch. We will press charges the next time she lays a hand on you. You can stay in Willie's room. We will look into the legalities of having you here full time should she cause any trouble."

"Why would you do that for me?"

Mrs. Martineli smiled. "Because we love you, Alex."

Try as she might, she could not stop the tears streaming down her cheeks. She tried to wipe them away. And then Mrs. Martineli pulled her close, holding her as only a mother can—in a shroud of protection. She felt her body sway back and forth as Mrs. Martineli rocked her and she continued to cry. Her tears weren't for the pain building up beneath her swollen eyelid, or for the aching rib which would be black and blue for weeks. Her tears were for the moment she had longed to have with her own mother, but would never have. Only now in the arms of a stranger it didn't matter she would never know that kind of love from her own mother. She had found it on her own.

* * *

"Trying to become the first human prune?" Mindy asked.

She peeked around the side of the shower curtain to see Mindy standing in front of the mirror applying make-up.

"I hope you don't mind. Willie's in the other bathroom."

Self-conscious of the tears streaming down her cheeks and her nakedness behind the flimsy shower curtain, she turned the water off. "Could you hand me a towel, please?"

"Sure." Mindy grabbed a towel off the rack and stretched her arm out forcing her to reach for it. She held the curtain in front of her the whole time. If she didn't know better, she would have thought Mindy was doing it deliberately.

"Thanks." She retreated behind the plastic curtain to dry off, and then wrapped the towel around her.

Mindy turned her attention back to the mirror as she reached for her robe.

With the robe securely fastened, she pulled the towel out and dabbed at her hair.

"Shit!"

"What?" She looked up in time to see Mindy grab a tissue and rub the giant blotch of mascara above her right eye into an even bigger smudge.

"Oh, God." She crumpled the tissue into a ball and threw it at the sink. "It's no use."

"Here." She took Mindy's chin in hand and found a clean tissue. She dipped it into the Vaseline and wiped the smudge away.

As she wiped, she remembered—

* * *

—Mindy prying her fingers from her eye and shouting, "Jesus Christ, you're bleeding." She explained her mother had a ring on as Mindy cleaned the cut out. It stung and she protested, but Mindy was just glad to see the cut would not need stitches. She put a Band-Aid on it and got some ice.

* * *

Mindy reached out and touched the scar above her eyebrow, as if she knew what she'd been thinking. She moved away.

"I'm sorry."

"Don't be." She threw the tissue away. "I think I got it all."

"I was just—"

"You know you don't need all that junk."

Mindy laughed, "You still hate make-up."

"I don't hate it. I just don't think you need it." She rarely used make-up. In college during basketball season it was just downright impractical, and Simon never seemed to like it. He liked "paint on his canvas, not his women." She couldn't argue with him because she felt the same way about Mindy. Mindy's skin was flawless. She couldn't remember a time when Mindy even broke out. Make-up just seemed like a waste of time and money. She closed the door behind her and dropped her pajamas on the bed.

There was a time when they could finish each other's sentences when telling a story or spend hours in a room without saying a word and know exactly what the other was thinking. Perhaps things didn't change as much as she thought they did.

She dressed in a hurry. As she pulled on her black nylons, she thought about leaving after the funeral. To be back in Simon's arms again where she belonged was all she could think about. She slipped her dress over her head and there was a knock at the door.

"Alex, you in there?" Willie asked.

She fixed her dress and opened the door. Willie stood dressed in a white shirt and black baggy pants, fiddling with a blue paisley tie. "Could you help me?" He marched over to the mirror, still fiddling. "Usually, I can do these damned things by myself, but today…"

She put her arms around him and took an end of the tie in each hand. "Don't laugh," she said into his ear, "this is the only way I can do this."

As she looped the one side of the tie around, up, over, and through, Willie was studying her in the mirror. She pulled the knot and straightened the tie. "There you go."

"Thank you."

"So, now you can help me zip my dress." She turned around and he pulled the zipper all the way up and closed the hook and eye. "Thanks," she said as she pulled the belt off the hanger and put it on.

"Have you seen Mindy?"

"Yes." She pulled the shoes out of the box and slipped them on. "I even talked with Mark a little."

"He's a great guy."

"I gathered that." She rummaged through her overnight bag searching for the earrings to match her outfit. "Willie, why didn't you tell me about Alex?"

He made up the bed—partially out of an obsessive need for order and partially to avoid the question. "What about Alex?"

Grabbing the other side of the sheet, she shot him a look which would make him cut the shit.

"The only Alex I know is you. There. Are you happy?"

She sat on the edge of the waterbed carefully and he sat beside her. "I tried to ask her when she did it, but she said it was none of my business."

She felt the need to change the subject. The thought of a child named after her was flattering, but the thought of it being Mindy's child, a child she'd never even met, whose life she'd never had the chance to be a part of... Even Mrs. Martineli didn't mention it in her letters. "Did you know your mother used to write to me?"

"She mentioned it."

"Did she also mention I never wrote back?"

He put his hand on her shoulder. "There's no reason to beat yourself up."

She knew he was right, but she also knew she should have at least written back. After all Mrs. Martineli did for her, she owed her more. "She must have thought I hated her."

"No, Alex, she never thought that." He squeezed her hand. "Look, you can believe what you want. But my mother loved you, and she knew you loved her. And whether Mindy talked about it or not, my mother knew you two had a falling out which is why you didn't come home. My mother thought of you as a daughter, I think of you as a sister, and as for Mindy...you'll have to work that out with her." He stood up. "And you're wrong about my mother, Alex."

"Wrong how?"

"You made Mindy so happy. Everyone could see she made you happy, too. My mother would have accepted your relationship."

"Willie—"

"You can think what you want, but I know I'm right. Now, come on, let's eat something."

"I'm not very hungry." She leaned over to pick up her purse.

"Well, I stopped for donuts and muffins. My mother would have wanted us to eat. So, I think we should make an effort."

He was right. Mrs. Martineli would have made a three-course breakfast for a day like this. She would have been bustling around the kitchen to avoid thinking about what was going on. Cooking was her escape. When she cooked she was free from everything and when people consumed her wonderful creations and sang her praises it was merely an added perk. "Did you get those crullers your mother loved?"

"Absolutely." He started down the backstairs.

"Well, those are light. I'll have one of those."

four

She watched as the mourners, clad in black, poured into the white-domed building on Main Street to pay their respects to Mrs. Martineli. The contrast of the white washed church and the bright morning sky against the people in black looked like a black and white photograph out of *Life* magazine.

Alex was happy to be out of the car, where she had spent the last twenty minutes sandwiched between Willie and Mindy. Mark rode in the front with the driver and if it weren't for Mark's constant chattering to the driver, the silence would have been deadly.

St. Sebastian's was her first encounter with organized religion. She had always believed in God, but when she moved in with the Martinelis, Mrs. Martineli took a first-hand interest in her religious growth. An old-world Catholic, Mrs. Martineli would attend Mass every day of the week and her children went on Sundays rain or shine.

On her eighteenth birthday, Mrs. Martineli gave her a card with a note inside that read: "In this materialistic world, we hope you will understand our love extends beyond those things which we can physically give you, and accept our gift of a mass to be said in your name this Sunday." That gesture summed up both their feeling for their religion and for her. That mass was the first time she took communion and the last until her wedding day.

The inside of the church was whitewashed as well. The floor was a light oak with a piece of blood-red carpeting running down the center and up three steps. The light oak altar was draped in a blood-red satin runner with a simple golden cross embroidered on the front. A wooden chair with a lectern in front sat to the left of the altar. Behind the altar and suspended above it was a huge crucifix and in the left-hand corner of the church about five feet off the ground on a shelf stood a life-size statue of the Virgin Mary. Both the crucified Jesus and the Virgin Mary statues were so life like, their eyes seemed to follow you. Alex remembered Mindy pointing it out early on, and it made looking at them difficult.

The coffin was in front of the steps on a rolling device. Father Castillo entered wearing a simple white cassock with a red stole. Five years ago, Father Castillo would have been about her age now. Then he was a young, high-spirited priest, who usually traded in the traditional collar and black shirt, for jeans, sneakers, and a blue shirt with white collar.

Father Castillo was the one Mindy used to confess to. Since he only ever gave her three Hail Marys and five Our Fathers to say, she knew it was a dead giveaway Mindy wasn't telling him about the two of them, which was all right by her, because she loved Father Castillo. He had a sharp wit and he was a tender soul. The years had been kind to him, as she was certain he had been to them. He looked much the same. As he stood behind the casket, she noticed despair in his eyes that she had never seen before.

Mindy genuflected near a pew in the front. Mark did not. That must have been a blow for Mrs. Martineli. Then again, if Mindy was happy, Mrs. Martineli might have accepted anything. Maybe Willie was right.

Taking a seat near Willie, she studied the sleek pewter coffin with silver handles. She thought about funerals and what a waste of money they were. When she died, she wanted her family to take the money they would have spent on a funeral and use it to live life to the fullest.

Father Castillo began the Mass and Willie rose to take his place for the readings.

She knew Mrs. Martineli would be in heaven now. But she wasn't sure her own mother would be there. All the threats of hell in the Catholic Church were enough to make you think about living a clean, honest life. But, if God was "all forgiving" then surely her mother would have had a chance. Perhaps she would finally meet Mrs. Martineli, and then Mrs. M. would kick her ass from here until tomorrow. She always said, "God help me if I ever meet that woman."

When the Martinelis took her in, her mother didn't even look for her when she didn't come home. No questions, no concern, nothing from the woman who gave her life. But if she and Mindy were going to be out late for any reason, the Martinelis wanted a full accounting. There were rules in their house, something she thought might be bothersome at first, having never answered to anyone. Instead she found she liked the structure, she liked the fact they wanted to know where she was not because they were nosey, but because they cared. And she realized despite her freedom growing up, she really did walk the straight and narrow. There was an inborn sense of right and wrong making her wonder who her father really was. Her mother used to work stag parties when she was younger. Maybe her father was just an engaged man sowing his last wild oats. None of it mattered after the Martinelis. Where Mrs. Martineli was warm and bubbling with love, Mr. Martineli was quiet and reserved. He was always very kind to Alex. He would go to all her basketball games and he'd help her with her political science homework when she had questions.

Mr. Martineli passed away in her first semester at school. Alex had just returned from an away tournament, exhausted and in need of a shower. Her roommate looked up from the book she was reading and said she had some bad news. "A guy named Willie called and said his father had a massive coronary and didn't make it." As her roommate went on to try and explain she didn't know how to get a hold of her, Alex grabbed the phone and dialed Mindy. But she had missed the funeral. Mrs. Martineli got on the phone and told her they had buried him that morning and there was no need to make the trip. Then she put Mindy on the phone and the pain in Mindy's voice tore Alex's insides apart. She had to do something. So she borrowed a friend's car and drove all night. Letting herself in the back door just before morning, she crept up the back stairs and opened the door to Mindy's room. Mindy had fallen asleep on top of her bed, fully dressed, tissue box clutched tightly in one hand, crumpled tissues all around her. She picked up the tissues and threw them away and then she pried the tissue box out of Mindy's hand. As Mindy stirred, she could see the streaks of mascara on her cheeks, obvious reminders of the streams of tears. "Mindy, I'm so—" But that was all she said before they fell into each other's arms and clung to one another until they were hoarse from crying and emotionally exhausted. In the morning it was Willie who woke them up. And the three of them spent the next two days trying to rouse Mrs. Martineli from the guest room, where she decided to sleep. She couldn't go back to their room. The sight of Mrs. Martineli like an abandoned child was devastating. She remembered Mindy saying, "They were together for thirty years. We've only been together for four and I can't imagine my life without you after this short time. Imagine thirty." She and Willie rearranged the master bedroom and Mindy slept in the room with her mother that first night. But it was Aunt Louisa who came and took her mother by the hand. She told them to leave them be for a while. No one knew what Aunt Louisa said, but whatever it was it did the trick. And by the end of the week, she and Mindy were back at their respective colleges forced to go on with the knowledge Christmas was just a couple months away and the family would never be the same.

Willie slid into the pew next to her and she realized Father Castillo was beginning his eulogy. He spoke about what a wonderful inspiration she was to the community with all of her volunteer work and what a wonderful mother she was.

"She created an atmosphere of love for her children, which is evidenced by the fine young people they have matured into…"

An atmosphere of love, for Mindy and Willie it was; for her it was a sanctuary. So, when she couldn't go home after Mindy broke up with her, she lost her center.

* * *

She had been sitting for Simon and he was growing increasingly agitated with her inability to sit still. When she told him to back off, he agreed to call it a day. As he cleaned his paintbrushes he inquired about what was bothering her. He had been the one to suggest living together over the summer. The idea seemed so natural to him. They got along famously, they could share expenses, save money. Plus he was certain his brother could get her a job for the summer, too. She had been uneasy with the idea at first. The idea of living with a man was not one she had really given any thought to in the past. But he wore her down with his arguments. And she trusted him like no one else at school, except for several teammates. So in the end they signed the lease on a small, two-bedroom apartment and lived together. She was surprised at what a great roommate Simon actually was. They seemed to balance each other, each liking the chores the other despised. In the evenings they would cook together, oftentimes simple meals, but occasionally something elaborate. She would sit for him while he painted and he would run with her in the mornings for basketball. She grew comfortable with him, but not comfortable enough to let anything happen. Mindy had broken her heart and as far as Alex was concerned no one would ever have the chance again.

* * *

The congregation was rising as Father Castillo said, "Let us offer each other a sign of peace."

"Peace." Willie leaned over and kissed her on the cheek and she could feel his tears brush against her cheek.

"Peace," she whispered back.

The woman behind her tapped her on the shoulder and when she turned, the woman engulfed her hand in an overzealous handshake. "Peace."

She smiled. "Peace be with you." When she turned back, Mindy was standing next to her, hand extended, waiting.

"Peace?"

She let her hand close firmly around Mindy's and stared into her eyes. The time had come for peace, for forgiveness even, and yet the word peace seemed to stick in her throat like a dry communion wafer.

Mindy leaned in and kissed her on the cheek and then whispered, "It's time, isn't it?"

Past time, she thought. She had no choice but to say, "Peace."

Mindy smiled and she thought, if only it were that simple. Mindy would never know the months of pain she suffered when she left. She agonized over their love affair. Mindy would never know how it hindered her relationship with Simon. She spent months pushing him away, because she was terrified of loving anyone again.

The choir sang a hymn she couldn't identify. *Poor, Simon. He put up with so much because of you. And what do we do once we make peace? We certainly can't pick up where we left off.*

They carried the coffin out of the church and the people followed in silence.

Another concept mystified her—the gathering after a funeral to eat, when the last thing in the world you wanted to do was eat. Then mingle with people and share each other's grief. Both Mindy and Willie had broken down at the gravesite. Instinctively she had moved toward Mindy, but stopped when she saw Mark steady her and hold her tightly against him. Instead she put her arm around Willie and let him lean on her for support. On the ride to the church hall, both Willie and Mindy leaned against her, as she was sandwiched between them. Willie's hand was entwined with hers and his head lay on her shoulder. She leaned her head against his and continued to blink back tears she had been fighting not to shed. She would cry at home or on the plane ride back. Probably sob like a baby, but not when others needed her to be strong. Crying was out of the question.

Mindy had moved close to her and carefully laid her head on the other shoulder. She shifted in her chair, not knowing what to do.

Alex looked around the room. She noticed Aunt Louisa, who had planned the entire funeral, swooping in from the moment they called and dealing with everything from the funeral home to the wake, thereby avoiding the grief that would eventually wash over her and pull her down in the undertow drowning her in a sorrow she was all too familiar with. She greeted everyone with a warm embrace, and a twist of the cheek for the younger ones.

Alex watched her twist the cheek of a little boy and remembered wanting to punch her every time she did that to her. "You can do it back," Mrs. Martineli would say, when she told her how much she hated it. She knew she couldn't. Still, just the thought of it made her chuckle as a teenager.

Dinner was simple. She and Willie polished off their wine and managed to push the rest of the food around on the plate. Willie had actually mixed his together in a multi-colored mess on the plate and then sat staring at it. She was getting ready to ask Willie if there was any more wine to be had when she felt a warm hand on her shoulder, and then Mindy whispered in her ear, "Take a walk with me."

Without a second thought, she rose and followed her past the crowd, past the hostess and out into the parking lot. They both took a deep breath and then there was a silence.

Mindy broke the silence. "You're still angry with me, aren't you?"

"I don't think this is the time to talk about it."

"Well, when are we going to talk about it?"

She really needed that glass of wine now. "I don't know."

"Would you feel better talking at home? Because we can leave."

"We can't just leave your mother's funeral."

"We can if I tell Willie we're going."

"But—"

"It's important, isn't it?"

"And your mother's funeral?"

"My mother would want us to make peace, Alex. I know that in my heart, and you do, too." She held out her hand. "Come on and walk home with me."

She conceded and Mindy went to tell Willie they were going. What exactly did Mindy have to tell her, she asked herself, and what exactly did she want to say to Mindy? She had known when it had happened, known for months what she would say. Sleepless nights were spent playing out their reconciliation. But as the months passed and Mindy didn't return her calls and her letters came back marked 'return to sender,' she knew—Mindy was gone.

* * *

And then her longing turned to rage. The one person she had trusted in this world had abandoned her and the pain was almost debilitating. She missed classes, practice, meals, tests, and instead she slept. She sent Simon away every time he attempted to rouse her from her sleep, until finally Simon picked her up, carried her down to the bathroom, set her in the bathtub, and turned on the shower. When the cold water hit her, soaking her and her clothes, something shifted. Initially it was her anger. She wanted to strangle him. And she had, tackling him in the hallway, and pinning him to the ground.

Drops of water fell off her hair and hit him in the face and he blinked. "Hit me if you want, Alex. I don't care. Just feel something, anything other than what you're feeling. It's been over two weeks."

And then, knowing as much as she wanted to, she could never hit anyone, not after being beaten the way she was, she just collapsed into his arms sobbing.

She felt people step over them, but no one stopped. At the time it made little difference, but in retrospect it seemed odd. Perhaps they didn't stop because Simon held her and rocked her. Then he helped her to her feet and took her back to her room. She sat on the bed looking at his newly drenched clothes, as he set clothes out for her on the bed. He told her to change and he'd be back. Then he took her to the diner and made her eat, and for the next several days he stayed with her—walking her to class, helping her with her homework, making sure she ate, until it didn't seem like work anymore. And the rage subsided.

* * *

Mindy reappeared within minutes. "I told Willie. Let's go the back way."

The back way was through the park. By foot it was shorter than the drive and certainly more scenic. The park was always a peaceful place for them. Sometimes they would go there to do their homework on nice days, or take a picnic on weekends just to be out of the house and by themselves. They would read to each other, or play Scrabble, or sometimes take off their shoes and wade in the stream. But at the time, it really didn't matter if they just lay together on the blanket and stared at the clouds; they were together and nothing else mattered.

"Alex, I've tried to think about what I would say to you if I ever had the chance to see you again…" Mindy stopped and turned toward her. "I've made mistakes, but of all the mistakes I've made in my life, leaving you…"

She held up her hand to stop Mindy. "I know you're sorry."

Mindy mumbled something like "you don't know how sorry," she thought, but she pressed on.

"In a lot of ways you did me a favor. I mean, I wouldn't have found Simon…"

"You really love him, don't you?"

"You seem surprised."

Mindy walked again. "A little."

"Why?"

"I guess I just never pictured you married to anyone other than…"

"What about you and Mark?"

"Well, we're happy…"

The sugar coating in her voice could not disguise the truth, Alex thought, but there was a genuine sense of joy as Mindy declared, "And we have two beautiful children."

"Mark showed me their pictures last night. They are lovely."

"You don't have any children, do you?"

"Not yet."

Mindy touched her arm, "But you really want them, don't you?"

"Simon would be a good father."

"And you would be a good mother, Alex. You shouldn't be afraid."

She pulled away; Mindy always knew what she was thinking, what she feared, what she wanted. She still knew. How could that be? "Mark seems very nice."

"He's okay."

"Well, I enjoyed talking with him."

"He said he enjoyed meeting you, too." She sat down on a park bench and patted the space beside her. "Sit for a moment."

She sat beside her. And then, after convincing herself it didn't matter, curiosity got the best of her, and she had to know. "Who are your sons named after?"

"Alex is named after you and Jordan is named after Mark's grandfather."

"You named your son after me?"

"I love you, Alex. I always have."

"You have a really funny way of showing it."

"I told you I made a mistake." She stood up and moved behind the bench. "Alex, I've wanted to get in touch with you so many times…but I figured you wouldn't want anything to do with me."

"Just the opposite."

"Even after what I did to you?"

"I would have ridden to hell and back just to be with you. But you made it perfectly clear you didn't want me. So, I shut myself off from people. I thought to myself, if they can't get in, then I can't get hurt."

"Like the hero in *The Knight Who Lost His Armor*."

"That's where the idea came from. Only it wasn't a princess who hid the armor, it was a prince."

"Prince Simon."

She tried to ignore the sarcastic tone in Mindy's voice. "He made me feel needed again and loved."

"So, I was right about him being in love with you." She sat down again.

"What difference does it make? I wasn't in love with him when you left me. I told you that then, and I meant it. Mindy, you were my whole world…" *What are you doing Alex?* She stood up and moved away from Mindy. "I wanted to see you to know if you were okay."

"But you just naturally assumed anyone stupid enough to tell you to stay the fuck out of their life wouldn't want to ever see you again."

"Basically."

"So I guess Simon is your whole world now?"

"Isn't Mark yours?"

"My boys are my whole world."

"Mindy, you never told Mark about us. Why?"

She looked horrified. "You mean you told Simon?"

"He's my partner. How could I keep a secret like that from him?"

"Mark wouldn't understand."

"You married someone who wouldn't understand."

"And you married someone who does?" She challenged.

"Mindy, there was no choice. When you left it was obvious. I was devastated. He figured it out."

Mindy touched her shoulder, "Alex, you have to believe I never wanted to hurt you."

She heard the sincerity in Mindy's voice, but she wasn't sure what she was supposed to say.

Mindy was going to talk for both of them. "I didn't understand then what I do now."

"Which is?"

She bent down in front of her. "I'd take it all back if I could."

"Mindy, we can't change the past."

"What about the future?"

She looked at the woman kneeling in front of her. She was still breathtaking. Skin flawless, eyes blue as ever and waiting for an answer. There was a fire in her belly and she was surprised at how much she just wanted to reach out, draw Mindy to her, and kiss those exquisite lips again. Or did she really want to just slap

Mindy. Whatever the feeling was, she was certain of one thing, she couldn't stay sitting there. "Why don't we both stick to the present for now?"

Mindy followed. It was apparent things weren't going exactly as she planned. "I wish I could just explain to you ..."

She just kept walking. "I don't think you should do that."

"But I want to..."

She turned to look at her. She already knew what Mindy was going to say and she knew that she couldn't hear it. Not now. Not ever. "Maybe another time."

Mindy reached for her face. "Will there be another time?"

She removed the hands from her face and held them for a moment. "Anytime you and your family are in New York. Look us up."

five

She had three drinks on the plane, her usual two to help her unwind, since she hated to fly, and a third one to help erase the dull ache that had started in the pit of her stomach from seeing Mindy again. By the time the plane touched down in LaGuardia she was feeling more than relaxed. But when the passengers departed, she became overly anxious to see Simon again. She wove quickly through the crowd until she saw him and her heart felt light again.

She set her bag down and threw her arms around him. His lips were waiting for hers and she felt his powerful arms close around her drawing her closer. She wanted to devour him, but he pushed her back placing both hands on her shoulders and drank her in with his eyes. Then he embraced her again and declared, "I'm glad you're back."

"Me, too."

He bent down to pick up her bags and told her he had some great news. As she followed him out of the building he insisted she guess. Simon liked to play the guess-what-it-is game; she, however, found it annoying at times. The last time she had to guess something big, something she'd never guess, was his first gallery showing. Her agent Roz had asked to see his other work and when she did she was so impressed she told her friend Cyndi, a gallery owner. Cyndi saw his work, fell in love, and wanted to be the one to 'discover' him. There were thirty pieces in that show; all but seven sold. Ten sold for five figures—the rest sold for four. All in all it was a lucrative first showing. Sometimes she would wonder how Simon got were he was so quickly. And then she would remember the six degrees of separation that make up anyone's life, but particularly those that are successful. At those times she would thank God for Professor Stiles, who set the ball in motion.

When they hit the parking deck, Simon said to look for Row G. She made several futile attempts to guess the mysterious news before spotting their blue Nissan Maxima at the end of the aisle.

"You were right. Row G," she said, pointing to the sign hanging directly over the car with a bright red C on it.

He laughed, "Well, what do you want? You're the writer. I's just a poor painter, ma'am."

"Are you going to tell me?"

Opening the trunk he set the bags in and continued to tease her. "Guess."

"You were commissioned to do a portrait of Madonna. That's my guess. Now fucking tell me already."

He escorted her around to the passenger side of the car and opened the door. "I was offered a commission to design a set for an off-Broadway show."

"Evidently," he began as he turned the car on, "the director saw my show last May and has been a big fan of your stories, so he's seen my illustrations, and he seems to think my style is perfect for his vision."

Last May's showing, she thought to herself, was the third in less than three years. In the art world there was quite a buzz about her husband. But a set design seemed to be a stretch. She asked what it entailed.

"I'll have to wait and see. But it sounds like something different. I think it will be fun."

"Sounds great."

"Would you look back for me, please?"

"Sure." She turned her head to see if it was clear and when it was, gave him the go ahead.

"Tell me about your trip."

She filled him in the details of her trip omitting not what she thought he didn't need to know, but more or less what she knew might hurt him. The trip had been a dangerous one, but necessary. She had missed Mr. Martineli's funeral through no fault of her own, but it had bothered her all these years, and what she felt for him was nothing compared to what she felt for Mrs. Martineli.

As he moved out onto the parkway he said, "I'm sorry about Mrs. M., baby, really I am."

She let her hand brush against his thigh and he reached down and took it in his. "Thank you. And I'm sorry I missed your show."

"Well, it's not like you haven't seen the stuff before."

"How'd you do?"

"Let's just say there's definitely room now to paint more."

She stroked the inside of his palm with her finger. "Will you be painting tonight?"

He squeezed her hand tightly to stop her. "We're not going to be doing anything other than explaining to the cops why we wrapped the car around a telephone pole if you don't stop that."

"Why?"

He smiled at her, "Ms. Russell, I do believe you are getting fresh with me, and you know it."

"What if I am?" She grinned at him and then stopped teasing knowing full well they would have to pull over soon and rip each other's clothes off if she didn't.

"Before the windows steam up why don't you tell me more about the trip?"

His wanting all the details was beginning to annoy her. She didn't want to talk about the trip. She wanted to forget the trip. She knew he wanted to know what Mindy looked like and if she was still attracted to her. But she didn't want to tell him. Not now and probably not ever if she could help it. She wanted to hear more about the show. She wanted to stay focused in the present.

He told her he sold seven out of the twenty pieces in the first evening, four the following, and Cyndi, the gallery owner, was certain the rest would be gone before the end of the month.

She was glad Simon's work sold so well, not just because it helped pay the bills but also because he was able to do what he actually loved to do. In the summers during school when he would have to work for tuition, there wouldn't be enough time to paint. He could spend every waking hour he wasn't working painting, but it would never be enough time. Now he could paint from morning until suppertime and sometimes several hours after and he was happy. Sometimes at night if he couldn't sleep, he would get up and paint. Converting the attic into a studio was the smartest thing they ever did. She wasn't as prolific as Simon. She tried to write every day for several hours, but sometimes the stories weren't there. Simon never had that problem. When she couldn't write she would ask to borrow his muse and he would tell her she was his muse. But she knew better. She knew that Simon was born to paint. From the moment he held a paint brush he was hooked.

Simon opened the door to their brownstone and she took a deep breath inhaling the familiar scent of home. She loved the old house. She never thought she'd like living in the city, but when Simon's parents gave them the money to buy the house, it made everything possible. They had a safe haven tucked neatly into a fast-paced city. For her it was the best of both worlds.

Simon carried her suitcase up to the bedroom and she locked the door and followed him. He deposited the suitcases onto the bed, turned around and bumped into her.

"Sorry."

She let her arms encircle him and looked into his glowing yellow-green eyes. "I'm not."

He laughed. "You weren't kidding in the car, were you?"

Her hands pulled his polo shirt out of his pants and quickly slipped under to the taut skin below. Sliding her hands up his smooth, muscular back, she eased the polo shirt off and let it tumble to the floor. His chest was hairless, which she liked, and finely chiseled from the weights he lifted every morning after their run.

"I think I should warn you I made dinner."

She kissed him, letting his moustache tickle her upper lip.

"Your favorite," he added between kisses, trying to maintain his cool.

She loosened his belt and undid the button fly jeans slowly while she trailed kisses down his neck.

"Chicken Florentine," he managed to breathe as she pushed his jeans down.

"Let's work up an appetite first." She smiled and unbuttoned her shirt. She had purposely not worn a bra and she let her shirt fall to the floor with the rest of his things.

He kissed her quickly, reaching for the zipper on her pants. "You're the boss," he murmured.

She took his head in her hands and guided his lips to her breast.

He responded, as he always did, taking her in with a passion which never ceased to amaze her. And yet, she could not seem to get enough of him.

She raised her head from his chest and kissed him. She wanted to feel him inside her again.

He caught her face in his hands. "Whoa, slow down, girl."

* * * *

She shifted positions so she was directly over him, letting her weight rest against him. His eyes had lost some of their yellow glow. They muddied slightly, as they did when he was deep in thought. "What's wrong?"

He kissed her lightly on the lips. "Alex, as much as I want to make love to you all night long, I need a little rest once in a while."

The difference between men and women, she mused. Mindy and I could make love all night long.

He let his hand brush against her forehead as he tucked a lock of her hair behind her ear, "Maybe we could just lie here and talk."

She let her cheek fall onto his shoulder and he wrapped his arms around her, keeping the warmth of the moment alive. Talk. From the time she left Mindy until the alcohol took effect on the plane, she had thought about all that had transpired. None of it made any sense to her and at the same time it made perfect sense. Mindy hadn't changed. She was the same woman she was five years ago. She thought it was almost as if the break up was a huge mistake Mindy had no idea how to undo.

She and Simon had changed over the years, as a result of success perhaps, or just each other's company. They had changed, if for no other reason than their direction in life. Before she wrote her first short story, she had no idea she would be a writer.

She and Mindy would plan their future together and she would be a basketball star. But when the pros came looking, she decided she didn't want to be on tour and away from Simon. Her knee had begun to give her trouble and the prospect of blowing it out in her first year terrified her. She wanted to settle down. She had found something she loved as much as basketball. She had found writing.

"Simon," she began slowly, "is it—I mean do you—"

He tilted her face toward his. "What, baby?"

"Are you happy with me?"

"Oh, honey," he sighed, "don't you know?"

She did, but she needed to hear it. "Just humor me, Simon."

"Okay, how about poetry? How do I love thee, let me count the ways…"

"I'm not being funny."

He sobered up. "She really got to you. Didn't she?"

"Don't be silly."

"Silly?" He sat up. "You come home, grab me, make love to me like a condemned woman, and then ask me if I love you, and *I'm* being silly?"

"You didn't answer the question."

"I love you. Call me crazy, but I always have, and if I were to venture an educated guess, I'd say I always will."

"Why?"

He sank back into his pillow. "Is this a trick question?" Then without waiting for an answer he turned it on her. "Why do you love me?"

"I don't know."

He grabbed his heart. "Ow—that hurts."

She kissed her finger and touched it to his heart. "I do know." She said. "I love you because with you I am part of something bigger than myself, and yet, I am also an individual. I can be myself." How's that for state-of-the-art bullshit?

"You want me to top that?"

She couldn't explain it to him. It wasn't a matter of topping it. She's spent the entire plane ride trying to find the answer. Why did she love Simon? Why did she love Mindy? Did she love Simon more than Mindy or Mindy more than Simon? Was it possible to love them both, but in different ways? With Mindy she could be herself and it didn't matter to her one way or the other if she was in a good mood or a bad mood. What mattered was she loved her no matter what. And then all of a sudden she didn't. So, she wondered now, was she really herself with Simon? Did she ever really let him in? Or was there a part of her holding back, a part she would never let anyone see again, a part of her that couldn't take that kind of pain again. "Look, you're the one who wanted to talk. So, answer the question."

"I said, talk, not discuss the inner workings and passions of our lives. There's a difference, you know."

He could be a real pest when he wanted to be, she thought, but he was adorable. "Should we discuss the weather?"

"Sure. Kick the machine into gear, and then stop it in mid-motion."

She laughed.

"Why do I love you?" He repeated the question out loud. "Let's see. You're very beautiful, even though you don't sit still when I try and paint you. You're very talented, and no one has inspired or challenged me creatively the way you do. You listen well. You cook well…well, relatively. In bed, well, you could kill a man who wasn't in good physical health with passion, but what do I love about you? Let me think."

"Okay, you win. Let's talk about something else."

"That didn't answer the question?"

She smiled. "It did."

"Good." He pushed her back and pinned her hands down as he kissed her. She could feel the weight of his body pressing down on hers and the tip of his growing erection against her thigh. "Want to have another go at it?"

"Another go at it?"

"I'm sorry the semantics of that approach weren't very eloquent or conducive to romance."

"Simon, I want a baby."

"Of course, that was also very blatant."

"I don't understand why we can't get it right."

He looked hurt, like she had wounded his sexual pride. "Well, I wouldn't say we can't get it right. Would you?"

"I'm sorry; that was a poor choice of words."

He softened. "Maybe it's just not the right time for us."

"Or maybe once was all—"

"Shh," he touched his finger to her lips. "I know it hurts, but it's bound to happen again. We just have to let it."

"Simon, I'm not getting any younger."

"I hadn't noticed."

"You've been sniffing too much turpentine."

"Well, it's a dirty job, but someone has to do it."

She pulled him closer and kissed him. "I missed you."

"Well, things were kinda lonely here without you." He looked deep into her eyes. "I love you so much, Alex. I just want to make you happy."

"You do." She closed her eyes as his lips found hers and tried to lose herself in the moment.

Later that evening her dreams dampened her happiness quicker than a strong gust of wind extinguishes a flame.

There was blood gushing out of the palm of her hand, spreading over the leg of her sweatpants. She curled up into the fetal position, shaking. And the red became fuzzy as tears filled her eyes.

"Jesus Christ!" Simon exclaimed as he entered the room. His sneakers crunched as he stepped on the pieces of glass littering the floor. "What the—" He bent down beside her. "Alex, what did you—"

He stopped when he saw her hand. "Oh, my God, you're bleeding!" He touched her shoulder as he knelt beside her.

She pulled away. "Don't touch me."

"Hey, I just want to help. That's all." His voice was soft, stroking her gently with his words. "Why don't you tell me what happened?"

"There's nothing to…" She tried to wipe her face with her hand and winced as the blood mingled with her tears. "Ow! God, just leave me alone."

He was moving about now, gathering the items he needed to tend to her hand. "I'm not leaving."

"Please," she cried.

He knelt and took her hand in his. "I only want to help."

"Don't you understand? No one can help." She pulled her hand away from him.

"They can if you let them." He seized her hand this time and wiped the blood from it. "Why don't you try me?"

"Because I want her!" She screamed and punched him in the chest. The punch was hard; she could feel her knuckles tingle. Though he barely flinched, she could see pain in his eyes replacing some of the concern. But he didn't let go of her hand.

"Well, she's not here. I am." He poured peroxide over her hand and she winced, trying to pull away as it burned into the open cut. "What went on here tonight?"

She tried to explain it to him, but it sounded stupid as it came out. One of her basketball friends had told her when she got pissed she broke things—plates, glasses, bottles, anything that would shatter. Just the shear exhilaration of breaking those items would help erase some of the pain. But she was sobbing now, and so what could have been a simple explanation turned into babbling.

He wrapped a bandage around her hand. "Take your time, Alex. Who told you about the bottles?"

The friend had said she would feel...cleansed, exhausted...she said it would make the pain go away. Simon knew she was in pain. She had been ever since Mindy left. She had no way of getting in touch with her. She wouldn't take her calls, wouldn't return her letters, her whole future had been yanked like a carpet out from under her. She would have tried anything to make the pain go away.

"There must be a whole case of bottles here."

"It didn't help." She cried. "It didn't help! I still hurt."

"I know." He said reaching out.

She pulled away from him. "No, you don't know." She looked at him. All he had tried to do for the past several weeks was comfort her. He kept trying to touch her, but she didn't want to be touched by him. She wanted Mindy's hands, Mindy's arms around her. It was Mindy's lips she wanted kissing her tears away. She didn't want to hurt him, but he need to know. "I just want it to go away. I *want the pain to stop, just for an hour or two, but it won't go away. It won't go away! It won't..."*

"Alex!"

Simon's hands were on her shoulders. She felt his fingers press into the muscles, holding her firmly against the bed so she would stop thrashing about. His voice was tender, but firm. "It's a dream. Wake up, honey. It's just a dream."

She let him pull her into his arms, seeking his warmth, his strength. "Just a dream?"

"That's all, baby." He stroked her hair and kissed her forehead lightly. "Just a dream."

"Just a dream." She kept repeating his words letting them calm her.

"That's better."

As much as she wanted him to soothe her now, to make everything all right, her stomach was churning violently and a part of her knew she wasn't just dreaming. She had a scar running across the length of her palm. She was aware of it when the weather was damp for long periods of time, as it would ache. For the longest time she believed it was something left over from her childhood. Simon told her he didn't know what it was from and Mindy wasn't around to ask. Mindy would have known, she told herself. But Simon had known only bits and pieces. She and Simon were strictly on a need-to-know basis. She had to keep it that way for a long time to protect herself. No one would ever do to her what Mindy did.

Slowly, she held the hand up to see the scar. The only light in the room was from the streetlight across the way. But she could see the faint line. She traced it with her finger, feeling the slight bump were the skin had met and knitted itself back together. And she gasped. "It was real." She whispered, and then she sought out Simon's eyes. Knowing he knew, had known all these years, she asked.

"I'm sure it seemed that way. Dreams are very vivid."

Even now he tried to pretend it hadn't happened. But she knew it wasn't a dream, but rather a memory she had buried so deeply it could only resurface in a dream. "No, it happened."
Simon kissed her forehead. "Okay, don't get excited." He pulled her back into a tight embrace. His razor stubble scraped against her cheek.

He had a lot of nerve, she thought, trying to comfort her when he could have just told her. "Was it a break down?"

"No," he said, as if the word could disguise the tone in his voice. "Well, maybe a little one," he admitted.

"Why didn't you tell me when I asked?"

He took her hand in his and traced the scar with his finger. "I'm sorry. I just wanted to forget that time in our lives." His eyes met hers. "It was wrong of me. I know. It's just there were some bad times that followed. I guess I just wanted to forget about it, too." He moved a lock of hair off her forehead and rested his hand under her chin. "You still love her, don't you?"

For the first time in a very long time, she had no desire to answer his question. But she had nowhere to go and his eyes were waiting. She wondered what he wanted her to say. Did he want her to tell him she never stopped loving Mindy? How could anyone believe love could be unconditional, that it could survive pain and suffering? That is how she loved her.

"I don't want to have to read it in your eyes, Alex. I want you to tell me."

"Does it make a difference?" She asked softly, trying to soothe him with her voice.

"There's something buzzing around in your head. Something dormant until now…"

"Even if there is something, I don't want to talk about it."

"We need to talk about it," he persisted.

She wondered why she could write so well, but when it came to speaking, she had trouble. "It doesn't have anything to do with you. I love you." She did love him. She had loved him these past five years. She would walk through fire for him. How could he not know?

He tried to explain their lives were linked so it did have to do with him. There was no comforting him. She could see that.

"You have an unusual way of keeping things inside and letting them build up for years like a time bomb. And then, bam!" He clapped his hands together for emphasis. "They all explode and it's not a pretty sight. I've seen it. And I don't mean the dream tonight, either."

"What are you talking about?"

"Nothing." He threw the covers back and got out of bed. He pulled his pants on quickly, all the while mumbling to himself. "I can't believe after all she put you through, after all we've been through..." He slipped on his shoes and shouted at her, "I just can't believe you still have feelings for her."

He rarely raised his voice to her. She tried to reach for him, but he pulled away. When she asked him where he was going he said he was going to take a walk. She tried to get him to stay. "Simon, I don't know what you're talking about."

"Yes, you do, Alex."

He was right. She did know what he was talking about. But she thought they weren't going to talk about it anymore and it seemed to keep coming up. "If you're talking about the miscarriage, I think I handled it pretty well considering..."

"I didn't say you didn't, but look at what it unleashed."

Always the word 'miscarriage' would open up a closet in the dark recess of her mind where everything had been shut and locked up. Then memories would tumble out on top of her. Only lately had she learned to step aside and avoid being buried in the rubble. She had tried to explain to him how she felt, but he couldn't understand. He would just tell her there was absolutely no reason to feel that way. When she would point out the statistics on battered children growing up to be batterers, he would tell her she wasn't a statistic.

"Simon, just because you love me doesn't mean I might not end up that way."

"But you don't have that kind of anger in you, Alex, and you know what it's like." He sat on the edge of the bed.

She touched his cheek, liking the softness of his beard under her fingertips. "Let's just let it lie." How could she ever explain the abuse to him. The scars she had were something that terrified him. The first time they made love she wanted the lights out. He assumed it was because she was shy, but she really wasn't ready for him to see the scars. Most of them could be passed over easily, but the ones on her back could not be disguised. She knew he felt them. She could see it on his face and she knew he wanted to ask, but he was afraid. In the morning, she awoke in his arms. He was looking at her and carefully tracing the scars on her back with his fingers. She could see his eyes cloud with tears. Kissing him lightly she told him it was okay, and then she told him what had happened and it terrified him.

Alex prayed he was right that all the anger in her heart had been laid to rest. Only Mindy could understand the true nature of the anger because they had both lived through it.

"It hurts me to see you torture yourself that way."

"I don't do it to torture myself, or to hurt you."

"Sometimes you just think too much. Just like I know what you're thinking right now, Alex. Talk to me, please. I want to understand."

So did she. How could she explain something to him she didn't understand herself? She tried to tell him he needed to be patient.

"I guess you're not really giving me a choice, are you?"

"No."

He stood up. "Well, then, I'm going for that walk."

"Simon, remember what your mother said about going to bed angry."

"That's why I'm taking a walk." He pulled the bedroom door closed behind him and she heard the quiet thud of his docksiders against the steps.

She rubbed the tip of her thumb back and forth over her scar trying to remember. Just like the genie pops out of the lamp, memories seemed to pop back into her head. Simon took her to the emergency room. The doctor stitched her hand and gave her something to calm her nerves. After that it was a blur.

Knowing Simon would be a while, she closed her eyes and tried to sleep.

She awoke at 3:15 a.m. When she reached for Simon, she only found an empty space in the bed. Her heart stopped for a moment, thinking something had happened to him. She got up and almost tripped over his shoes. When he wasn't in the kitchen or the family room, she knew exactly where he was.

He was slapping a thick coat of gesso onto a canvas when she went up behind him and slid her arms around his waist. "I reached for you and you weren't there."

His back stiffened. "Now you know how I feel."

"That's not fair."

"What's not fair about it?"

"I am here for you." She rested her cheek against his shoulder.

He took her hands from around him and turned to look at her. "Alex, I could take you back into our bedroom and make love to you all night and all you'd be thinking about would be Mindy!"

"That's not true." She tightened her hug, but he kept his silence. "Simon, talk to me."

"When I'm ready I will."
She let go of him. "Oh, now you're being childish."

He set his paintbrush down and turned to face her. "And you're not?"

"I don't know how I feel, God damn it."

"So maybe I can help you set things straight."

"No pun intended?" She was the one pulling away now.

"Alex, I'm not just your husband, I'm your friend. Remember?"

"How could I forget?"

He pulled away, and brushing her hair back off her forehead, he looked directly into her eyes and asked again, "You still love her, don't you?"

She couldn't answer him. She loved her at one time more than anything or anyone...but she thought it was a long time ago. And he was right, Mindy had hurt her. She hurt her more than she imagined anyone could. But despite all that she loved her.

But she loved him too. How could he not see that?

"You do." He pulled away.

"Simon, I love you."

"Alex, I need to be alone right now."

He was closing off. He didn't do it often. But when he did it was best to back off. And she had no right to be angry with him; he was only reacting to her. She could try to lie to him, but he would see right through that. "All right." She pulled the studio door shut behind her.

six

She stepped out onto her stoop and realized it had been raining for a while. Where a downpour would draw out smells from the earth in the country and the distinct smell of worms and dirt would fill the air, in the city the odors lingering in the air were man-made. The smell of urine would permeate the air on less-traveled streets; garbage sitting in dumpsters would waft out filling the air with a sickeningly sweet, overripe stench. Puddles would form at the corners of streets—the kind of puddles that made one think even the most chivalrous gentlemen would not have a cape large enough to allow passage without drenching your shoes. Fortunately jay walking in New York was a fine art.

She opened her umbrella and walked out into the pelting water. She debated hailing a taxi to preserve her blue rayon pants. But walking always gave her a chance to think and, as usual, she chose to put another mile on her sneakers.

Simon had been acting very bizarre and was locked in his studio again when she left. Since they'd married Simon had never locked his studio but ever since she returned, his daily routine took an alarming pattern. At eight he would rise, run with her in silence, lift weights, shower, grab something for breakfast, and retreat into his studio until seven, when he would resurface for dinner. The dinner would be conducted with a minimal amount of conversation, just enough to remain civil. And then he would retreat to his studio again until eleven when he would return to their bed.

She could not imagine what he was working on. All she could surmise was the level of energy he was expending. Simon was always an artist first, a man second. When he worked, art flowed through his veins, his heart beat at a different rate, and all other life forms around him ceased to exist. Occasionally, he would become almost obsessed, but he hadn't in quite a while.

At first, she would get frightened seeing how drained he would get, how distant he seemed, but on those nights when he returned to their bed they would have sex, and then he would wrap her in his arms and sleep. She had thought since the talking ceased the sex would stop, too. But, she had learned the difference between fucking and making love. Simon had taught her that. When he was obsessed with his work the sex was different, it always had been. Simon was an attentive lover, and in their first days together he had been slow and gentle, taking his time, making sure she wanted his mouth on her, his hands on her, in her. She remembered feeling his penis harden against her thigh and then it seemed like hours before she felt him inside her. When he finally did enter her, she had already come twice, once in his mouth and then again as he explored her with his fingers. He moved slowly, looking deep into her eyes for approval of the one sexual act he thought was new to her, and then he slid inside. Her legs wrapped around him, fingers pressed into the muscles on his shoulder blades and they found a rhythm. And she remembered him crying out, "Oh, sweet Jesus!" just as he came.

But on the nights he painted, the sex was raw. At first it had scared her. Not because it was raw, but because it was more one-sided than usual. On nights Simon wasn't himself, she felt she could have been almost anyone lying beneath him. There was hardly any foreplay just enough to get her wet, minimal eye contact, no holy incantations when he came, and she was never satisfied. But when it was over he would gather her into his arms, pulling her back into his chest until there was no space between them, lock his arms around her and whisper in her ear, "Thank you." Or sometimes, "I love you, Alex."

She had asked to see the painting and he told her she had to wait until it was finished. She knew there would be no further discussion, no persuasion, for when Simon made up his mind there was no changing it.

A glance around the café told her Roz would be late as usual. She stepped into the ladies room immediately and changed her shoes. Then she washed her hands, brushed the hair back off her forehead, straightening the kinks blown in by the wind, and went back into the dining room to wait for Roz.

In what had become a habit, she informed the waitress she was waiting for Ms. Glasgow and the waitress showed her to the table. She had spent the entire morning watching children's cartoons to prepare for the meeting. Unfortunately for Roz, her three hours of television had done nothing to convince her to make this deal.

"Would you care for something to drink?" the waitress asked.

"A glass of chardonnay, thank you." She noticed she was a lovely girl, with dark brown hair pulled back into a single braid trailing down her back. Her eyes were a light chocolate color and she had a pleasant smile. It struck her that she rarely looked at women any more. There used to be a time when she looked all the time. Mindy used to punch her in the arm and tell her to stop. And then she would tell her she could window shop as long as she wasn't looking to buy. Both of them knew it was a game they played, as they adored each other.

"Glass? Make it bottle!" Roz exclaimed, kissing her cheek before sliding into the chair across from her. "I'd apologize for being late but it's so fashionable, I just can't get used to being on time."

She studied her friend dressed in a white linen suit with a black silk blouse opened to the third button to reveal just a hint of cleavage. Her brown hair was cut short, parted at the side and spiked a bit at the top. She wore dangling earrings that looked more like small wind chimes than actual earrings. Since the day she had met her Roz's age remained a mystery, despite the lines beginning to form under her brilliant blue-gray eyes. Her manner and the way she carried herself had a certain sophistication peppered by a youthful playfulness.

"But seriously," she continued, "I do hate being late for you. Especially with a deal like this sitting in my pocket. Have you had time to think about it?"

"I'm fine, and how are you, Roz?"

Roz laughed and her eyes danced.

She had no doubt Roz could play the game, but she had never played it with her. She remembered the first meeting.

* * *

Dr. Stiles had sent her the manuscript and then she and Simon had taken the bus into New York.
The waiting room was overly modern and fairly antiseptic—like a doctor's office, almost. The receptionist, a gaunt young woman with long red hair and leopard skin cat-eye glasses, wore a form-fitting dress leaving nothing to the imagination. Simon tried initiating a debate on whether or not cat woman, as he so aptly called her, was wearing a thong or going commando. She

understood he was trying to keep her relaxed and amused, and he was doing a good job. Then cat woman called her name and she rose slowly. Simon wished her luck and she followed cat woman back into an office overlooking Fifth Avenue. Roz rose from behind a huge wooden desk overflowing with manuscripts and took Alex's hand firmly in her own. She didn't remember too much after that initial handshake, other than she liked Roz immediately. Maybe because she reminded her of Professor Stiles, maybe it was her quick wit, or maybe it was just a feeling she could trust her. Even though Professor Stiles had said it was a long shot, Roz was pleasant enough to look at Simon's illustrations. She respected the fact that Roz would humor her and play out the scene for her college roommate's sake. But when she cleared a space on her desk to let Simon lay his portfolio down, and flipped through his sample pages, she grinned from ear to ear. They both left her office with a very large legal document in hand to read.

* * *

"Did I forget the pleasantries? How silly of me, but you know how I get when I'm excited."

"All too well."

The waitress brought a bottle of chardonnay, poured into Roz's glass as she fumbled through her briefcase. Roz tasted the wine and nodded, and then the glasses were filled.

She sipped her wine as Roz outlined the proposal for her. She had promised Simon she would pay attention and keep an open mind, but she really didn't find this as flattering as everyone else seemed to think it was. Having no children made her books almost like babies to her, and the fact she and Simon worked on them together made them even more precious than she ever imagined they could be. But Roz seemed impressed with the two individuals who wanted to option the book. The waitress returned to take their order but they had to send her away confessing they hadn't even looked at the menu.

Once they had ordered, Roz settled back in her chair and smiled. "Alex, can we talk?"

"We can try."

"I am very excited about this."

"I hadn't noticed."

"Please, darling, this is the only excitement I've had in months."

"I find that hard to believe." Roz was the kind of woman men loved, and invariably they would flock to her when she walked down the street. The mystique was one she shared with Mindy.

She laughed. "Well, I suppose this is a slow season for love. Anyway back to the subject at hand. This is the first substantial offer that would take us to another level. I don't have to tell you children's authors are under paid. This is a very substantial offer, Alex. I brought the paperwork, a first treatment, and story boards for you to take a look at."

A large manila envelope was placed on the table beside her and Roz refilled the wine glass. "Of course you'll want to take them home and read them."

"You're sure you don't want me to read them now?"

"Could you?"

"No problem." She picked up the manila envelope and undid the clasp.

"Actually, I know you'll want Simon to have a look as well."

"If I can pry him away from his studio."

"What's this? Trouble in paradise?"

"No. Paradise seems to be holding up remarkably well…"

"Because you know if you ever tire of him I will be more than happy to take him in."

"I doubt I'll tire of him."

"True. Perfection is hard to tire of."

Perfection, she thought, interesting Simon appeared that way. On some level he was really perfect, but no one was totally perfect, were they? "Since you brought the subject up—" She ran her finger around the edge of her wine glass as she decided whether or not to ask her question. Roz had a certain wisdom and understanding about people and situations, the same wisdom that Simon had, and that she possessed at times, but never when it concerned her own situations.

"I'm asking you this because you've been in love more than once."

"Now, you have my attention. What?"

"Do you think you can be attracted to someone you had a relationship with a long time ago?"

"Of course." She set her glass down. "How long ago?"

"Five years."

"If it was a very passionate relationship it could withstand any amount of time. Especially if you parted on good terms..."

"And if you didn't part on good terms?"

She looked at her for a moment. "Why do you want to know?"

"Just curious."

"Thinking about changing your genre? Writing an adult novel perhaps?"

She had thought about it several times. Simon even encouraged her to, but she still wasn't ready to bare her soul to the world. "No."

"And you're not thinking of leaving Simon?"

The waitress returned with their food and set it down before them. She just shook her head to indicate no.

"Well, when they leave me, I tell myself it's over." She cut into her crepe and took a bite, then moaned a sigh of approval.

"So you wouldn't feel anything?" She took a bite of her seafood salad while she waited for an answer.

"Darling, you know me. What I say and what I do are two very different things."

"Then it's perfectly natural to feel something, even if you don't want to?"

"Attractions are funny things, my dear." She held out her fork with a piece of crepe on it, "Try this. It's exquisite."

She took the fork and let the cheese and crab melt in her mouth awakening every taste bud. "This," she said handing back the fork, "is terrific."

"Isn't it?" She took another bite, followed by a sip of wine. "As I was saying, attractions are funny things. Some come, some go, some get better with age, and I guess the answer is yes. But it would have to have been a very strong relationship."

"Thank you." She took another bite of her salad and wished she had ordered the crepe. "Now, tell me more about this cartoon venture."

" 'Drop it, Roz.' I can take a hint."

She filled both their glasses with more wine. She thought, Why be so damn cryptic? Just tell her. "I'm sorry. I don't mean to play games with you. It's really not my style."

"No, it isn't. And you have piqued my curiosity."

"It killed the cat, you know."

"Why, Alexandra, I do believe you have a few secrets. Don't you?"

"Doesn't everyone?"

"Mmm." She took another sip of wine. "Well?"

"Before Simon, I had a lover. We were both very young and…"

"He dumped you?"

"Sort of."

"Oh, do tell." After a moment, and several sips of wine, Roz said, "Okay, I'll tell you. Since you don't strike me as the May-

December type, and you turned down a pro basketball contract, I'm going to say he was a she."

"It's not public knowledge. But, I'm certainly not ashamed of it either."

"Does Simon know?"

"From the beginning." She took another bite of her salad, amazed at how good she felt for actually admitting it. "I couldn't be with someone who didn't know who I really was."

She watched as Roz fought the urge to smile. "And she's back?"

She explained the situation and finished by saying, "Don't get me wrong. I love Simon."

"I have no doubt about that."

She picked up her wine glass and set it back down. "I don't really know what I'm trying to say."

Roz couldn't help herself now. She was smiling. Alex thought of Mrs. Martineli who used to say, "She looked like the cat that swallowed the canary." This was the first time she knew what that meant. Roz reached over to fill her wine glass and finish off the bottle.

"What is so funny?"

"Nothing, Alex, really."

"What?"

"I just think it's interesting you have a past." She raised her glass. "Somehow it makes you more human."

"What exactly do you mean by that?"

"You never say much about your past. It's as if your life began the day you met me, that's all."

"Well, that's not true."

"I know. I'm just saying it's interesting to know you actually did have an adolescence that's all. Now I understand your writing a bit better."

The waitress returned to see if everything was all right and they stopped their conversation long enough to tell her it was wonderful.

Roz kept going. "I can see why you went straight for Simon though. True perfection is hard to pass up."

"I'm glad I didn't pass him up."

"Really?" Her eyebrows were raised now. "It sounds like you're questioning."

"No." *Yes, you are Alex; don't lie to the woman.* "I guess I'm just nostalgic."

"Nostalgia is fine, darling. Just don't forget what you have in the present."

"I'm not, Roz."

"Well, enough of this. I'm certainly not going to lecture you; you're a big girl now. You know what you're doing."

If only that were true. I don't have a fucking clue what I'm doing. She felt like she was drowning in a flood of old feelings. She was treading to keep her head above the water, but there didn't seem to be any outlet. She was trapped.

"Have some more to drink."

"Are you trying to get me drunk?"

"How could you say such a thing, Alexandra?"

"You keep filling my glass. I know you know I don't want to hear about this cartoon thing. Do you think you can ply me with alcohol?"

"I'll ply you with whatever it takes to get you to take this deal. It's good for your career and it won't be bad on your bank account either. Think franchising!"

"Or yours." She said raising her glass.

"I'm going to pretend you didn't say that." Roz laughed and went on to tell her the two young filmmakers were NYU grads who had gotten some serious funding to start their own animation company and her book would be their first project. She brought along videos of some of their work and reminded her how she started out.

She explained to Roz she was afraid they would do what so many filmmakers did when they got their hands on a book, "fuck it up."

"You are not the first author to utter those words. And I'm sure you won't be the last. Alex, fear is a very healthy emotion for an artist. It keeps you on your toes."

"If I wanted to be on my toes, I'd have taken up ballet."

"Touché."

"If I promise to think this over, will you stop harping on it?"

"Promise?"

She crossed her heart with her finger. "You have my word."

"All right, then. We can change the subject."

"What about Simon's illustrations?"

"Simon's not a cartoonist." She took a fork full of her salad.

"No, but he created the characters."

"You created the characters, my dear." Roz reminded her.

"You know what I mean."

She did and she agreed to discuss it if Simon felt the need to pursue it, but she wanted her to just take everything home read it over, look at it, and think about it for a few days. "Don't make any rash decisions."

"Yes, ma'am."

"And watch that ma'am thing. Dessert?"

"Absolutely."

seven

She arrived home to find the mail on the kitchen table as usual. On top of the stack of bills and magazines sat a rose-colored envelope with familiar handwriting on it. The corner of the envelope was smudged with paint Simon had tried to wipe off. She smiled at the idea of him holding the envelope up to the light to see if he could read the contents. Setting the letter to the side, she opened the bills, put them in order of importance. Then she opened a can of diet soda and took the pile of mail into her study. She stuck the bills on the desk in the 'to be paid' pile, set the magazines on the coffee table, and folded Mindy's letter so it fit in her back pocket. Then she went upstairs to Simon's studio.

Sting's voice drifted out from under a crack in the door, and she stopped to listen a moment.

Simon was singing at the top of his lungs on the other side of the door, "Free, free, set them free. If you love somebody…" His strong tenor voice was more suited for a Sondheim or Porter tune.

Knocking on the door, she let him know she was back. The music was turned down and Simon asked how things went with Roz. She told him they had homework to do. She tried to see the painting again, but was turned away. As she turned to walk away, she heard him ask, "What did Mindy have to say?"

"Don't know. Didn't open it yet."

"What are you waiting for?"

She pulled the letter out of her back pocket. The contents strained against the envelope suggesting it was a long missive. "I'm not sure."

He was standing in front of her now, closing the door behind him. A streak of cadmium red ran the length of his left cheekbone, fanning out under his eye. His white tee shirt splattered with paint from a lifetime of painting, clung to his body, which had a thin coat of perspiration on it making him look downright shiny. He reached down and took the letter from her hand and sniffed it. "I bet it's a love letter."

"Grow up." She snatched the letter back from him and noticed there was fresh paint on the envelope. "Simon, look what you've done."

"Sorry. I didn't realize. Here." He pulled a paint rag from the back pocket of his faded Levi's and wiped as much paint off as he could. "Here." He handed it back to her. "I'd kiss you, but I think I have paint on my face."

"You do. But, I wish you would anyway."

"That's what I was afraid of."

She raised her hand to swat him and he caught it in his clean hand.

"Just remember, the other hand has paint on it," he cautioned. Then leaned over and pecked her lightly on the lips. "Let me know what it says."

You call that a kiss? "I will."

He released her hand and disappeared back into the studio.

She took the letter into her bedroom, turned on the radio, and sat on the bed. Carefully she tore open the envelope trying not to damage the multiple pages. Then she discarded the paint-covered envelope in the trash.

The notepaper was also rose-colored with embossed roses around the edges. She unfolded the letter and read.

Dear Alex,

Willie and I have been going through Mother's things, so I am still at home. If it can really be called a "home" after both of your parents are dead. If it weren't for Willie I don't think I would have made it through this last week.

And I wanted you to know how much it meant to me, to us, to have you here again. I never thought I would see you again. I'm glad I was wrong. It's too bad it took my mother dying to bring us back together. I think she would be happy to know we were talking again. She always loved you like one of her own. You know that, don't you?

Mark and I are going to take the house. It's what my mother left us. She left the guest cottage to Willie, since he's already living there, but she thought since we had the children, we should have the house.

We won't move until the end of summer, but we want to be settled by the fall so Alex can start daycare here. Mark feels we should move, and so does Willie, but I'm not so sure.

I had to write and tell you I'm so glad we are on speaking terms again. I hope when we get settled into our new house you will come and visit. I'd so love for you to meet my children. And Alex is a big fan of your books; it would be such a thrill for him to finally meet you.

And I look forward to spending time with you when we don't have anything clouding our time together. I hope this finds you well, and I'll hear from you soon.

I love you,
Mindy

Setting the letter down on the nightstand, she lay back, sinking into her pillow, and thought about what the letter had really said. If, in fact, she had said anything at all other than she was glad they were friends. I love you, Mindy. What was that about?

Then she thought about visiting Mindy at the Martineli's house. Simon would love that. He always wanted to know where she had grown up. He'd walk into the room she used to sleep in and take one look at the waterbed and know she had lied to him about waterbeds all these years.

She sat up, tucked the letter back into her pocket and went down to her study. Her computer hadn't been used in days and pages of *The Reluctant Knight* were scattered across the desk. Settling into her chair, she quickly tidied up the desk, making neat stacks of papers and bills, and turned on the computer.

Accessing Word, she opened a new document and typed:

Dear Mindy,

You letter came in the mail today and I decided to reply right away. I would think going through your mother's things would be difficult, especially since you two were so close. And I'm not at all surprised your mother left you the house. It will probably be a good move for you financially—more money to tuck away for your children's education now. However, I can understand your trepidation. There will be some adjusting to your mom not being there.

I met with my agent this afternoon to discuss "The Great Cartoon Caper" as Simon so aptly named it. She left me several videotapes, a treatment, storyboard, and contract, all of which will probably sit on my desk for several days before I have the nerve to open them. On some level this is what an author wants to happen in terms of money, but on another level I feel as if the story wouldn't be mine anymore. Perhaps it's just my insecurities showing through. Who knows? At any rate, I guess I'll have to check things out to be fair to all involved.

I haven't finished the latest installment in my children's series, but when I do I will share an advance reader's copy with you.

I hope all goes well for you in the move, and Simon and I will try to visit. I would love to meet your children. Take care of yourself and give my love to all.

Alex

She ran the letter through spell check and reread it quickly before printing it. A bland response, nothing at all like the letters they would exchange in college before the break. Writing to Mindy in those days had been a cleansing experience for Alex. Mindy's letters were equally passionate.

Pulling the stationery from the printer, she took out a pen, scrawled her name across the bottom and was debating whether or not to rip it up and start all over when Simon appeared in the doorway.

She didn't look up at first. She knew he was there from the scent of his lavender shampoo drifting into the room. She looked up to see him leaning against the doorframe, hair still wet from the shower. He was buttoning the blue paisley shirt tucking it into the wrinkled navy chinos. *Would he ever learn to hang them up properly?* she thought.

"What are you working on?"

"Just responding to the letter."

"What did she have to say?"

She recapped the contents of Mindy's letter as she folded hers and stuffed it into an envelope.

"Sounds like a nice letter."

Knowing the effort he was exerting made her love him even more. "It was."

"So, sounds like things turned out pretty well."

She peeled a stamp off the sheet and stuck it on the envelope and addressed it. "I suppose they did."

"Good."

"What are you doing showered and changed?" She teased as she looked at the time on her Swatch. "It's only four twenty-five."

"I suppose I deserved that." He sat down on the couch and tied his brown oxfords.

"I didn't mean it to be as smart-assed as it came out."

He smiled. "Sure you did."

"So, answer the question."

"I'm suddenly very hungry and I thought we could get some Chinese."

"You finished it, didn't you?"

"Pretty much."

She jumped out of her chair. "Well, let's see it."

He caught her around the waist and held her firmly against him. "Food first."

She protested, but to no avail. Finally he had to silence her with his lips. When he pulled away he whispered, "Trust me."

His hazel eyes were muddied with thoughts.

"But, when we come back, right?"

He crossed his heart with his index finger, "Scout's honor."

They went to their favorite Chinese haunt about three blocks away. Dinner was nice. They forgot about Mindy and the tension they'd been dealing with. They even flirted as they shared a plate of steamed dumplings, General Tso's chicken, and Szechuan shrimp, feeding each other with chopsticks. They talked about the cartoons he had watched as a child. Simon loved animation.

One of the things she found fascinating about Simon was his incredible mind. He was on the dean's list every semester at college. He could talk intelligently about almost any subject. But when he talked about art, you could see he understood it in the way a woodworker understands how to work with the grain of the wood or an architect understands how to keep a thirty-story building from toppling over on itself. He understood how paintings were made. He could look at a painting and dissect it, telling you what style it was painted in and how much the artist truly knew about painting. She looked at a painting and responded to the subject matter, but Simon could go beyond. He could look at a piece he didn't particularly like and still respect the craft. He could spend entire Sunday afternoons at the Met, and they did, staring at the great masters' works. They went to gallery openings in the Village to see the competition. As far as she could tell Simon painted like the masters. His subject matter might have been new but his technique was as old as Raphael.

She felt Simon challenged her. He pushed her to write, to understand her craft. She never felt she had the grasp on writing that he did on art. But his passion spurred her on and she wanted to understand writing the way he understood his art. She read constantly, thinking nothing of spending several hours a day immersed in a book. Simon would occasionally read something she had recommended just so they could talk about it. But mostly he read about art.

On Friday nights they would go to the movies come rain or shine. They would see everything from foreign films to the latest Pixar creation. The only criterion they had for choosing a film was that it be interesting. Once in a while they would succumb to choosing a movie for the star or the director, but they tried to see as many different kinds of films as they could.

Perhaps their life had become routine with their certain rituals, but that was what made it comfortable. She liked that the people behind the counter at the café around the corner knew she wanted mocha gelato and a cappuccino before she even opened her mouth to order, just as she enjoyed sitting in the same back corner booth of the Chinese restaurant. It gave her a sense of ownership.

She never quite knew what to expect when Simon finished a painting. That night was no different. She couldn't imagine what had kept him holed up in the studio. The last time it had been a painting of his brother, Peter, and himself. The piece was hauntingly beautiful. In it, two little boys held each other. The younger of the two had scraped his knee and the older brother was comforting him. One look at the canvas and you were overcome by the amount of tenderness and love. He had called it "Brothers." She was certain they would keep it, and they did. It hung in the living room above the sofa. Simon wouldn't even put it in the show, despite Cyndi's pleas.

Stopping in front of the studio door he reached in his pocket for the key. "Now, I want to tell you I've been working on it since you got back and I want your honest opinion. If you don't like it, you'll tell me, right?"

This, too, was a ritual, she thought. The "I love you and it means the world to me what you think" dance he did with her. And ultimately why? Why seek approval for his art? He knew he was talented and would paint what he wanted anyway.

She, however, needed his approval. When she finished a story she would be on pins and needles until Simon read it. When he laughed, she would want to know at what; if he made any sounds at all, she would want to know what they meant. Until finally, one day, he promised to read her stories, but only while she did something else.

She made the promise and the door was unlocked. Simon stepped into the dark room. Moonlight streaming through the skylights cast shadows on the easel in the center of the room. She breathed deeply letting the familiar aroma of oranges from the paint remover fill her nostrils. The smell comforted her, as she always associated it with Simon.

"Close your eyes while I flip the light on."

She did as she was told and then she opened them when she was told. Looking at the canvas in front of her, she felt her chest tighten. And as swiftly as it was unveiled, a stabbing pain above her right breast seized her and she needed to reach over and massage it with her fingertips.

For several moments she tried to fathom what she was seeing. Somewhere along the synapses to the brain the message was getting lost. Words were not forming, and she knew he was waiting for her to say something. She stood stunned by what she was seeing. On the canvas in vibrant colors were two naked girls locked in a passionate embrace. The two girls were lying on burgundy sheets. She knew the painting was of her and Mindy and the resemblance was eerie. Mindy lay on the bed holding her. Her head rested against Mindy's breast and her arms were locked around Mindy's waist. Mindy's hand rested in her hair, and the other cupped her arm. The sheet covered her back and Mindy's waist. The girls were obviously basking in the afterglow of sex.

Turning to look at her husband, who stood there, hands in his pockets studying her, she felt a flash of anger. She hated the fact he could crawl inside her head the way he did. Wishing she could just run from the room, she found her feet wouldn't move.

"You hate it, don't you?"

"Is that how you see it?"

"That's pretty much how it was. Isn't it?"

She couldn't look at the painting any more. Instead she looked at him. "I'm not sure what you want me to say."

"Whatever you want to say."

"What's it called?"

"The First Time."

That was it! "I can't do this with you, Simon."

She pushed past him and out of the studio and took the stairs down to the second floor. Once on the second floor she caught her breath. She could hear his footsteps behind her and she went into the bedroom and shut the door.

The painting was like looking at a memory so strong and vividly etched into her brain she would never forget it. And the quiet beauty of the painting was what plagued her. She knew how Simon felt about Mindy, and yet he painted that.

He was knocking at the door and calling her name. She just sat down on the bed and crossed her arms. The nerve. What did he think she would say? And how could he paint something like that?

"Talk to me. Please."

Talk to you. I'll talk to you. Give you a good old piece of my mind. She stood up and went into the bathroom and shut the door behind her. He had done the painting to make her talk; she knew that now. And when they did, he would pretend he didn't know it would upset her.

The door opened and she could hear him outside the bathroom door now.

"Don't be so childish. Let's talk."

She opened the door and looked at him. "Fine. You want to talk. Let's talk, Rembrandt. Why don't you start with why you did the painting?"

"Certainly not to upset you."

"And what part of it did you think wouldn't upset me?"

He looked down at his feet. "I just paint what's there."

"That's a pretty god-damn funny thing to be in your head."

"Why, you think you're the only one to think about it?"

"In the light you painted it, yes. Why would you think about it that way? It looks so beautiful."

"You want it to be ugly?"

"In your eyes, yes." She crossed her arms and sat on the bed.

He sat next to her. "Why?"

"Simon, I know for a fact you don't see it that way. I know there's a part of you that wishes you were the first love I ever had."

"No." He reached for her hand. "I don't need to be the first. I just need to be the last."

"You are."

"Now who's not being truthful?"

She stood up. She had had enough of this shit. "Well, I certainly hope you're not planning on keeping it."

She held her hand up to stop him from saying anything else. "Simon, don't. It's your way of communicating, I know. You're hurt and you're pissed off at me. I get it, okay? I just wish you would learn to communicate with words."

"I've tried talking to you."

"So now, what? Shock therapy? Save it, Simon. I don't want to talk about it."

"You're going to have to some time, Alex. We can't go on tip-toeing around each other."

"You are going to have to back off, Simon. And I mean it."

"Fine. I'm backing off." He started walking backward to the door. "But, just remember something, Alex. We stood together in a church in front of God, our family and friends, and we made promises to each other."

"You think I don't know that?"

"Sometimes I wonder." He pulled the door closed after him.

She fell back onto the bed and found herself staring at the painting above the bed that he had done of the two of them. Painting really was his method of communicating, she thought...

* * *

He had been anxious for her to return from the away game to show her something, she knew from their conversation earlier in the day, but now he bounded up the stairs to their second floor apartment and she was hard-pressed to follow. "Simon, I just played two grueling games of basketball. This is not the time to take up marathon running."

He apologized and then drew her into his arms and kissed her passionately. She protested since she was still sweaty from the game—something he never seemed to mind, but something that made her crazy.

He moved to his easel and took the cover off the painting. "Voilà!"

A 24 x 30 canvas sat on the easel and she stopped short, thinking for a moment she was looking into a mirror. The painting was of the two of them, she in her basketball jersey, Simon standing behind her in his paint shirt with his arms wrapped around her.

"Wow!"

"I thought we could hang it above the bed in our new house."

She turned to look at him. "I was only gone for a couple of hours. Did I miss something?"

"No. I could have sworn I told you about the new house when I asked you to marry me."

She managed to catch her breath. "You never asked me to marry you."

"I didn't?"

"I'm relatively certain I would remember."

"That must explain this." He reached into his pocket and pulled out a small black box. "All day long I've been wondering what this thing in my pocket is." He held it out to her. "This must be yours."

She had a feeling he would ask her some day from their conversations lately, but she never dreamed he would do it before they graduated. "Simon, are you?"

"Take it."

She let her fingers close around the soft little box, and then carefully opened it, making sure nothing was going to pop out. The diamond caught the light and sparkled. The clear gem was surrounded by tiny rubies set in a white gold. She realized as she looked at the delicate ring she actually had hoped this would happen.

"I bet it would look even better on your finger," he said as he took the box out of her hand and slid the ring onto her finger. "See? I was right."

She cleared her throat. "Doesn't a question go with this?"

"Hmm. Let's see." He opened the box and shook it around. "Doesn't look like it."

"So, if there's no question, then what do I say?"

"Good point." He bent down on one knee and took her hand. "Alex, you are the only person I want to wake up next to for the rest of my life. Would you do me the honor of letting me be your husband?"

She tugged at his hand, pulling him up to his feet and into her arms. Then she touched her lips lightly to his. "Nothing would make me happier."

* * *

"Alex, talk to me, please." Simon was sitting beside her on the bed looking down at her.

"Huh?"

"Where did you go?"

"Just thinking."

"About the painting?"

"I just don't quite understand why there is so much love in a painting dealing with something before your time, something that—if you stop and think about it long enough—had a very strong effect on our relationship. And not in a positive way, I might add."

"What do you want me to do? Look back on it with an anger that won't change those events? It's a painting, for Christ's sake! When you write a story about us or something having to do with us, I don't ask you why you wrote it the way you did." He stopped to catch his breath. "There was lot about that time in your life, whether you believe it or not, that prepared you for me. Just the fact you could open up to Mindy…" He turned toward her. "I'd be lying if I said I didn't want to be your first love. I think when you find the person you're meant to be with it's a natural feeling. But if I had met you first, even in high school, would I have had a chance? If you hadn't known Mindy, you would have still been living with that woman."

The way Simon handled the abuse wouldn't have been any different when he was younger, so he probably was right, she thought. The abuse made Mindy crazy with anger, too. But only on one occasion did she have to wrestle Mindy to the floor when Mindy wanted to go over to the apartment with a baseball bat and kill her.

* * *

Every muscle in her body ached as she tried to hold Mindy down. "She deserves to die." Mindy kept saying over and over. And she had to convince her violence didn't solve anything, which wasn't an easy argument to make considering she, too, had wanted to kill her on more than one occasion. When Mindy saw the pain in her eyes she realized she needed to stop struggling because she was hurting her. "Oh, my God, I'm so sorry," she murmured as she wrapped her arms around her and held her. They stayed that way for a very long time, Mindy rocking her in her arms and kissing the top of her head as she cried. "I should have been taking care of you." Mindy whispered, "I just get so frightened of losing you." She just hugged her tighter and told her everything would be okay.

* * *

"I don't mean to upset you." Simon's chin was on her shoulder and he was talking into her ear.

She shifted slightly letting him put his arm around her and pull her back into him.

"Why must it always be words with you?"

She wanted to answer him, but she had no idea what to say.

"You know, I don't always see things in words."

He said that, but it wasn't true. He knew exactly what he wanted to convey and he found the way to put it on the canvas.
"I don't know about that," she said, turning her face to look at him. "You seem to have a pretty clear picture of things and I don't think you have a problem putting a picture into words."

"Now you know why I didn't want you see it before it was done."

"I'd have ruined your perspective." She took his hand in hers and eased him forward until she could feel his chest firmly against her back.

"I'm sorry."

"There's nothing to be sorry about."

Yes, I think there is. "I'm really scared right now."

"I know."

"And I don't mean to hurt you."

She tried to concentrate on the warmth of his arms, on the solitude of the moment. They had lain this way so many times before and she had thought they would lie this way so many times again. But as she closed her eyes, she saw the dim light of the moon streaming through the skylights onto the painting. The girls gazed into each other's eyes the very same way she and Mindy had looked into each other's eyes.

"Simon?"

"Hmmm?"

She tilted her head toward his. "How do you know that's the way the girls would look at each other?"

"I don't. I only know that's the way I look at you."

He was right. "Is that the way I look at you?"

Simon's eyes darkened for a moment. "Sometimes."

There wasn't much left to say. They just held each other that night, each caught up in their separate thoughts, but unable to let go of each other.

Simon had been so patient with her. He never told her how he felt; he wanted to be sure she felt the same way. She remembered that night toward the end of their junior year when he had taken her to a gay bar on the outskirts of Pittsburgh.

* * *

When they walked in, the music assaulted them, its volume ready to blow out your ear drums, the bass making the floor shake. The tune was one of the more popular Boy George songs. The room was a mirrored square with a bar in front as you entered and a bar at the farthest end of the room. Flashing purple and pink neon strips hung over the dance floor and blinked sporadically. A disco ball hung in the center of the room and there were flashing lights of all colors. Simon offered to get her a drink and as they sat at the edge of the bar sipping their beers a very attractive blond woman walked by and undressed her with her eyes. She felt uncomfortable sitting there with Simon. Before she could recover another woman asked her if she'd like to dance. She looked at Simon for an excuse not to, but he just smiled and said, "Go ahead."

Before she knew what was happening, her hand was in the stranger's and they were on the dance floor. The stranger's features were striking. Dark brown hair brushed the tips of her shoulders and her skin was tanned to a golden brown. Her eyes were the color of a cup of hot chocolate, and as she felt them on her, she felt warm just as if she'd been sipping the chocolate.

The woman moved closer to be heard. She introduced herself as Sarah and asked her name. She watched as her taut body moved in time with the music and she struggled to remember her name. When she finally told her, the woman said, "Beautiful name for a beautiful woman." She felt her cheeks begin to warm. Sarah was drinking her in with her eyes—taking her time— and her looking was like touching. Sarah lingered for a moment on her breasts and then moved her eyes further down her body.

She looked around for Simon and saw him sitting at the bar, sipping his beer and talking to a gorgeous black man next to him. Occasionally he would look over to where she was, but looked away when she tried to catch his eyes.

Sarah was moving closer. She whispered into her ear again. "I'm into software."

Not sure she wanted to know, but trying to keep the conversation going, she said, "What?"

"For computers." She smiled as she explained she designed video games for arcades and computers. Sarah inquired after her profession. When Sarah heard she was a basketball player, she knew immediately who she was.

She felt uncomfortable as Sarah moved closer and as she tried to keep some distance between them she bumped into the dancer behind her. She apologized and Sarah used the opportunity to pull her closer.

"I really love this song, don't you?" Sarah asked as she pulled her into her arms so their bodies were touching. She felt her body snap to attention as Sarah slid her thigh between her legs. "Relax," Sarah smiled, "I don't bite," and then added, "unless you want me to."

She pushed past Sarah and ran from the bar. Once outside in the cool evening air she took deep breaths and tried to slow her heart down. She felt a hand on her arm and she jumped.

"Alex, it's okay. It's only me," Simon said.

She turned toward him and had to stop herself from punching him.

"Did something happen in there?"

"What the hell did you bring me here for?" She yelled at him.

"I thought you wanted to get out."

He was wearing his blue paisley shirt with loose fitting jeans that hadn't quite ceased to be blue. She noted how attractive he was in that outfit. He was a handsome man; she had begun to notice that. Perhaps it was the moonlight beginning to come out lighting one side of his face, leaving the other half mysteriously shadowed that made him appear different to her. She recalled the length of time he had spent preparing to go out that evening, and she looked directly at him and said, "Are you gay?"

"What?"

She repeated the question.

"I heard you the first time." He was agitated and he made no attempt to disguise it. "Is that what you think?"

"I don't know what to think." All she knew was she didn't want him to be.

"What could possibly make you think that?"

"You don't date anyone. You knew about this place…"

"Everyone knows about this place."

"I didn't."

"Oh, well, then, of course, I must be gay." He threw his hands up and walked toward the car.

"There's no reason to be upset, you know. It's not like I accused you of anything I haven't done." She said following him

He turned so abruptly she had to stop to keep from bumping into him. "You think I'm upset because I think being gay is something awful? I'm upset because you don't know."

"I don't know what?"

"Precisely." He walked toward the car.

This time she had raced to keep up with him. "Simon, I'm sorry. The last thing I want to do is fight with you."

He slowed down and turned. "Why?"

"Why don't I want to fight with you?"

"Yeah."

"Because you're my friend."

"Oh." He turned his back to her again. Only this time she heard the pain in that single word and she was paralyzed with the same pain. She had hurt him, which was not what she wanted to do. He was so good to her. If it weren't for him she probably wouldn't have made it this far. How could she have been so thoughtless? He wanted her to tell him how she felt. That's what he meant when he asked why. He wanted her to say she loved him and she knew that.

"Are you coming or what?" He called from the car.

Simon was opening the passenger side of the car and as he turned to walk around the car, she cornered him. Before he could say anything she grabbed him and kissed him. Surprise was quickly replaced with passion as they kissed deeply. Then his arms were on her shoulders and he pushed her back and simply stared at her.

She had to know she felt something physically before she said anything, and standing there in the moonlight trying to breathe again she felt the pounding of her heart and the queasy anticipation. "I don't want to fight with you, because I love you, Simon."

His hands dropped to his sides and he fell back against the car.

She reached out to steady him. "Are you okay?"

He shook his head and sat down on the car seat.

Bending down in front of him, she took his hands in hers. "What's wrong?"

There were tears in his eyes when he looked at her. "I've wanted to hear you say that for so long. I just never thought I would."

She reached up and brushed her palm against his cheek, wiping his tears away. "Then I guess if I told you I wanted to make love I'd have to call the paramedics."

He smiled and drew her toward him and whispered, "God, I love you, Alex."

eight

Willie's bus arrived at three o'clock and she met him at the Port Authority. Stepping off the bus, he looked like the picture so vividly painted in her mind. His tan blazer, patched at the elbows, tie disappearing into the third button of his denim shirt, and jeans covering the top of an old pair of converse high tops. He juggled a tattered suitcase, a small leather portfolio, and a hang-up bag. She took the hang-up bag from him as he kissed her on the cheek.

"You look great!" she exclaimed, kissing him back.

"And you look marvelous, my dear." He said in his best Billy Crystal voice.

"Well, let's blow this Popsicle stand."

"Good idea," he concluded, following her up the escalator to the main floor.

Once out on the street, they flagged a cab and headed uptown. In the cab Willie told her all about his freelance job. He would only be staying for a couple of days, but he was hoping to use the money from this job to upgrade his computer equipment and buy his daughter some new equipment of her own. He filled her in on the house situation and how Mindy was doing. She listened intently. When the cab pulled up in front of her house, she pulled a ten from her wallet and handed it to the driver. Then she helped Willie carry his stuff up the stairs to the door. As the cab whisked away, she pulled keys out of her pocket and opened the door.

"You've painted since I was here last," Willie noted as he set his things in the hallway.

"Every now and then we have these spurts of domestic energy," she confessed.

"It's a great job."

"Thanks. Come on," she picked up his hang up bag, "I'll show you to your room."

She started up the stairway with Willie in tow. She stopped in the doorway of the guest room. She hoped Simon remembered to put the sheets on the bed and a fresh set of towels out. Surveying the room quickly, she noted he had. Willie bumped into her, sending her sprawling onto the bed.

His apology was followed by the thump of his bags as they tumbled out of his hands.

She pulled herself up on the bed laughing.

He gathered his bags together and placed them on the bed. "I should have remembered you don't come in here much."

"You shouldn't have to remember my idiosyncrasies."

Clearing a space beside her on the bed, he sat down next to her and squeezed her shoulder. "It will happen again, you know."

"Thanks." She patted his hand. "The important thing now is it's a guest room, and you are the guest."

He turned and unzipped his suitcase. "I brought you something," he announced as he produced a very large package and handed it to her.

"Willie, you didn't have to…"

"Just open it."

She tore the paper off the corner and exposed a silver frame surrounding a charcoal mat. Further tearing revealed a smaller copy of the photograph that used to hang above her bed.

"I wanted to give you the original, but Mindy wouldn't let me touch it, so I copied it for you."

"I can't believe you still had the negative."

"Are you kidding? If you had played pro that would be worth big bucks now. Not that it's not worth anything now."

"This is great. Simon's going to love it. Thank you. Let's go get a beer and I'll show you what we've done with the rest of the house."

"Where's Simon?" Willie asked, as she pulled two bottles of beer from the refrigerator.

"He's meeting with the producer of an off-Broadway show about a set design."

"That sounds pretty exciting."

Scrounging in the drawer for the bottle opener, she said, "Yeah. Evidently the set needs to be a piece of sculpture, so they want to hire a real sculptor, not a set designer."

"What about the cartoon caper?"

She handed him his bottle. "Well, I have to admit I haven't really looked at the stuff yet."

"Alex," he scolded.

"I know. I just can't get used to the idea, but I did promise to look at the stuff, so I will." She asked if he wanted anything to go with the beer and he assured her the beer was enough.

So she took him up to Simon's studio to show him the new painting. She was anxious to see his response. On the way up to the third floor, he asked if she thought Simon would paint a portrait of his daughter so he could have it around when she wasn't with him.

"Ask him," she said as she opened the door to the studio. "He hasn't done any in while, but since you're family, who knows?" She took the blanket off the painting and stood back so Willie could get a full view of it.

His eyes widened for a moment, and then he took a very large sip of beer. Tucking his left hand into his pocket and grasping the beer tightly in his right hand, he moved a bit closer to study it.

She nursed her beer as she waited for a comment of some kind. But Willie's lips failed to move, other than to scrunch up slightly and then straighten out. She waited until she could stand it no longer.

"Well?"

"Wow!"

"Wow?"

"It's amazing."

"How's it amazing?"

"It looks just like the two of you."

"I noticed that too. Anything else?"

"What do you want to know?" He asked, adopting a British accent, not unlike many of the critics Simon dealt with. "How I feel about the style, which is somewhat different from his other pieces, or whether I think it will be hanging in a museum centuries from now." He topped the last sentence off by downing the rest of his beer, and then holding out his bottle. "Or whether I want another beer?"

She took the bottle. "Smart ass."

"What's it called?"

"Tell me what you think it's called."

"Alex, I'm not good at guessing games. All I know is Simon is not only a hell of a good painter; he's a good catch for you."

"What makes you say that?"

"There's a lot of love in that painting…I just think you have something special and you shouldn't let it go."

What would make you say that? "I wasn't planning on it."

"Good. Now, what's it called?"

"The First Time." She tried to pinpoint the new tone in his voice. She hadn't heard that tone before, and she wasn't entirely sure she wanted to hear it again.

"Can I have that beer now?"

"Willie, don't you think the painting is weird?"

"Weird how?"

"Why did he do it?"

"I can't answer that." He pushed his hair back off his forehead. "It bothers you, doesn't it?"

"Wouldn't it bother you?"

"I don't know."

"You are such a fucking *guy*." She covered the painting back up.

"What the fuck does that mean?" He followed her into the kitchen. "Alex, if you want to talk about it. Let's talk about it."

She opened the refrigerator and took two beers out. "I just can't believe you don't think it's weird."

"It's a very beautiful picture."

"Yeah, if you're some stranger off the street looking at it. But knowing what you know…"

He moved behind her and put his hands on her shoulders and massaged. "You need to relax. How about some basketball?"

She spun around to look at him. "Basketball doesn't cure things, Willie."

"No, but it releases stress. And I think you could stand a little stress reduction right about now."

"You're pretty quick to want to get your ass kicked again."

"A bit harsh don't you think. Considering I could beat you blindfolded."

She reminded him he had a short memory span.

"Well, let's see how short. Get the damn ball out and let's play."

She knew he didn't want to talk about things. Basketball was his way of getting out of it. But she also knew it would take her mind off other things, so it might not be such a bad idea.

She slipped her arm around his shoulder. "You know, you have this hang-up about beating me at what the sports-casters have called 'my sport.' It's somewhat disturbing, don't you think?"

"And who taught you how to play the game?"

"So now you're fucking Yoda?"

"I brought clothes. Let's change and find out."

While Willie changed into the clothes he brought for their rematch, she dug out her lucky high tops. All of her shorts were already packed away, so she settled on a pair of lightweight sweats, and her tattered "Property of Pitt Athletic Department" tee shirt.

Willie put on an oversized muscle shirt and gray gym shorts and left his Converse on. Willie was still in great shape for his age, she noted. His legs were still as muscular and hairy as they had been in his youth. "Great legs." She whistled at him as he came down the stairs.

A tinge of red rose to his cheeks. "You're awful."

"No, I'm not." She opened the door and started walking toward the playground five blocks away, dribbling the basketball as they walked.

They passed the neighborhood stores and cut behind the school to the playground. The gate was always open during the day, so they walked right in.

Several girls were climbing on the jungle gym, talking and giggling as they maneuvered their way around the iron framework. In the far corner, a mother was pushing her daughter on the swings. A group of prepubescent boys and girls was using one of the two basketball courts. One team had fluorescent markers tied around their waist to separate them from the other team.

"Isn't that great?" She pointed at their game.

"What?"

"It's a pretty fair mix over there." She tossed him the ball. "Come on."

"Hey, don't we toss to see who goes first?"

"Don't look a gift horse in the mouth." She winked at him and took her place at center court.

He dribbled the ball outside the court. "Are we playing full court or half court?"

"Your call."

"Well, we haven't played on a full court in a while. So, full court it is."

"Okay. Hang on for one sec." She reached into her back pocket and produced a bandana she proceeded to tie around her head to catch the inevitable perspiration. "Which side is yours?"

"I claim the fence side." Willie said with great determination.

"Okay, anytime."

He dribbled toward the hoop near the fence, but she was at his side, letting him get close enough to shoot before pivoting in front of him, arms raised to block any shot he might try. He moved the ball back and forth as he tried to find an opening to shoot, but she was like a mirror image matching his every move. Finally, he tossed the ball up and it bounced off the backboard.

She caught it before he could get to it. As she dribbled down the court at breakneck speed, she thought, basketball was so much easier than writing. Basketball was for her what art was for Simon. Willie was trailing her. Before he could block her, she shot and scored. "One, nothing," she announced and tossed him the ball.

"I have to at least let you think you still have it, don't I?"

"Let's go." She egged him on.

He started to dribble and she watched the muscles of his legs rippling beneath the pressure of his strides as he raced down the court. She started after him, debating whether or not to weave in and out to make his offense harder. She'd let him run a few feet and then pop up in front of him. He'd dodge her, run several feet in the other direction, and then have to stop when she appeared in front of him. About four feet from the basket, she planted herself so unexpectedly he stopped and held onto the ball. "Shit!" he exclaimed as he realized he had to shoot.

The ball twirled around the edge of the rim several times before falling off. She caught the ball and decided to take her time. Instead of racing down the court she dribbled slowly. Willie was all over her, reaching for the ball every chance he got. Every time his hand shot out, she would move the ball behind her back and continue to dribble. She watched with amusement as his lips tightened with frustration. The one move Willie could not execute was the one she was so adept at and it made him crazy.

When she reached the basket, she faked him out on her first attempt to shoot; on the second attempt the ball swished through the hoop. "Two, nothing."

The game continued that way for the next six shots and then Willie came back. He got four in a row, dancing around the bottom of the hoop every time chanting, "Yes."

The kids playing on the other court gathered around to watch. They hadn't bothered to separate, as she thought they might, into one sex cheering for their own, but they stayed in their groups. Every time Willie would make a point, a sea of fluorescent orange waves would be seen, and they jumped up and down and cheered.

Somewhere during the game their age peeled away, like layers of unnecessary clothing. This must be what they mean by déjà vu, she thought.

Willie was one point away from her now and the time had come to end his streak. She stuck to him like glue, mirroring every move he made. Even the sweat pouring down his face and coating his body seemed to be dripping down hers as well. As he moved to shoot, she reached up, smacked it out of his hand, and took it. Cheers from the crowd filled the air and she let the rush that comes from having the crowd behind you carry her down the court to the other side. She dunked the ball before Willie could even reach her.

"Seven to five!" Her fans called out.

She turned to look at Willie, who was bent over, hands on his knees, catching his breath. "You want to take a break?" she offered.

"I'm fine." He stood up.

"Well, I need one." She sat down on the bench.

"You're not going to stop," several voices asked at once, "are you?"

She laughed, "Listen to them."

"We're playing to twenty one." He called out.

A boy with dark curls and mocha skin approached her. His muscle shirt hung on his body exposing his scrawny frame and his shorts hung below his knees. But his face was beautiful. His dark eyes glowed underneath eyelashes long enough to walk on. He smiled as he held out a squeeze bottle and she knew who he reminded her of—a woman she had played with in college. He was too old to be her son, and she probably wouldn't have had one, but if she had he would look like this. "You want something to drink, lady?" he asked.

"Thanks." She smiled back at him, took a squirt from the bottle, and handed it back.

One of Willie's fluorescent children approached him, a towheaded little girl, holding out a plastic cup with a yellowish liquid. "Mister, you thirsty?"

He took the cup from her and tousled her hair. "Thank you." Then he emptied the cup and set it town on the bench.

"Ready?" he asked as he stood up.

"Let's do it." She tossed him the ball and took her place on the court. Willie came back, sinking two baskets in a row.

That yellow liquid was good shit! She could hear her side chanting now. "Go lady, go lady," echoed through the air. As she wrapped her hands around the surface of the ball, she knew the game was over. Any thoughts she had entertained of letting Willie win were gone. Basketball was her game. Willie may have taught her how to play it properly, but even before Willie, before Mindy, it was her game.

Willie put up a fight, prolonged the struggle, but he couldn't stop the inevitable. She sank the last shot and her crowd went crazy. Willie's fluorescent bunch gave him the rest of the sports drink and told him he played a good game.

The dark-haired boy approached her again. "You're really good, lady. We play here every Saturday. Do you think you could teach us some of those moves?"

"What's your name?"

"Charles."

She smiled. Charles. The teammate he reminded her of was named Casey. How appropriate. "Well, Charles, I'll think about it."

"Cool."

She clapped Willie on the back. "Come on, old man, let's hit the showers."

He laid his head on her shoulder. "Christ, you don't give an inch, do you?"

She ruffled his hair. "Not on the basketball court."

He sighed, "I need another beer."

"You shower first, and then I'll get you a tall one."

"Maybe two."

"You can have as many as you want, Willie."

Willie had three beers and a bag of nacho chips before Simon returned home to find them freshly showered and waiting to go out to dinner. He shook Willie's hand, kissed Alex on the cheek, and smiled at the two of them. He could see their hair was still damp, "Couldn't stay off the court, could you?"

"It's all him." She said pointing at Willie.

"Well, I guess we should get going, then. I imagine you two are pretty hungry."

She was glad they were going to the café around the corner. She had been thinking about their salmon since she searched the cupboard for something to snack on until Simon returned. Dinner was enjoyable. She was happy to see Simon and Willie get along so well. With Willie at her side, she felt a sense of family she had missed these past few years and she was glad to have him there.

They returned to the house and sat in the living room looking at Willie's portfolio. Simon had opened a bottle of merlot and they sat on the sofa with Willie in the middle turning the pages and giving the background on each photo. She had a nice buzz going, but not enough to miss the power of Willie's photographs. Willie had always known his way around a camera. She remembered photographs he had taken of Mindy when he was only seven or eight were stunning. But black and white photography was his true passion. Willie could set one of his black and white photographs down next to the most vibrant color photograph and one would be drawn to his. His understanding of light and shadow had always amazed her.

One of the last pages was a photograph of a family of four. Two boys stood in the middle holding each other's hands. Their other hand reached up to cling to the adult next to them who were cut off from the waist up. She recognized the boys from the photos Mark had shown her and she saw the high school ring on the mother's hand. Willie offered no comment with the photo and was ready to turn the page, when she set her hand on it. "What made you cut the parents off?"

"Do you think the photo needs them?"

Simon had just taken a sip of his wine. He set the class down on the end table beside him. "It's exceptional the way it is."

She understood what they were saying. The photograph didn't need the parents. She needed to see the parents. She wondered what Mindy looked like with her children and with Mark.

Willie moved her hand and turned the page. "I'd be happy to take one of the two of you."

"We'd have to pay you." Simon said.

"Don't be silly."
"Alex?"

She drained her glass of wine, suddenly very uncomfortable. But she said, "If you'd like to." Simon seemed genuinely intrigued with the idea. She remembered the photographs he had taken of her with Mindy. She loved those photos; now they were packed away in the attic. Simon said she should throw them out or burn them, but she could never bring herself to destroy them.

Later that night, when Simon was fast asleep, she pulled back the covers and grabbed her robe. She went up to tiny room next to Simon's studio that they used for attic space. The light bulb hanging from the ceiling cast just enough light to see the boxes stacked on either side of the room. The photographs were in an old wooden box, where she had always kept them. She found the box and set it on the floor in the middle of the room directly under the light. She blew the dust off the lid of the box and opened it.

On top of the photographs lay a stack of love letters. Simon had wanted her to burn those, too, but love letters were for keeping. She pulled an envelope from the pile and opened it.

September 5, 1981

My Dearest Alex,

Hi, I got your letter this morning – I'm so excited, I've read it about ten times already. I was in history class and I was going to stay after to talk to the professor, when I realized my mail would be there, so I ran to my mailbox instead. I got a letter from Mom, something about a campus show, and one from you. I can't tell you what show they're doing, and I haven't even read the one from my mother.

Thank you for sending me your class schedule. Mine is enclosed. My professors are okay. They're so different from our high school teachers, but I guess you're finding that out, too. I have this one guy for political science who doesn't wash his hair (gross!) and another one who reminds me of Mr. Rogers. I keep expecting him to sit down, take off his shoes, and put on his sneakers.

My roommate is okay. I'm not sure she likes me much. She's very boy-crazy and wants to score at every frat on the hill ... God, I miss you. I miss you more than words can even begin to tell you. I want you here or me there. There's so much I want to share with you I just can't write it all down, or talk about it over the phone.

I miss your arms around me at night when I try to go to sleep. I hug the bunny you gave me, but bunny doesn't hug back...bunny doesn't smell like you, or feel like you ... I better stop before I get too horny. It's only the first week of school, and I can't wait until break to see you again. I have a campus job in the admissions office and I'll send you the money to get home if you're short. Don't let me down...I need to be in your arms again...I love you so. Mindy.

She slid the letter back into the envelope and back into the pile. Then she picked up a postcard marked 8 September 1981 with a rubber band around a cassette tape. The card read:

"I don't want to wonder where my life would have gone without you...you are so important to me." And her writing, *"at the risk of being un-original, I saw this and had to send it to you. I am also enclosing a tape of love songs I made for you. Please, listen to them at night before you go to sleep and think of me. Love, Mindy. P.S. Bunny still doesn't hug back.*

Turning the tape over in her hand she read the titles of the songs. Then she rubber-banded the tape and the postcard back together and put them back in the box. Looking at the postmarks—all about two days apart—she skipped ahead in the stack and pulled one out from November 1981.

Dearest Alex,

I'm so glad we spent our break together. I needed so desperately to be in your arms, to feel your kisses...I can't believe when we make love, it's always so wonderful, and I never want it to end. I can't believe how empty I feel when you're not by my side. All my friends are beginning to think I'm a real crackpot because I don't want to go out every weekend and pick up guys. I've tried to tell them I really need to study and do well, because I want to graduate top of the class. Some of them buy it, but I know some of them don't.

Why couldn't I have picked your college? It would be so much easier, knowing I could room with you, we could hold each other at night, and make love whenever we wanted. That we could help each other study, like we did in high school, read books to each other…I must have been a fool. I wonder if I could transfer. My mother might understand. Send me some literature on your school so I can see if I could transfer without much trouble. Just think about it. We could be together.

My body aches for you—and I miss the way you make me laugh. I miss everything about you. I'm so lonely here! Please write me soon. Love. Mindy.

Folding the letter, she put it back in its envelope.

There was a time after they parted, where she thought she had imagined all that transpired between them. She read the letters again and again, searching for some sign, something to explain what happened. But when she thought about ending it she wrote less often.

She opened the last letter.

15 December 1982

My dearest Alex,

Finals are almost over and I'll soon be in your arms again. I can't wait. I miss you so very much, and I've gotten you something terribly exciting for Christmas. I can't wait to see you open it.

Setting the letter down, she picked up the small velvet box in the bottom and pulled out the diamond stud. She remembered how excited Mindy was when she gave it to her.

Mindy had waited until they were alone in her room. The other gifts Mindy had gotten for her were under the tree in the living room ready to be opened in front of everyone. She opened the box and saw the diamond.

"It's too much," she said.

"It's not enough," Mindy said. "I tried to buy you the world, but it wasn't for sale."

Reaching up, she felt the second hole in her ears. It had closed long ago when she removed the earring, but she could still feel where the hole had been.

She picked up the faded Xerox copy jammed in the bottom of the box and read her own words.

"Dear Mindy,

I don't understand what happened between us. I've spent the last two months trying to make sense of it all. I have read your letters over and over again until I probably could recite them by heart. I have listened to the tapes you sent me. I have thought about our time together...my imagination has cooked up all kinds of crazy scenarios. I need to know what happened.

I meant every word I said to you, every word I wrote, and my feelings for you have not changed. I would not have let you into my heart if I did not think we would be together forever. Please help me to understand. I need to know. Even if you don't understand the reasons yourself...please share them with me. I beg of you. Forever, Alex.

"Forever." An English teacher in high school had told them, "Never put anything in writing you don't mean. The written word is more powerful than anything else there is. Thus, the term 'the pen is mightier than the sword'. Once you put it in writing, it is there forever. People will be able to read it over and over again." Mindy was in her class; she had heard all the warnings, too. The first time she gave Mindy a card, Mindy had asked her if she remembered what Mrs. Finch said and she assured her she did.

She knew the rules. She knew what she was writing. She must have meant it. She closed everything back up in the box and sat in the center of the room staring at it. After all this time why did it matter, she asked herself. She had tried to put her childhood behind her, as far behind her as she could get it. And she had succeeded until the funeral, or at least until the miscarriage. When she lost the baby she remembered for the first time feeling the need to track Mindy down, knowing Mindy could comfort her in a way Simon couldn't. All Simon saw now were the scars on her body. Mindy had seen some of the open wounds. She had cleaned them, bandaged them, and tried to ease the pain. Mindy understood her fears. They had talked about raising children when they got older. Raising a little girl together. They talked about artificial insemination and who would carry the child, what they would name it. Her name would have been Zoë, the Greek word meaning life. That was when she was going to be a professional basketball player and Mindy was going to be the curator of a museum. They had planned, as all young couples do, to be successful, to have lots of money to be able to do whatever they wanted. Mindy was convinced her mother would embrace their child just as she would embrace them. Alex was afraid to take the chance. She had waited so long to have a mother, she couldn't risk losing the one she had found. In retrospect she knew Mindy was right. Mrs. Martine li loved them unconditionally.

The doctor tried to explain to Simon she had miscarried because she was too afraid to carry the baby to term. But Simon could not understand. She had wanted a child so desperately; she had been so elated when the doctor told her.

"Wow, what a depressing place to be sitting." Willie exclaimed.

"Did I wake you?"

"No. I can't always sleep, plus I think the cheesecake is keeping me awake."

"That was a pretty big piece."

He patted his stomach. "Tell me about it. What are you doing up here?"

"Just looking at some old stuff."

He looked at the box. "Photographs?"

She realized she hadn't even looked at the photographs in the box. "Among other things." Tucking the box under her arm, she said, "How about a bit of brandy to help you sleep?"

"That sounds nice."

In the study, she pulled the brandy out of the liquor cabinet and poured two glasses, while Willie starred at the wooden box she had set on the coffee table.
"Here." She handed him a glass.

"Funny," Willie said taking the snifter. "I never pictured us sipping brandy."

She sat down next to him. "I'm the one that needs a friend now."

"Alex, this place... I mean, what you got here..."

"Willie, I want a friend. Not a lecture." She let herself settle back into the sofa. "I just need some time to sort some things out. Usually I talk to Simon, but he's so threatened by all this...and he's worried, Willie. I can see it in his face."

"Does he need to be worried?"

"If I could answer that, we wouldn't be sitting here, would we?" She took a sip of the amber liquid and let it warm her from the back of her throat to her stomach. "Simon and I have been together for four years now...friends before that. He stood by me through thick and thin and now all of a sudden these feelings that have been dormant are re-awakening. I know your sister feels something, too. I felt it when we were in the park and I ran from it. I don't want to lose what I've spent so much time building."

"So don't."

"It's not simple, and you know it." She took another sip of the liquid. "What kind of life could we have after so much time, and with her children?"

"I can't answer that..."

"You think we have nothing in common...nothing we could talk about, let alone share. In my wildest dreams I never thought Mindy would settle for being a housewife. Not that I think there's anything wrong with that…it's just not how I saw her. She was going to set the world on fire."

"She didn't have a chance. She got pregnant so fast and they got married." Willie set his snifter on the coffee table. "She did have one article published in a journal, something she'd written her senior year. I thought she would pursue it to a graduate level, but then she married Mark and had Alex."

"Would you like another?" She reached for his empty snifter.

"No. One is my limit."

"Even if we have nothing in common from the day we parted, we would still have everything in common from the days before. Mindy was such a big part of my emotional development. I can't imagine what my life would have been like if I hadn't met her. If you're family hadn't taken me in."

"Sometimes I wonder if you'd be alive."

"And if I was, would I just be another dysfunctional adult roaming around?"

"Well, I'm glad we knew each other then. It was nice having another sister, and when you think about it, you were such a jock it was like having a little brother, too." He leaned over and kissed her lightly on the cheek. "And I meant that in the best possible way."

Warmed by his tenderness, she smiled at him. "I'm glad we're still friends."

"Me, too." He stood and stretched like a cat, reaching up for the ceiling, loosening all his limbs. "I think we've done enough talking for one night. Why don't we try and get some sleep?"

She agreed, promising to go upstairs after she rinsed the glasses out in the kitchen.

Sitting on the edge of the bed, she studied Simon, who was fast asleep. Covers around his waist, on his back with his left arm flung over his face and his right arm over his head dangling through the brass headboard. She watched as his chest rose and fell with each breath. She had been happy with Simon these past few years. After

Mindy left her, he was the only lover she had, with the exception of Casey. She rarely thought about Casey. Cassiopeia was a basketball teammate at Pitt. She smiled as she remembered how easy it had been to maintain her feelings for Mindy, even though half the women on the team were lesbians. Being the only two freshmen on the first string, she and Casey got close pretty quickly. She helped Casey study for her tests, since she was having trouble passing some of her classes and she had to keep her grade level up to keep the scholarship. Casey was actually smarter than she thought she was. She just had terrible study habits. Mostly she helped organize her and explained certain things Casey found confusing. She made her get a dictionary so she could look up any word she didn't understand. Casey would tease her about "the big-ass red book she had to lug around."

* * *

She noted the clock on her dresser flashed a time well after midnight when the knock came at her door.

"It's me—Dunk."

Dunk was what everyone had called Casey when they discovered her untapped talents. She opened the door and was swept up into large black arms lifting her off the ground in a bear hug.

"Thank you! Thank you!" she shouted, and then set her back on her feet. "I went to the science lab and the grades are posted. Thank you. Thank you!" She shouted again as she lifted her off the ground again and kissed her on the lips.

"Dunk!" Was all she could manage to say.

"Sorry." Casey set her down. "I'm just so happy. You don't know how it is. I'm the first one in my family to make it to college."

She closed the door and took Casey's coat. "I know what that's like. I'm glad I could help."

Casey produced a bottle of champagne. "I thought we could celebrate?"

She set the bottle down on the desk and told Casey it was just midterms.

Casey sat on her desk and she in her chair. "Why don't we save this for finals?"

"Okay." Casey stared down at her for several moments. Neither of them spoke. She had no idea what Casey was thinking. She could feel Casey's eyes on her body and they seemed to burn. Casey's light chocolate skin was smooth, her tiny taut curls just cropped, which only made her high cheekbones and large brown eyes more striking.

"Maybe we could still celebrate." Casey said.

"I have some beer." Before she could move to get it, Casey swung her chair around and placed a hand on either thigh.

"Girl, we don't need no alcohol." She rose to her feet, hands still on her thighs. Casey kissed her tenderly on the lips.

Casey had a reputation for being loose, and she was not going to be just a notch in someone's headboard. "Dunk, I don't think…"

"Did I say anything about thinking? You're lonely and I'm lonely." Casey's long fingers danced up and down her biceps.

"Maybe we shouldn't…"

Casey's arms slipped around her waist and pulled her closer. She wrapped her legs around Casey's slender frame. They were entering dangerous territory now.

"Why? You don't want to?"

She did want to. Who wouldn't? "I don't take these things lightly."

Casey traced her lips with her fingertip. It was all she could do to think, as Casey whispered in her ear, "Too bad, because I want you somethin' fierce."

Skilled fingers slid under her sweatshirt and moved up and down her spine. She could smell the coconut soap Casey bathed with. Casey kissed her again, a long, hot smoldering kiss that made her blood rush. Her hands found the taut, muscular back. "And, I think you want me, too." Casey smiled.

Alex wanted to talk, to say something, but her throat was tight and dry...all she could do wa s let Casey undress her. Part of her wanted to stop, but the other part wanted to know what Casey felt like, what she tasted like. Casey was right; she had been lonely. And she did miss a woman's touch.

Maybe they would be together now, she thought, but calling out Mindy's name as she climaxed put a real sense of closure to the physical part of their relationship. They had remained friends, treating that night as something better left in silence. Even after college they exchanged Christmas cards and an occasional letter.

* * *

She had remained silent when she and Simon began making love. She was afraid to repeat the incident, so many months passed before she let herself make any noise at all. This was absurd, she told herself, why was she torturing herself like this? She had to get some sleep. Nestling her head against Simon's chest, she tried to relax. She missed holding someone in her arms. Feeling Mindy's back rise and fall against her breasts, kissing the back of her neck. She had tried these things with Simon, but it just wasn't the same, so she stopped trying. Now she rested in his arms, which was nice once in a while, but it wasn't the same.

nine

Simon delivered breakfast in bed. "Thought you might be hungry," he said as he set the tray in front of her. He had made eggs just the way she liked them. The hash browns were browned to a crispy golden brown and the toast was lightly buttered. He had eaten while he made hers, as he usually did. But he added an extra cup of coffee to the tray for himself.

She smiled at him, stretched, and sat up. "Thank you."

"I gather you didn't sleep well."

"Why would you say that?" she asked as she stabbed a piece of egg with her fork.

"Willie said you were up for the better part of the night."

She set the fork down. What she thought was a loving gesture was turning out to be a fishing expedition. "Willie has a big mouth."

"Maybe he's just concerned."

"There's nothing to be concerned about. I just have some thinking to do."

"Alex, we *have* to talk about this."

"I don't know what to say to you," she took a sip of juice. "I wish you would just let me work it out."

"But we always work things out together."

She moved the food around on her plate as she studied him. Why was he crowding her like this? Did he always crowd her and she never noticed before? Didn't he realize the reason they always worked things out together was because he insisted they did? There were a lot of times she would have let things just lie, but Simon lived for resolution.

"All these feelings I'm having are probably just the result of opening an old wound. I'll stop bleeding soon enough and everything will be just fine."

"*The Lost Princess*, chapter three. Don't use stuff from your stories with me."

"Simon, leave it alone."

"Well," he set the paper down on the bed and stood up, "I guess I'll go up to my studio and work."

"Why don't you?" she suggested. "I'll be in my study."

"Whatever," he sighed and left.

She set the tray aside and pulled the covers back. She would shower and get dressed and then go to the study to read some more letters, or write, or something.

Pulling on a pair of sweatpants and sweatshirt, she ran a comb through her wet hair, picked up the tray and started down the stairs to the kitchen.

Willie was busy chopping onions. He stood at the island in the middle of the kitchen surrounded by fresh vegetables, humming. "What are you making?" she asked, depositing her tray near the sink.

"Thought I'd make some spaghetti sauce and some fresh gnocchi. It's still your favorite, isn't it?"

"Yes."

"My interview isn't until 3:00 and it shouldn't take too long. I figured I'd curb some of my anxiety…unless…"

She held her hand up. "No basketball."

"Can't blame a guy for trying."

She opened the refrigerator and took out a can of diet soda. "I'll be in my study working…"

"You mean reading."

"Willie…"

He held up his hand. "I know. I know. Shut up and cook."

"See you in a while." She closed the door to her study and went to the couch. Reaching for the box of letters she crossed her legs and sank into the corner of the sofa. Setting the box of letters squarely in her lap, she carefully opened it and pulled one out.

November 30, 1981

Dearest Alex,

My history professor is incredible. She knows so much about everything and she really pushes me. I thought I would hate that, but it's so stimulating. I'm learning so much. I'd like to get a job in a museum when I get out of college or maybe even teach. Boston is a really great place; the only problem with Boston is you're not here. I can't wait until you visit and I can show you all the sights. You are going to love Quincy Market and all the historic sites. Maybe we could live here after school. We haven't talked about where we're going to live. Is Pittsburgh nice? Maybe we could live there, if you like it better. I don't really care where we live as long as we can be together. Well, I'd love to write to you forever, but I have an English paper to write for my Shakespeare class. I miss you more and more with each passing hour. Christmas will be here soon, I pray. 'Till I'm in your arms again—
Always,
Mindy

Folding the letter she set it back in the box and picked up another one. She turned the light blue envelope over in her hands as she asked herself what the point of this exercise was. Was it to prove they loved each other? That their love was as strong as any great love? There was no reason to even question.

She'd taken solace in Simon's arms for years, taken refuge in his love. She didn't keep in touch with many people. She spent her days writing, signing books, lecturing, cleaning, attending openings with Simon, and just spending time with him. They were each other's whole world.

This was the first time since the miscarriage that she had difficulty speaking to him. This was the first time she needed someone else to talk to. Willie was not the answer. Casey kept popping into her mind, but she hadn't seen her in ages. Could she just call her out of the blue?

Setting the box down on the couch, she went to her desk. She knew Casey was in New York running a bar somewhere in Greenwich Village. Going through the bottom drawer of her desk she found the last Christmas card, called information, and got the number. She placed the call and was surprised at how thrilled Casey was to hear from her. She invited her over that afternoon without a second thought.

She changed into a pair of jeans and a denim shirt, tucked some money and tokens into her pocket and her keys in the other. She had enough time to stop by the corner bakery for some fresh pastry before jumping on the subway.

Casey sounded excited when she called. She thought they might be able to see each other sometime later that week, but Casey sensed she needed a friend so she invited her to join them for lunch and some videos. 'Them,' she recalled, referred to Casey and her partner Anne. She had never met Anne but she remembered seeing her name on the Christmas cards about two years ago.

She got off the subway at Bleecker Street and followed the directions she had scrawled on a piece of paper. The apartment was on the top floor of a brownstone on a tiny street right off of Christopher. She found the appropriate buzzer and pressed it. Then she climbed three flights of stairs to the top floor.

Casey greeted her with a warm embrace, lifting her off the floor. In one moment all the time that had past between them melted away and they began exactly where they had left off. Casey guided her to a chair and introduced her to her lover, Anne. Anne was a petite blond woman dressed in sweatpants and one of Casey's sweatshirts that practically reached her knees. Her long blond hair was pulled back and tied neatly in a ponytail; she had slightly pudgy cheeks and eyes the color of coffee with cream.

"It's nice to meet you," she smiled, taking her hand. "I've read all your books.'

There was something intimate about a handshake. When a person had a limp handshake she immediately thought they were weak and/or sneaky. Anne's firm grasp immediately endeared her.

"I'm sure that Dunk told you to say that, but thank you."

"Dunk? I've never heard her called that before." Anne laughed, "Casey did buy the first one for Emma, but my daughter is very picky and she loves them."

"Thanks." Casey clapped her on the back. "I'm not going to hear the end of that now, you know?" She turned to Anne and said, "Alex was never good with compliments."

Suddenly she became aware of the box she was holding in her hand and she held it out toward them. "This is for the two of you."

"How sweet." Anne took the box and went to the kitchen.

"Thanks, Alex."

She was curious about Anne's daughter and asked how old she was.

"Five." She set the box of pastry in the fridge and then sat down in the chair resembling a satellite dish and almost disappeared into it. "I'm hoping she'll return from her birthday party down the block in time to meet you."

"I'd like that."

"Have a seat." Anne said, "What I'm sure Casey failed to tell you when she invited you was it's her day to cook, which means we'll be ordering take out for lunch, shortly. I hope Chinese is okay with you."

She settled into the tan leather couch and looked around at the apartment. The amber tone on the walls and chestnut woodwork lent warmth to the room. On the one wall there were large African prints, and on the other wall sepia photographs framed in dark wood frames. Casey and Anne had taken family photographs and blown them up. A half bookcase chock-full of books separated the living room from the kitchen. "I really didn't come here to eat, so anything would be fine with me."

"How about a soda, tea, beer?" Casey offered.

"Soda would be fine."

"So, Alex," Casey called out from the kitchen area where she was opening the refrigerator, "what's wrong?"

"That's it babe, cut right to the chase." Anne laughed, "Casey was never one for small talk."

"I remember." She took the cool glass of soda from Casey who sat beside her. "I also remember she was never big on commitment, but you two have been together for..." she tried to recall the Christmas cards.

"Three years." Anne beamed. "She just needed to meet the right woman."

"Casey never told me what it is you do." She realized even though she was nervous about talking about her problems, she wasn't just stalling for time she was genuinely interested in their life together. Casey had never written in great detail about their life together only about how happy she was.

Anne explained she ran a small computer shop offering services like resume writing, typing, and faxing. Casey told her she ran her Aunt's bar, but they were thinking of trying to get out of the city.

"It's not the best place to raise a child," Anne said. "But, on the other hand, where would we go where people wouldn't bat an eye at two lesbians raising a child?"

"I don't know. I never thought about it. I guess you don't have many problems here. Do you?"

"Emma has been lucky. One of the teachers in her school is a lesbian, and she's having a baby in a couple months."

Casey seemed excited to add that the teacher was so loved the students were more disappointed she would be on maternity leave than concerned about how she got pregnant in the first place.

"That's great."

Casey placed a hand on her knee. "Enough about us. I know you looked me up for a reason."

She felt the tender warmth of Casey's hand through her jeans; she saw the genuine concern in her eyes. For a moment she wasn't sure what to say. She had spent all her time with Simon rarely confiding in other people. "Usually I can talk to Simon, my husband," she explained for Anne's sake, "but lately, well..."

"Try starting at the beginning, Alex." Anne said.

"I'm not sure where that would be." She took a sip of her soda as she tried to collect her thoughts. "You see I'm not exactly sure why I'm here...other than because I've been wondering..."

"Thinking about switching back?" Casey asked.

Switching back, interesting choice of words...had she switched? Was she bisexual? No, Alex never believed...she always believed it was a question of love. "I wouldn't have put it that way, but yes."

"Well, I don't have any doubts. In fact, I was quite surprised when you married Simon. But, Simon is so gentle and artistic...and effeminate."

Was Casey saying she married Simon because he reminded her of a woman? She never thought of him that way. But he was gentle in ways most men she knew weren't. There was nothing feminine in his appearance. "I'm not sure Simon is effeminate." Alex said to Anne, "I've always thought he was very masculine."

"Honey, he's an artist. He's gentle, considerate. I bet he never scratches in public."

"Casey," Anne scolded, "why don't we hear what Alex has to say before cataloging her husband for her."

"Thank you." She tried to relax into the sofa. "So how do you know if you're a lesbian or not, or if you just had an experience?"

"Are you happy with Simon?"

"Until the funeral I thought I was extremely happy."

"The funeral?"

"The mother of a friend of mine."

"Your ex-lover?" Anne inquired.

"I guess you're right. I should start at the beginning. When I was young," she began, "I met a girl. I say a girl, because we were both only teenagers at the time. Anyway her family sort of took me in. And, well, I was in love with her and it turns out she was in love with me. Shortly after, we became lovers. It seemed like the most natural thing in the world at the time."

"The plot thickens." Casey picked up Alex's glass. "More soda?"

"That would be nice."

"I'm going to order Chinese. Anything you like or don't like?"

"Not big on red meat or fried rice. Anything else you want is fine."

"You know what I like, babe," Anne added and turned to Alex, "Go on."

"Where was I?"

"How long were you lovers?"

"Oh, until sophomore year at college when she ended the relationship, quickly and very cruelly."

"Still feel something for her, don't you?"

She looked at Anne. "I thought these feelings were dead. I thought Simon had erased them all. I thought our love had been replaced."

"You can't replace love, Alex. No two loves are ever the same."

Anne was right. You can't replace love. That is what she had tried to do. But she loved Simon; she knew she did. She just didn't love him the same way she had loved Mindy.

"Does she still carry a torch for you?" Casey called out from the kitchen.

"I never thought so, until I saw her."

Anne shifted in her satellite dish. "Is she with anyone?"

"She's married—not too happily, though, I might add. He seems nice enough. The kind that doesn't scratch in public."

They both laughed.

"They have two children, and get this: she named her first child after me."

"Ooo-eee! Call out the fire trucks, girl!"

"What?"

"That's Casey's way of saying she still has the hots for you. Do you want her back?"

That was it, wasn't it? That's what this was all about. "She tore my heart out," she tried to explain. "You must both think I'm crazy."

Anne's voice was soft and comforting, probably the same voice she used to soothe her daughter when she was upset. "There's no reason to think you're crazy."

"I can't believe this is happening to me."

"Why not?"

"My life was in such perfect order. I mean, I'm successful — something I was never sure I'd be. If it weren't for Simon, I never would have ever tried writing."

"My experiences with men leave something to be desired, but your Simon sounds incredible," Anne said.

She was right. "He is." Simon was a prince in every sense a little girl dreams of. And she had been buying into the fairy tale for the past few years. She had allowed herself to become his princess, a role she never thought she'd play. With Mindy there were no roles, there were no princes or princesses—although Alex sometimes fancied Mindy was the princess and she was the suave debonair type.

"That's true," Casey said, handing her another soda. "He is a prince among men."

"I know. I love him. I've loved him for four years…I just don't understand how seeing Mindy after all this time could awaken feelings and make me question my love for Simon."

"Still waters run deep." Anne said softly.

"Alex, has Mindy indicated to you that she wants to get back together?"

"No. This is all just the confusion of seeing her again after all these years and making peace. Well, we said we made peace, but she never did explain why she left me…only if she could take one moment in time back that would be it."

"Sounds like she wants you back to me." Casey rose and moved over to where her wallet sat. "If you'll excuse me, I've got to go down and pick up the food around the corner."

Maneuvering out of her satellite dish, Anne took the money from Casey. "I'll go, babe. Stay and talk with Alex."

"You sure?"

"Yeah, Dunk." She chuckled at her newfound knowledge and then kissed Casey on the lips.

Warmth swept over her—they looked so natural together. She wondered if she and Mindy looked that way.

"Thanks. You know, no one has called me that in years. Now I won't hear the end of it."

Alex apologized but secretly she was amused.

"Well," Casey sat in the satellite dish, "I can understand why you can't talk to Simon about this."

She looked at Casey's long legs touching the floor and thought it odd that while the dish owned Anne, Casey owned the dish. "You said before you were surprised I ended up with Simon…why?"

She leaned forward and rested her elbows on her knees. "Because of what happened between us."

They never talked about that evening. Their friendship went on as if nothing had happened. They had made a silent pact to forget it. Now she was breaking the silence and she had to let her know. "Maybe if I hadn't been such a jerk…"

"Alex, I wasn't ready to settle down. I meant what I said about it being a casual thing."

"Is that what you thought about our friendship?"

"No, and you know it. We would have probably slept together for a while; it was nice."

Her cheeks flushed. Casey's candor brought back the memory so vividly. "You mean until I called out Mindy's name?"

"Yeah, nice until that point." She smiled. "And don't be embarrassed. I knew your heart belonged to someone else, but Alex you were so hot."

"Me?" She sought out Casey's eyes to see if she was kidding.

"God, girl, every red-blooded lesbian on that team wanted you. You didn't know?"

She had to admit she didn't. "And you don't know that."

She laughed, "Yes, I do. You don't think people talked about the great white hope?"

She hated when they called her that. It just perpetuated the myth white girls can't play basketball and she was some mysterious exception to the rule. She also found it hard to believe the other girls would sit around and talk about her in a sexual way. "Well, I wasn't the only white girl on the team."

"Alex, why can't you accept the fact you're a desirable woman? Take a compliment for a change."

She couldn't think about a locker room of women sitting around talking about fucking her. That was one image she could have lived without. "We need to change the subject."

"All right."

"So, if you weren't the settling down type, what made you change for Anne?"

"It just happened that way." She drew her legs up into the satellite dish and crossed them Indian-style. Casey's body relaxed as she discussed her favorite topic—Anne. "I met Anne when she was coming out of a very ugly divorce...she was just a straight woman that needed someone to talk to..."

"It's hard to tell your girlfriends in the suburbs your husband gets off on beating the shit out of you," Anne added as she entered, arms full of paper bags.

"Let me help you." She offered, taking one of the larger bags.

"I'll get the dishes," Casey announced rising from the satellite dish.

"I wandered into Casey's bar. I'd run away from my husband...taken Emma to my brother's for safe keeping." She opened the bags and began setting the cardboard containers out on the counter. "Casey would listen to me for hours and when I need to cry, she held me and I never felt so safe." Anne opened the carton of rice and offered it to her.

Casey handed her a plate.

"She was so gentle. I never knew she was a lesbian until she told me and it didn't make any difference to me." She reached over and took Casey's hand. "Thank God, it didn't."

"So you were straight?" She examined the contents of the container, chicken and garlic, sweet and sour shrimp and curried chicken. She took a spoonful of each.

"I prefer to call it living in the dark ages." Anne smiled as she handed her a mug and a container of hot and sour soup.

"Thank you. I love this soup. When did you know?"

"Sit over here." Casey motioned to a place where she had cleaned off the coffee table. She took her things and sat on a corner of the couch.

"Slowly, over time, I realized I was falling in love with Casey. That I'd had these feelings in the past, before in high school, but I was always too afraid to act on them. And Casey was so wonderful. She never made a play for me."

"No. You made a play for me."

"And I've never regretted it." She kissed Casey's hand.

"Do you think it had to do with the abuse?"

"A lot of people might think that, but I don't." Anne sat beside her.

She took a bite out of her curried chicken and when she was through savoring the heat of the curry, said, "I'm sorry. I hardly know you and I'm asking all these questions."
"It's all right, Alex." Anne touched her hand. "I don't mind talking about it."

Casey plopped on the floor across from them. Her plate was heaped with food and Alex remembered just how much Casey could pack away. When the team was traveling they used to have a pool to see if anyone could guess how many helpings Casey would eat. She was one of those people that ate slowly and ate a lot. Everyone would be finished and she would still be eating, and she would sit at the table having seconds and thirds.

"I only ask, because…"

"Alex was abused, too." Casey finished the sentence for her.

She looked at Casey. "I never said anything. How did you know?"

Casey moved the food on her plate around. "Those scars on your back, Alex. I can only imagine."

Her head was spinning. "Did the whole team know?"

"No. Alex, I only knew because—"

Their eyes met and Casey raised her eyebrows.

She took a sip of her soda. She could feel the color rising in her cheeks.

"You don't have to pretend around me." Anne said, "I know Casey had a busy past. What's done is done."

"That's very mature. I think." This was not the most awkward moment of her life, but it was close.

Casey reached across the table and pushed a stray hair out of Anne's eyes. "Because you know there's only one woman for me."

Anne's face lit up.

Anne turned to her and said, "I bet you would like to change the subject. Wouldn't you?"

She nodded as her mouth was full.

"Do you think the abuse is what drove you into Mindy's arms?"

"No." She had to admit it had nothing to do with the abuse. It never had. "I wanted her from the moment she first said 'hello' to me."

She remembered the first day of social studies class. The teacher played a game. They all had to write on piece of paper what they wanted to be when they grew up and place it in a hat. Then he walked around with the hat and everyone picked a piece of paper. The assignment was to find out whom the paper belonged to. She looked at the pretty handwriting on the paper and read, "I want to be a historian." To this day she could not explain how, but she knew it belonged to the beautiful girl sitting by the window. She noticed her when she walked in the room. The stunning brunette had smiled at her before she took her seat and her heart skipped a beat. As everyone walked around asking questions, she took a deep breath and walked over to where the beauty stood sandwiched between a tall lanky blond who looked like he would eventually grow into his body and a beefy football player who had no neck. She excused herself and held the piece of paper out. "I believe this is yours," she said. Sea blue eyes looked up from the paper and she felt warm all of a sudden. "How did you know?"

She had no explanation— she just did. The girl was intrigued, she could tell, and in that instant they were hooked on each other.

"We were destined to be with each other," she said.

"I like to hear that better than us turning to women when men abuse us."

"It was my mother who abused me."

Casey dropped her fork and it bounced off the coffee table. There was a long period of silence. Anne replaced the fork and looked at Casey. She imagined the two of them were trying to fathom what they had just heard. Finally Casey looked at her, "Your mother did that do you?"

She nodded. "I don't know who my father was. I doubt my mother even knew. But as you say, when you're abused by men you turn to women, so in my case wouldn't men be safe? I mean not that anybody… "

The phone rang and she let out a sigh of relief when Casey rose to get it.

"It's probably Emma."

"How did Emma adjust to the two of you?"

"It's funny—I stayed with him when he hit me, but the minute he laid a hand on her—I was out of there. And she loves Casey. She sees I'm happy. Children can sense when a parent isn't happy, even when they're very young."

"That was Mrs. Peterson." Casey sat back down, "She said she'd bring Emma home when they were finished. They rented a Disney flick and all the kids were pretty engrossed." Turning her attention back to Alex she asked, "You don't have any children, do you?"

"No." But Mindy does, she thought. "Simon and I have been trying. I guess it's not the right time for us."

"Best thing that ever happened to me."

"I never pictured you with children."

"She's wonderful with Emma," Anne said. "Could you pass the soy sauce?"

"Certainly." She handed her the packets of sauce. "I'd like to meet Emma sometime."

"Well, you'll have to come back another time."

"I'd like to come back. I'd like to see your bar sometime, too."

Casey smiled, "You do know it's a women's bar."

"I expected no less."

"It's a lot of fun," Anne said.

"Was it a women's bar when your aunt ran it?"

"Yes. Only I think it was more militant."

Anne dumped the small amount remaining in the hot and sour soup container into her mug. "You said you really like this."

"Thanks."

"Alex, does Simon know you're confused?"

"Simon knows everything." She dipped her spoon into the soup, but not before noticing the concerned look on Anne's face.

"You don't think he'd harm you in any way…"

"Anne, the one thing I know is that after what my mother did to me, no one will ever treat me that way again. Isn't that how you feel?"

"Absolutely."

Casey wiped the sweet and sour sauce off her mouth with her napkin. "Besides, Simon wouldn't hurt a fly."

"It's so hard to read him these days."

"That doesn't sound good."

"Well, I know he's threatened and he's scared, but then he went and painted this..." How to describe it? "Well, its two women locked in a passionate embrace."

"What?"

"It's incredibly beautiful, these vibrant colors melding together in sensual curves...and don't you think it's weird he painted it?"

"Maybe he's trying to tell you something."

"What? He keeps telling me I love her. And I keep telling him I love him and...and I don't know what I'm doing."

"Maybe you don't have to do anything, Alex. If you're happy with Simon there's no reason to do anything."

"Can I ask you something?" Casey set her fork across her plate and looked directly at her.

"Could I stop you?"

"Did we lose those last three games sophomore year because of this Mindy chick?"

"Casey!" Ann scolded.

"Yes."

"I've always wondered what the hell happened to you then. She totally blew your concentration."

"Enough, Casey."

"No, Anne, you don't understand. This woman is like a god on the basketball court—especially for a white girl."

"Like a god." Alex laughed. "I just play the game."

"Do you still play?" Anne inquired.

"Once in a blue moon." Alex looked at Casey. "Do you still play?"

"She coaches at the community center."

"You should come play."

"Maybe. I beat the shit out of my friend yesterday and I had forgotten how good it felt."

"Always does." Casey smiled.

She glanced at her watch. She wanted to take it off and fling it across the room, but she knew she had to get back uptown.

"I'm so sorry, but I have to run."

"Don't go."

"I have to get home because I have company. I wish I didn't have to go." She rose to her feet. "I want to thank you both for listening."

"Anytime."

"It was a pleasure meeting you, especially after reading your books."

"The pleasure was mine." She extended her hand to Anne and took Anne's firmly in her own.

"I hope we'll see more of you."

Casey walked her to the door. "Anne's right you know. You shouldn't be such a stranger. It's a small island we live on."

"I'm starting to realize I've really cut myself off. I need to get back in touch with some of my friends."

"Well, anytime you need to talk, no matter what you decide." Casey pulled a card out of her wallet and handed it to her.

She turned the card over in her hand and noticed it was a card for the club.

"You're welcome anytime. Please come and check the place out."

"Thanks," she kissed Casey on the cheek, "I'm going to take you up on that."

Taking the stairs two at a time down to the street, she decided to take the subway rather than a cab. Their apartment was incredible, she thought to herself; not different than any other couples she knew with lofts, only their loft was so warm and cozy. She thought about what they had talked about as she descended the subway stairs. Thought about how she had wanted Mindy from the moment she saw her. She hadn't felt that way about Simon. She didn't even realize she was in love with him until he took her to the gay bar. She had begun to think about him sexually but not for long…and not with the same longing she had for Mindy.

ten

"Where did you go?" Simon asked as she entered the kitchen. He was wiping off the counter.

Probably cleaning up after Willie, she thought. "I went to visit an old teammate."

"Anyone I know?"

She had never told him about that evening with Casey so she could tell him without any repercussions.

"How is she?"

"Great." She opened the refrigerator and took out a diet soda.

"What did you talk about?"

"Basketball, her aunt's bar, college...did Willie go to his interview?"

"About a half hour ago."

She let herself smell the incredible aroma in the room. "Dinner is going to be wonderful. Should I make something for dessert?"

"Willie made flan."

She sat down at the kitchen table. "That's my Willie." The rich aroma of the simmering sauce reminded her of Mrs. Martineli and she felt her throat constrict. "This smell takes me back."

"I don't think you've been anywhere but back for days." Simon mumbled as he left the kitchen.

She didn't rise to go after him, like she normally would have. She didn't want to. When she fought with Mindy they would never chase each other. They'd let each other go, knowing they each needed their own time to alone to cool down. Simon had a tendency to run after her, making her crazy at times. As a result she learned he wanted her to go after him. If she didn't go after him he would pout about the house. The habit was something that boggled her mind. Even though she didn't want to hurt him or have him pouting about, she couldn't make herself get up and go after him.

She rubbed her temples, which were beginning to pound. The beginning of a tension headache was descending on her. She felt the tension in her neck and knew if she didn't take something now she would end up lying in a dark room with her head packed in ice. She didn't get them often, but when she got them they were debilitating. She knew enough to get the ibuprofen out of the kitchen cabinet. As she dumped the three brown pills into her hand she reached for a glass to fill with water and knew she would have to put an end to this confusion. If she lay quietly in her study for a bit they would take effect and hopefully nip the migraine in the bud. She set the glass in the sink and went into the study.

The answer was simple, she told herself as she kicked her shoes off and stretched out on the couch. She wouldn't see Mindy again. She had built a life with Simon these past couple years. More than that, she had taken a vow—a vow supposed to last forever. She closed her eyes and tried to clear her mind—something she thought would be difficult to do, but perhaps the lack of sleep or the sheer mental exhaustion let her drift off into a dreamless state.

Willie woke her up in time for dinner. The meal was amazing. Willie had truly mastered his mother's culinary skills and recipes. But she said very little, sticking to simple compliments. They ate in silence for a while, not out of awkwardness, but more out of respect for the food itself. She let Willie dominate the conversation when they did talk, inquiring about his freelance work, how his meeting was, and more.

Willie rose to clear the table off and Simon told them to go and talk and he would clean up.

"Are you sure?" she asked.

"Yes."

"Okay. Let's go into the living room."

Willie followed Alex into the living room and sat down in one of the wingback chairs. "You're making him crazy, Alex. You know that, don't you?"

"I'm not trying to." She pulled out a Simon and Garfunkel CD and put it on. "I've been thinking about it, and everything was fine until I saw her again. So I think the solution is quite simple."

"And what's that?"

"I won't see her." She sat down in the other wingback chair and closed her eyes listening to the lush harmonies.

"What are you going to say if she tries to visit you?"

"I'm busy, we have plans…something."

"Well, if you think that's the answer, then I'll go along with you. I won't tell her what we talked about. I don't want to be in the middle of the two of you."

"Quite noble of you."

"I'd call it a survival technique."

"Look around you, Willie. I don't have it bad here. I was happy as a clam until the funeral, so I must be happy, right?"

"Alex, sometimes the past should be just that."

"I think you're right about the past." But she really wasn't convinced. She just knew she had to do this to protect what she had. She owed that much to Simon. "Hey, Willie, do me a favor and challenge Simon to game of Chess. It'll give me a chance to do the dishes right, and it'll take his mind off of stuff.

Willie followed her into the kitchen.

"Hey, Simon what about a games of Chess?" he asked.

"Go ahead, Simon. I'll finish up."

"Are you sure?"

"Yes." She took the dishcloth from him and kissed him on the cheek. "Go ahead; you know I can't give you a run for your money like Willie can."

"Okay."

She watched as they went into the living room where the chessboard was set up, then turned her attention to the dishes. It wasn't that Simon didn't do a good job. She just wanted to do something mindless so she could think about how she would go about avoiding Mindy. Fortunately, they lived far enough apart, so it wasn't like she'd just show up on the doorstep. She would stop writing to her, keep her at a good distance. Christmas cards and birthday cards should suffice. If Mindy wanted to visit, she could always be busy. If they didn't see each other, then there would be no threat to Simon. She knew he was threatened the evening she came back. How could she ease his mind?

She didn't want to have these feelings; they just surfaced on they're own. How could she explain them?

"Simon, take it easy," she heard Willie say.

"I'm trying, Willie. It's not easy, though."

She moved closer to the archway, so they couldn't see her, but she could hear better.

Simon was talking. "I knew when you called this might happen. It's the first contact they've had since the initial break. I took all the psych courses in college. I know exactly what's happening and I've tried to understand. But, she won't talk to me…"

"I think she doesn't know what she's feeling. Simon, can you understand that?"

"Don't defend her, Willie; she's a grown woman now. She could talk to me."

"Well, I've tried to talk to her, and I haven't gotten anywhere."

"Of course you didn't. She didn't talk to you either. She went to talk to some old basketball buddy she occasionally swaps Christmas cards with."

"Maybe she needed a different perspective."

"I'm her best friend, Willie. We talk about everything. We always have. But, now, it's like she won't let me in. I just want to know."

"You're afraid she's going to leave you, aren't you?"

"I don't know what she's going to do, Willie. That's what's frightening. Not knowing how she feels."

"I can't tell you what she's going to do, Simon. I have no idea. I thought you guys had this great thing going on here."

"I did, too."

"She's been with you a while…I don't think she would blow it."

"It's like your sister has some mystifying power over her. I knew when I met Alex she and Mindy were lovers. It was written all over her face. I didn't want to fall in love with her, Willie. I really tried to stay distant. I didn't think I'd ever have a chance, and then when they broke up, Alex turned to me. She talked to me, cried on me. I put her back together, Willie. Your sister really destroyed her."

"I know."

"And now I feel like I put her back together just so she go could back to the person who ripped her apart."

"Have you told Alex how you feel?"

"Not in so many words."

"Maybe…"

"Willie, she knows I'm scared out of my wits right now. She could at least tell me something, anything."

She couldn't tell him. She just couldn't. She went into her study and closed the door. She didn't want to hear anymore. The last thing she wanted to do was hurt Simon. But, she did know. If only she hadn't gone to that damned funeral.

eleven

Willie left and she immersed herself in finishing the book. Things with Simon calmed a bit. She'd put the letters back in the attic and tried to put Mindy as far back in the recesses of her mind as she could get her.

Simon started work on the off-Broadway show and was busy researching his design. Sculpture was really his second love, painting his first, but he was adept at both. The show was about an artist and his obsession with his art. She found the script a bit dark, but Simon was fascinated by the challenge.

Roz had called several times about the cartoon venture. She wasn't making her happy by putting her off, but she was afraid to have her stories translated into cartoons. They were so personal. Roz told her they were universal, but it was like relinquishing control of your children and having a stranger raise them. The tapes sat on her desk along with the storyboards in an envelope. She moved it around on her desk, but she refused to open it. Instead, she piled all the bills and correspondence on top of it.

Casey called to see how she was doing and to invite her to the bar. She promised to go down when Simon went away on business. Aside from the show, he had several interviews with museums to display his work. Casey convinced her to play basketball. They met at her community center on an off night. Being indoors made it seem like a regular college game only without the rest of the team. She'd almost forgotten what an outstanding player Casey was. Casey gave her a run for her money. They were pretty evenly matched. Casey won the first game and she won the second; they left the third for another day. It was amazing she could play so well after not playing for so long. Since college, aside from her morning runs with Simon, her exercise regimen amounted to swimming laps at the health club three or four times a week. In the summer she and Simon would strap their bikes on the car and go up to the Berkshires to ride ten to twenty miles and stay in the Red Lion Inn so they could sit on the porch and sip Long Island iced teas at sunset. Once in a while they'd see a show at the theatre festival or drive up to Tanglewood with a picnic and listen to the music. But mostly they would just relax on the whitewashed

Victorian porch with huge columns. After a day of riding it was nice to kick back in a rocker and just watch the tourists go by and after several Long Island iced teas they'd go up to the room and if they had enough energy they'd make love. If they didn't they'd just fall asleep in each other's arms.

After the basketball game, they went for Afghan food with Anne and Simon at a small restaurant on St. Mark's. They sat on cushions in the dimly lit window booth, drank the bottle of merlot Simon had brought from home, and ate fried turnovers, tandoori chicken, basmati rice, Afghan bread, and eggplant. Anne and Casey seemed to really enjoy Simon, as most of her friends did. They seemed to hit it off right away. Anne was particularly fascinated in hearing about Simon's artwork. Simon loved to talk about art so that made the evening go quickly. She loved watching Anne and Casey together. Aside from their habit of finishing each other's sentences, they seemed to complement each other perfectly.

Anne and Casey had to call it an early evening because they had to pick Emma up at the babysitter's. Simon suggested walking uptown. She let her hand slip into his as they walked, enjoying the familiar warmth as he told her how much he enjoyed meeting Casey and Anne. He remembered Casey from college, but he had never spent any time with her.

She asked him what he thought about gay couples having children and he told her he felt children needed two people to love them. It didn't really matter who those two people were. He wanted to know why she asked, and she told him she had been thinking about Emma. He seemed content with that answer, but the truth was she had been wondering ever since she met Casey and Anne about Mindy's children. They had talked about children when they were together, as if it were the most natural thing in the world. Mindy had wanted them to get Willie's sperm and have her carry the baby; then it would have both their genes. She was totally convinced when the time came it would be an easy thing to do. Alex was not convinced, but then she was never convinced she should be around children.

Simon talked about his sculptures and she found herself letting his excitement sweep her back into the moment.

They stopped at a deli along the way and Simon bought her a single red rose. She looked at him. His burgundy shirt was tucked neatly into his khaki pants. His belt matched his light brown sandals. He did clean up well, she thought. He smiled and his eyes sparkled. She loved the way his hazel eyes would change color. He leaned over to kiss her and she clung to him, smelling the musky cologne he always wore. She cherished his smell. Sometimes he would arrive home and she would know it before he said a word because she would smell his cologne in the air. She realized he really was a romantic at heart. She also realized that the night was only beginning for them.

twelve

Simon had left for a business trip. He was interviewing with a museum in Chicago to have some of his works shown. Sometimes she would tag along, but she had already been to Chicago several times and it wasn't one of her favorite places. She told him she would use the time to go over her line edit and follow up on some correspondence. The line edit she knew would take very little time. Her editor Gillian, rarely had too many edits and the ones she did havewere always excellent. Alex rarely argued with Gillian, because Gillian seemed to be able to get inside her head and adopt her voice when she edited. Today was no exception. She breezed through the edit, making the changes Gillian suggested. She had just closed the file when the doorbell rang.

The sight of Mindy on the other side of the door—overnight bag in hand—as she pressed her eye to the peephole was like a blow to the chest knocking the wind out of her. She stopped to regain her breath. Her hand found the cool glass door handle and she managed to turn it.

"Surprise!" Mindy called out as the door opened, and fell into her arms.

Soft curls caressed her cheek; breasts pressed against breasts; sweet perfume filled her nostrils. Her throat tightened as she realized just how much she had actually missed this.

"I hope you're not too upset with me for not calling."

Pushing Mindy back quickly, she tried to compose herself and asked, "So, what do I owe this surprise to?" Her heart was racing. Thoughts whipped around her brain like the tea cup ride at the carnival, making her dizzy. This wasn't happening, she tried to tell herself as Mindy spoke.

"I would have called, honestly, but it was so spur-of-the-moment. Willie went off to California on a shoot and Mark took the boys on a Cub Scout retreat…and I thought why not use up some of our frequent-flier miles?"

"What would you have done if I wasn't home?"

"Visited some friends from college that settled here." She stood in the doorway. "May I come in?"

Danger, danger, warning, Will Robinson.

"Alex?"

"Yes, of course." She reached down and picked up Mindy's overnight bag. She wasn't expecting it to be so heavy for an overnight stay. Mindy pulled the door shut behind them.

"This is a lovely place. Too bad it's in Manhattan."

She remembered New York was the one place Mindy never wanted to live when they talked about living in different cities. But after living there for a couple of years, she found it hard to imagine living anywhere else. "Actually, it's perfect for us. Come on, I'll give you the ten-cent tour."

She led her around the house listening to the usual comments about furniture and the artwork, but she wasn't paying attention. The smell of Mindy's perfume filled the air, the scent used to drive her wild. All she could think was, *she's here…what do I do now?*

"And this is the guest room." She placed Mindy's bag on the bed. "I'd have put clean sheets on the bed if I would have known you were coming."

"I'll make it up later if you tell me where the sheets are. This is a lovely room. The clouds are fantastic." Her eyes settled on the photo of Alex shooting basketball. "I see Willie gave you the photo."

"Really, he said it was a copy—said you kept the original."

"I've always loved that photo. It's like you're flying. You were so amazing when you played."

She felt her cheeks warm. "Well, why don't we go downstairs into the study and chat? I have to turn my computer off."

"Were you writing something new?"

"Just going over the final line edit."

Mindy shrugged.

She had just spoken a foreign language, but she didn't feel like explaining. And Mindy was already on the next subject—asking where Simon was.

She told her where he went and why and Mindy seemed very excited. She wondered for a moment if Mindy's enthusiasm was for his good fortune or for his timely absence. "Yeah, I'm very proud of him. He really is quite amazing."

"Does he have any work I could see?"

She thought about the painting in the studio. "Not right now."

"Could I use your powder room?"

"Sure. It's just right through there," she said, pointing the way. "I'll just go down and shut my computer off."

"I'll meet you downstairs."

"Okay." She moved down the stairs quickly, wanting to get away from Mindy as fast as she could. Ever since she walked through the door it was all she could do to not stare at her. She had already memorized the outfit Mindy wore. Navy rayon pants and a blue blouse with a delicate floral pattern with flecks of red and gold. The blouse was open to the third button. Around her neck was a tiny gold cross, a cross Alex had given her on their first Christmas together. Her skin was still flawless.

Stopping in the hallway, she checked her reflection in the mirror. At least she had put on her jeans without the holes in the knees and a navy polo shirt instead of her usual sweat clothes. She buttoned the shirt up to the collar, and ran her fingers through her hair, which was slightly tousled. Then she went into the study.

Mindy arrived as she was shutting the computer down.

"I really don't want to take you away from anything."
"You're not," she admitted. "Have a seat. I just want to put these papers away."

"Okay." She sat down on the edge of the sofa. "This is really a lovely room. Did you decorate it yourself?"

"Yes."

"Are those all your awards?"

She saw the genuine look of awe as Mindy looked at the wall of plaques lining the opposite wall. Simon had insisted she hang them. "They're nothing really, just some children's organizations that honored me."

"Don't say that's nothing," Mindy scolded, as she crossed to get a better look.

"I don't think they're nothing. I just..."

"Get embarrassed easily," Mindy said. "I remember."

She put the line edit back in the envelope and tucked it in her desk drawer as Mindy studied each award.

"Very impressive," Mindy said as she crossed back toward the sofa. "You are extremely talented, you know."

She could feel her cheeks burn. "Could we change the subject, please?"

Mindy laughed. Then she let her hands sweep over the stack of magazines lying on the coffee table. "Do you really read all these?" she asked as she pulled an issue of *Ladies Home Journal* from the pile.

"Sometimes when I watch TV. Not too often."

She laughed, clearly amused at something she was reading. "Listen to this survey. The Hidden Woman, her life and desires."

"They have some doozies in there."

"Let's take it."

"I don't think so."

"Come on, it'll be fun. Get a pen."

It beat making small talk, she thought, as she reached for a pen and then sat down beside Mindy. She remembered how the two of them would lie on Mindy's bed and take the surveys in *Seventeen*.

Mindy folded the magazine so the first page of the survey was flat. "'Do you enjoy cooking?' No. You?"

"Most of the time."

"Really?"

"I'm no wizard like your Mom was, but I'm not bad."

"She was amazing, wasn't she?"

"Yes." She saw Mindy's eyes were filling with tears and she wanted to change the subject. She leaned over and read the next question. "'Do you like cleaning?' What, are they crazy?"

Mindy smiled. "They must be." She looked at the next question, "'Favorite entertainment activity?' Well, definitely the movies. Is that still yours?"

Alex nodded.

"'How often do you watch TV?' Four or five hours a day. You?"

"You really watch that much TV?"

"Yeah. Why?"

"I just watch it once in a while. Simon and I either do something in the evening or I end up reading or writing."

"Hmm. Must be nice. 'How would you describe your figure?'" Mindy continued. "And listen to the choices: a) fat, b) hippy, c) full bodied, but attractive, d) good figure, or e) too thin." She stood and did a full turn. "Well, what do you think?"

Given permission to look, she did. She followed the curve of Mindy's neck down to her breasts, which were slightly larger than she remembered—probably since the birth of her children—to her flat stomach. She could feel Mindy's eyes on her and looked at her face in time to catch her smiling. *Do they have a fantastic category?* she thought, and then swallowed before she said, "Good figure."

Mindy's face lit up. "Thanks. And you, there's no question about it. You have a great figure." She checked the appropriate boxes and continued to number five.

"'Favorite facial feature?' I think the eyes have it." She didn't wait for Alex to concur. "'Least favorite feature?' I think it's my hair, and you don't have any bad features."

"My chin." Alex said.

"Your chin is perfect. I'll just make another column for you." She scrawled 'none of the above' underneath the question and checked it. "'People you socialize with most?' Friends, for me."

"Simon."

"Okay. I guess we can put him under family. 'Where did you meet your husband/boyfriend?' College for both of us. ' What is the biggest problem you have with your husband/boyfriend?' Let's come back to that one. ' Is there anything you haven't told your husband/boyfriend about your past?'" She flipped the page to the next question.

But before Mindy could read it aloud, Alex asked, "Why didn't you tell Mark about us?"

Mindy looked into her eyes. "I...didn't know how."

"I didn't mean to put you on the spot. I'm sorry. What's the next question?" She leaned over to read. "'How would you rate your sex life?'"

Mindy chuckled.

"Is there a twenty-five?"

Mindy's laughter stopped. "It only goes to ten."

"Then it's a ten."

Mindy slammed the magazine shut and placed it back on the coffee table. "You're right. This is stupid."

"'Did I say something wrong?'"

"No."

"Are you sure?" she inquired, noting how somber things had suddenly gotten.

"Yeah."

Must have been the over-rating of my sex life. Why not just tattoo a big sign on your forehead—off-limits. "Well, why don't I get us something to drink?" *Drinks are probably a good idea.*

"That sounds good."

"You choose."

"Do you have any wine?"

She suggested the open bottle of merlot in the kitchen. The phone rang as she entered the kitchen.

"Hey, baby, did I catch you at a bad time?"

"No," Alex lied.

"You sound a bit funny."

Why did he have to be so damned perceptive? "Just finishing up my line edit."

"How's it going?"

"Slow."

"Too bad. But I guess you'll have more time now. It looks like I'm going to be delayed another day. They want me to meet the museum's board of trustees tomorrow and I can't exactly say 'no.' I'm sorry."

"Don't be silly. Just go in there tomorrow and show 'em your stuff."

"I will."

"Good luck."

"I miss you, baby."

"I miss you, too."

"I'll call you when I know what time my new flight will be."

"I'll be waiting."

She let the receiver fall back onto the phone and took a deep breath. She should have told him. She should have insisted he come back right now. The last thing she wanted was to be alone with Mindy and yet here she was. Puttering around to fix the drinks she told herself it would be okay. Making Simon come back before he cut a good deal would have been selfish. She could handle this.

She set the tray with the two wine glasses and a bottle down on the desk and reached across into the right-hand drawer where she kept cocktail napkins. Mindy had moved into a corner of the sofa and she noticed she was crying.

"Mindy, what's wrong?" she asked, sitting down beside her and holding out a glass of wine.

"Nothing." She wiped her eyes with her hands and took the drink.

"Here." She offered her a tissue from the box at the end of the table.

"Thanks." She blew her nose. "I guess I just let the words of the song get to me."

"Oh," she turned her attention to the last chords of Barry Manilow's "Weekend in New England." 'And when will I hold you again.' If it was the words, then she was right about Mindy's feelings. But, she didn't want to believe that. She watched as Mindy shredded the tissue into tiny pieces. "Are you and Mark—?"

"No."

"Then, what?" She took the bits of tissue out of her hand.

Mindy locked onto her eyes and held them captive for what seemed like an agonizingly long time. She wanted to look away but she could feel Mindy searching. She noticed Mindy's throat quivered.

She sat back for a moment. What was she trying to see? What could she possible be thinking that would cause such a flood of tears?

"Can I put on a CD?" Mindy asked as she moved to the bookcase and leafed through the CD collection.

"Of course." She joined her and helped her pick out an Indigo Girls CD, which she put on the stereo. Mindy leaned against the bookcase studying her as she put the case back on the shelf.

"Mindy, if you're having some sort of problem, you know you can talk to me. I mean I know we haven't talked in quite some time, but..."

"It's not a problem."

She clicked the 'on' switch and the soft strings of their guitars filled the room. She turned to look at Mindy.

Tears were sliding down her cheeks and Mindy turned her attention to the floor.

"Mindy," she let her hands close around Mindy's face. "What is it?"

After a moment Mindy whispered, "Don't you know?"

"No. Tell me."

"It's you."

"Me. But I..." Suddenly Mindy's lips were pressed firmly against hers. Burning with an unquenchable thirst, Mindy tried to drink her in. She had forgotten what a sweet taste Mindy had. Memories appeared in her head like a multi-colored slideshow. The two of them together...the first time they made love...her back as she left...Simon's face! Letting go of Mindy's face, her palms found Mindy's shoulders and pressed them trying to push her away.

Mindy fought the pushing until she shoved so hard she sent Mindy back several steps. The only word she could form was "no," which she exclaimed loudly.

"But you responded."

Stupid! Stupid! She crossed to the coffee table and downed the rest of her drink. "I didn't mean to."

"But you did." Mindy moved toward her.

"I love my husband!" she shouted—stopping Mindy in her tracks.

"I wish I could say the same. But I can't. Alex, I've never stopped…"

"Don't say it," she cautioned as she moved toward her desk and refilled her wine glass. "Please, don't say it."

"But it's how I feel. I never meant to hurt you."

"But you did."

Mindy reached for her hand.

She pulled away, noting the pain in Mindy's eyes as she did. She had never seen that look before and it sent a chill through her.

"I didn't want it to turn out this way. I should have never left you."

She felt her heart soften. "Mindy, let's not do this."

"We have to do this, Alex." She buried her face in her hands to muffle the sobs.

Alex tore several tissues from the box and handed them to her.

Mindy grasped her hand.

She was looking into Mindy's eyes. Before she knew it her finger brushed against Mindy's cheek, catching a teardrop. "You would think after all these years I wouldn't be affected by your tears." She felt her armor shift a bit.

Mindy kissed her palm tenderly. "I want you, Alex," she said quietly. "I always have."

She felt Mindy's fingers burn against her palm, but before she could pull her hand away Mindy's lips touched hers. She remembered how soft and gentle her kisses could be. How good she felt in her arms after all this time. Yes. This was it. This was where she belonged. She closed her eyes as Mindy pulled her closer. She opened her mouth to welcome Mindy's tongue and she let her arms encircle Mindy's neck.

She could feel her stomach somersault as she tried to stop. She had to stop it. Mindy's hands were pulling her shirt out of her pants when she caught her by the wrists. "Mindy, I can't." She gently pushed her away.

"But you want to. I can feel it."

There was no point in lying. "Yes, I do. But I can't do this to Simon."

"Why?"

"Because I've built a life with him and I'm not going to give that up. I've worked too hard to get it."

"I wish I had found someone like your Simon. Someone to understand me the way he understands you. But, only you seem to be able to do that."

"We did have something special."

"Yeah."

"Mindy, stop crying. Please."

"When I went to college, I realized what a fantasy world you and I lived in."

"What are you talking about? Everything I felt for you was real."

"Oh, the feelings were real enough, but society would never accept them. I didn't think I could give up being able to walk down the street hand in hand, being able to tell everyone who you were and what you meant to me."

"But we never told anyone in high school."

"It was easier not to. You were always by my side."

"You broke up with me because we couldn't hold hands in public?"

Mindy continued to cry as she explained. "I had a roommate in college. I thought we were close, but I was wrong." Her tears seemed to wash away her age and she appeared to be seventeen again. "Shelley was her name. Anyway, she found your letters to me, along with my diary and she read them when I was in class. I'll never forget her face as long as I live. She looked at me as if I had committed an axe murder or some other heinous crime. And when I tried to explain I loved you more than anyone or anything she said it was an abomination of God and I would rot in hell and she couldn't be my friend anymore."

"She sounds like an ass."

"Alex, she was going to go to the dean and try to have me expelled. She told the sorority I was pledging all about it and they dropped me like a hot potato. No other sorority on campus would touch me when they found out. Then there were my friends. When they found out they acted like I was a leper or something. No one talked to me. I don't know if it was the pressure of pledging the sorority and they were told not to talk to me or if they were just homophobic."

"I guess the thought they weren't really your friends never crossed your mind?"

"I had to tell them Shelley was lying. I told them you wrote the letters, but they were your feelings, not mine. When they asked about the diary I told them I wasn't writing my actual feelings, but rather keeping notes for a story. Your letters gave me the idea."

"You what?"

"I was doing so well, you know…my grades were top notch. There was too much at stake. Shelley was threatening to call my mother unless I went to the Director of Residence Life and got a new room assignment. I had to do it, don't you see? I told the Director it was all a misunderstanding. Shelley had made a huge mistake and I didn't want my mother hurt by such accusations. She agreed with me. You understand, Alex, don't you?"

ButAlex didn't understand.

"Well, don't just stand there looking at me."

"What should I do, Mindy? Say it's okay?"

"You had it easy. You played on the fucking basketball team. Everyone knows they're all a bunch of dykes. You could have told the world you were gay and no one would have cared as long as you were scoring. It wasn't like that in Boston. Jesus Christ, you know how uptight New Englanders are? I had no one to turn to. And if she told my mother, how could I explain?"

"She would have understood."

"You don't believe that, Alex. You know it would have killed her."

"In some ways, yes, but I also know how much she loved you. The sun rose and set on you, Mindy. You know that. Especially once Willie dropped out of college."

"I couldn't take that chance."

"You mean you couldn't take that chance for me?"

"Alex, my world was coming down around me. I wasn't thinking about you. Can't you understand? Maybe if you'd lived through what I lived through, you'd feel differently. It was a very ugly thing. Having people love you one day and hate you the next. Can't you even accept I was young and stupid? I was trying to save my neck. I never realized the price I would pay."

She wasn't sure what Mindy was looking for. What did she want her to say? "That's okay, Mindy, I understand you had to sell me out"?

"Don't you remember how I cried the last weekend we were together? Every time we made love I knew I would never know your touch again. Alex, I never thought I'd turn out this way."

"What way?"

She took time forming the word and then, like a bad piece of candy, she spat it out—"gay."

"Funny, I never thought of myself as being gay. Well, not for long. I decided it was just a question of love."

"Well, I know I'm gay."

"How do you know?"

"I knew when I was little. And now, well, Mark tries to please me in bed, but all I can do is close my eyes and pretend it's you."

Don't tell me this. This is not what I want to hear. She poured more wine into her glass and downed it. "Have you told Mark how you feel? Not about me, about not being satisfied?"

"Don't be silly."

"Mindy, I'm sure if you told him he would try something different. It's a matter of sensitivity, that's all."

"He's not very sensitive."

"Well you have to help him learn how to be sensitive."

"It's not the same, Alex. You were always so wonderful."

Well, if I was so goddamned wonderful, why'd you sell me out, Mindy? "I was crazy about you. I would have done anything to please you. I met Mark and I know he's crazy about you, too."

"Alex, I married Mark because that's what you were supposed to do. Grow up, get married, have babies…that's what society expects."

Alex filled her glass again. She was looking for the buzz to dull the pain, but it wasn't coming. "That's bullshit and you know it."

"I had to date Mark. If I didn't start dating someone they would have known I was lying. We dated for so long, Mark just took it for granted I would want to marry him."

"So you married him out of some social obligation?"

"I married him because you married Simon."

"You married him out of spite?"

"No, Alex. I thought marrying him was my only choice. I had thought I might…it doesn't matter what I thought. You married Simon and I married Mark. End of story."

"You thought you might what? Come back to me?"

"I know you still love me, Alex; I could feel it just now when you kissed me."

"I never denied my feelings for you, Mindy. You were my first love and I learned a lot from you. You taught me how to open up and give, willingly. And I've never regretted a moment I spent with you."

"But you love Simon."

She didn't like Mindy's tone. "People move on." *Or at least they try to*, she told herself.

"And yet you respond to me. Why?"

"A part of me still loves you," she said.

"And I need you."

Touching a finger to Mindy's lips, she continued. "You didn't let me finish. I can't be what you want."

"Just this once."

"You don't want it to be just once."

"You're right. I want it to be forever. But, I'll take just once."

"Mindy, we're both married now. There are other people to consider. Not just the two of us."

"We're the only two people in this room, Alex. We're the only two people that matter to me. I don't understand why we can't be happy."

"I am happy."

"Are you, Alex? Are you really happy?"

"Yes."

"Then why'd you kiss me like that if you're so goddamned happy with Simon?"

Good question.

"I'll tell you why. Because you never stopped loving me, just like I never stopped loving you." Mindy took the glass of wine out of her hand and moved closer to her. "Why can't you just let your heart guide you?"

"Listen to me, Mindy; if you wanted to spend the rest of your life with me, you should have spoken up a long time ago, instead of walking out of my life. Because when you walked out, Simon was there, and he cared, and he loved me. And in time, I realized I loved him, too. And I'll be damned if I'm going to ruin something so good because after all these years you decide that you feel the same. It's too late for us."

"Don't say that."

"I have to say that. Mindy, you have a husband, children. Have you thought about them?"

Mindy sank into the sofa. "So you don't give a fuck about me?"

"Don't twist my words. You know exactly what I mean. I think maybe we could be friends again, and I do still care about you, but what we had physically together—that's a memory now. That's all it can be. And we shouldn't try and resurrect something that's been dead for years."

"Oh, if it's so dead why did you warm up so quickly?"

"Because in my mind it never ended the way it should have. You and I were supposed to be together. I wanted that more than anything in the world. But you ended it, Mindy. You. And whether you think it's a mistake or not, you are the one that made it. You broke my heart."

"Don't say that."

"Why not? It's true."

"Alex, I can't take it back. If I could, I would. I told you what happened."

"And that's supposed to make everything better? No, Mindy, not this time. This requires more than a simple apology. I'm sorry you had a jerk for a roommate and she did a number on your head. But, I always thought you had more strength."

"What?"

"I never would have betrayed you like that."

"You sound like a martyr."

"And you're going to try and tell me we didn't understand the consequences of our relationship being exposed? That we kept it a secret all those years just for the hell of it? That you snuck into my bedroom or vice versa because it was fun to sneak around? Don't play stupid with me. It's not becoming."

"Well, there's a little color in your cheeks these days. Looks like my little Alex has finally developed a temper."

If anyone knows your buttons, she does. Keep your cool, girl. "If you think this is anger, honey, you haven't even scratched the surface," Alex warned.

"You were always so afraid of being angry. What's the matter, afraid you'd end up with your mother's temper?"

In an instant her palm tingled and she watched as Mindy touched her red cheek in disbelief. She couldn't breath. She looked at her hand, but it wasn't hers. It couldn't be hers. Her body shook as she gasped for air.

Mindy's arms were around her. "Jesus, Alex, I'm sorry." Mindy rocked her, "I didn't mean… you're nothing like her. Nothing."

The comparison was brutal. Even though she had never hit anyone in her life—had never dreamt she could—she had hit Mindy hard.

And in that instant her whole world blew apart at the seams. The only thing keeping her from crumbling to the ground in a ball were Mindy's arms around her.

"I didn't mean it." Mindy whispered over and over as she rocked Alex. "I swear to God. It's okay. I deserved to be slapped."

"No one deserves it," she managed to choke, and then the tears came.

Mindy was crying, too. "Oh, God, Alex, don't cry. Please don't cry. I didn't know what I was doing then. Can't you understand? I would never leave you now. And I know I hurt you. It breaks my heart to think I could have ever hurt you. I'd take it all back if I could."

Then Mindy's lips were on her cheeks, kissing each tear away. "I'm sorry. I'm so sorry." She whispered over and over again as she kissed the tears away. "I never should have said that. Never." Mindy's arms tightened around her and their bodies melted into each other's.

She wasn't certain whose lips found whose first, only that they were kissing, tenderly at first and then with a hunger. And all the anger and all the pain and hurt became logs in the fire, adding fuel to a passion erupting in such an explosive manner the resulting flame took several hours to douse.

At first she felt reborn—then thoughts of Simon crept into her head. She felt confused, guilty, and ashamed.

thirteen

Mindy kissed her on the cheek as she stirred. "Morning," she smiled.

She could not mirror Mindy's happiness. Quickly, she maneuvered out from under Mindy. "Is it?" she asked as she started toward the bathroom. She needed a shower. Mindy was behind her; she knew it, but she closed the door between them anyway. Couldn't Mindy sense she needed to be alone?

"Hey, what's the matter?"

"I need a shower."

"Well, I know this great trick with a bar of soap."

How well she remembered that trick. She met her reflection in the mirror. *Well, stupid, what do you have to say for yourself?*

"Was that a yes?" The doorknob turned and she reached over and locked it.

"No."

"What's the matter with you?"

Not an unfounded question after the night of lovemaking they had just shared. Her nipples were tender and her bottom lip was slightly swollen.

"I need to be alone."
"Why?"

"Please, just leave me alone," she said as she stepped into the shower. She turned on the water hoping to drown out any further questions Mindy might have. The warm water raced over the tension starting to form between her shoulder blades the moment she woke up. The water pounded on her back helping her relax. She closed her eyes and prayed the water would wash the night away. Lathering up three times she scrubbed her skin raw with the washcloth until it tingled.

Roz would know what to do. If she made it to her office before eleven, she would have time to see her. The time was probably nine. She had been checking the time all morning when she couldn't sleep. Stepping out of the shower and reaching for a towel, she knew she had to get dressed and get out of the house. Roz would know exactly what to do.

Mindy was waiting for her when she stepped into the bedroom. She wished Mindy could take the hint and leave her alone.

"You turned awful shy, all of a sudden," Mindy remarked as she stepped back into the bathroom to change.

"What time is it?"

"Nine-fifteen. Why?"

"I have a meeting with my agent." She dressed in a hurry, pulling on a pair of khakis, a beige turtleneck, and one of Simon's black sweaters. *Might as well wear his clothes while you can*, she told herself. "So I have to run out."
"Too bad. I was hoping to spend the day in bed."

"There's food downstairs," she offered, trying to find the holes in her ears to put the gold hoops through. "God damn it. I can never do this."

"Let me."

"That's okay," she said, dropping the hoops on the sink. She needed to maintain her distance. Dropping to her knees by the bed, she reached under and retrieved her sneakers.

"Well, I guess I should get dressed."

She looked up at Mindy's naked body. Why did she have to be so beautiful? None of her thoughts made any sense any more. Her mind was like a bad Monty Python script with bits and pieces of different sketches flying in and out. She was holding on by a thread and she knew it.

The bed! The sheets had to be changed before Simon came home. "Shit!" She pulled the sheets off the bed and stuffed them into the laundry bag.

"Destroying the evidence?"

The tone in Mindy's voice did little to make her feel any better. She flung the clean sheets at her. "Just help me."

Mindy dropped the sheets on the bed. "Why should I?"

Nine-fifteen in the morning was never a good time of day for her to begin with, but she was not accustomed to losing her mind at that hour either. She hadn't put that on the calendar for this morning, and by God, she was going to prevent it if she could. "I would appreciate it," she said sweetly, "if you would give me a hand, since I seem to be running a little late."

They made the bed in silence. She slipped through Mindy's arms, avoiding a kiss not meant to be a good-bye, grabbed her bag, and started down the stairs. Subway tokens were in the study. She stopped in the doorway wondering if she had enough time to pick up the articles of clothing scattered around the room. And she knew she would never look at the couch the same again. Grabbing the coins off the desk, she raced from the house. Breaking into a run the moment her feet touched the sidewalk, she raced the four blocks to the subway. Roz would know what to do, she told herself over and over. Besides, she had to speak with someone before she saw Simon again.

By the time she reached the twenty-first floor of Roz's building she felt a bit calmer. Just the calm before the storm, she told herself. Beverly Anne, Roz's assistant, greeted her with the usual overzealous manner. She told her Roz was on the phone with an important client and she'd have to wait, and then flashed a smile Crest would have paid money for.

Roz was seated behind her mahogany desk, mulling over some papers, phone pressed tightly to her ear, when she burst in. "Not now, Beverly Anne," Roz said without lifting her eyes from the paperwork.

She dropped into the chair opposite Roz and drummed on the arms of the chair.

"Absolutely not, Oscar. I told you once the contract is signed, you have to be prepared to put out. It's been over six months and you have not even discussed an idea with them, let alone shown them an outline." She put her hand over the receiver. "Beverly Anne, please, I'll buzz you when I'm finished, sweetheart."

"I'm not Beverly Anne."

Roz looked up at her and mouthed, "What are you doing here?"

"Advice." She replied as Roz continued to chew out her client. She looked around the eclectic office Roz kept. The walls a burnt sienna, the floors were a light oak with an inlaid pattern framing the room. In the corners of the room sat a large leather sofa, two Victorian chairs, and an oriental coffee table with a marble top. Underneath the furniture lay a well-worn Oriental rug. Among the photographs of her with various authors and her awards were the trophies from her various excursions. A large black mask carved out of wood, with huge eyes and a gaping mouth, sat strategically between the photo of her with the greatest horror writer of the 20th Century and the one with the African-American poet laureate. A large medieval tapestry woven in rich tones of burnt orange, amber, brown, and blue depicting a unicorn in a field of flowers covered the wall by the door. Behind her desk was a window serving as a wall. Looking out at the buildings looming like giants next to this one, she wondered what her life would have been like if she had never come this far. Would she have found her voice?

"Don't call me again, just do what you promised them and write the damn book." Roz set the receiver down, shoved her papers back into the folder, and deposited it in her outgoing tray.

"You don't make appointments anymore?"

"Sorry."

She smiled. "Lucky for you I have a light morning."

"Good."

"Something is obviously bothering you. I hope it's not one of your books."

"I wish it were." Her mouth suddenly felt dry. "Do you think Beverly Anne could bring us some water?"

"Do you want something stronger?"

"How about a pill to turn back time?"

Roz pressed the intercom and asked Beverly Anne to bring in two glasses of water and to hold all calls. Then she stood and walked to the other side of the office where the sofa was. "I think you'll be more comfortable over here."

"I think you're right." She sank into the sofa next to her. For a moment she wondered what she was doing there. Roz couldn't help her. No one could. She had dug her grave. Simon would know the minute he saw her. She had sacrificed everything for sex and now she was living out a fucking Greek tragedy.

"Alex, you burst into my office unannounced to talk to me and then you just sit there."

"Sorry." She met Roz's inquiring eyes, but she still couldn't talk. Beverly Anne appeared with a tray containing two water glasses and a pitcher of water.
"Thank you," she said, taking a glass and downing half of it in hopes it would loosen up her throat.

"I'm expecting a very important phone call from London. Please make sure they can be called back."

"I will." Beverly Anne left. Roz set her glass on a coaster on the antique coffee table and took her hand. "If I were to have this pill you want to turn back time and I gave it to you, exactly what would it erase?"

She looked at the slim hand holding hers with the perfectly manicured nails. She had come this far, and now she wasn't sure what to say. "I told you about Mindy?"

"Briefly."

"Well, she came to visit." She looked at Roz. How could she really explain what had happened? She didn't want to.

"And Simon is gone and you and Mindy fell into bed again. Is that it?"

"I don't know what to do."

"And you want me to tell you what to do?"

"Would you?"

She released her hand. "And if I did, would you listen?"

"It depends on what you told me."

"That's what I like about you, Alex. You're honest. What is it you want me to tell you?"
"I don't know."

"I don't buy that. But we'll play it your way." She took a tug off her drink. "Well, answer me this, did you enjoy it?"

"I don't think that is the issue here."

"Should I take that for a yes, or are you going to answer the question?"

"Okay. It was nice…familiar…who am I kidding? It was fantastic. Roz, what am I going to do?"

"Do you want to keep sleeping with Mindy?"

"No."

"You're sure?"

"Hello, I'm married to Simon."

"I know. But, sweetheart, one does not necessarily have to do with the other."

She was lost now. "What are you saying?"

"That you can have feelings for both. Did you think about Simon when you were with Mindy?"

"You don't leave anything to the imagination, do you?"

Roz reached over and pulled her hands apart before she twisted them into a knot and kept a hold of her hand. "You want me to help you or not?"

"I thought about him when I tried to stop her, and afterwards...but it all happened so...no I didn't think about him." She felt her stomach begin to spin like a dryer set on tumble. Her back snapped to attention as the pain sliced through her shoulder blades. The migraine would follow if she didn't relax. "I was in a time warp. All these feelings I thought had died years ago suddenly snapped to life."

"What I'm gathering from this broken dialogue is you and Mindy spent the night passionately making love without a thought of Simon, even though you did not consciously want the night to end that way. Am I on the money?"

She nodded.

"Now, isn't this the bitch who dumped you in college?"

"Don't call her that."

"So what did she get out of this evening? Home Wrecking 101, or are there still genuine feelings there?"

"I thought the feelings were over. She tried to make it perfectly clear when she left. Now, all of a sudden, after all these years she says she made a mistake and she's always loved me. She went so far as to tell me she fantasizes about me when she's with her husband."

"Laying it on a bit thick. Don't you think?"

"But, I know when she's lying. And the scary thing is she was telling the truth. They don't get along at all. I don't really understand why he worships her."

"Did you worship her?"

"She was everything to me. Mother, sister, lover, friend." Alex looked into Roz's eyes. "Is that sick?"

"Not at all."

"Roz, I don't want to hurt Simon."

"I'd say it's a bit late for that, Alex." She reached over and wiped the tears starting to run down her cheek. "You don't need to tell him if it's not going to happen again."

"He's going to know when he looks at me."

"Probably."

She set the water glass on the table. "I just want her to go away."

"You think so, don't you?"

"What do you mean?"

"If you just wanted her to go away, you wouldn't be here. You'd have sent her packing and you'd be thinking about how to minimize the damage with Simon."

"That's what I thought I was doing."

Roz laughed. "That's what I love about you, Alex. You want to do the right thing so desperately you don't acknowledge what you feel."

"I don't know what you're talking about."

"She's in your system, Alex. She always has been. You can see it when you talk about her."

"Look, I don't want to have these feelings. I love Simon."

"I know. I've seen you together. You're very good together. He's good for you and you are good for him. But you seem to be under the impression the human heart is only big enough to house one love. And how can that be, Alex? If that were true then no one would remarry; no one would date after their true love left; no one would have affairs; there would be no battles over a maiden's hand. Face the facts, my friend: you're human."

"I know that."

"No. You don't." Roz poured two glasses of scotch. "You think you have to be something more. You have ever since I met you." Handing a glass to her, she sat down again beside her. "Drink it."

"It's not even noon…"

"And a little late in the game to be thinking about rules, don't you think? Just drink it, Alexandra."

Obediently she took a large sip and felt the warm liquid burn as it slid down her throat into the spin cycle. She watched as Roz sipped hers.

"I sympathize with your plight, Alex. You think since your mother didn't love you, you have to make the world love you."

She wanted to protest but she had no energy to. The split in her back was beginning to close with the alcohol. She could have stopped Roz's dime store psychology, but some of it was ringing true.

"I wish I could tell you what to do, Alex. But only you can know what is right for you. Your Simon is a wonderful man. One of the finest of his gender I've met."

"So, why are these feelings so strong?"

"Let me show you something." Moving toward her bookshelf she took down a photograph of herself snugly nestled in the arms of a young brown-haired, olive skinned gentleman in the back of a sailboat.

She studied the picture. They made a beautiful couple, both glowing in each other's presence. "He's handsome."

"Demetrius was his name. I met him in Greece. I was traveling with my lover, Tim. We had been sleeping together for four years, and I had been faithful, but Tim never wanted to tie the knot. It was just understood we were going to grow old together. Anyway, Tim had a very bad case of sunburn and I went into a shop to buy something to put on it. I bumped into Demetrius—literally—knocked the items he was carrying on the floor. I bent down to help him pick them up and our eyes met and it was like I had known him forever. We started talking and one thing led to another. I thought I was head over heels in love with Tim, but he couldn't compete with Deme." She put it back on the bookshelf.

"What happened?"

"Fate makes decisions for us sometimes." She poured herself another scotch and took a very large sip. "He drowned at sea. It would have been two and a half years…"

"I'm sorry."

"I never wanted to hurt Tim and I agonized over that for a long time, but there was no fighting the attraction to Deme."

"So you're saying I should stay with Mindy?"

"I'm saying you should do what makes you happy, Alex. You have to decide what that is. And you are the only one that can know that."

"I thought I knew," she sighed, "but now, I'm not so sure."

"Whatever you do, remember you are the author of children's books. If you choose Mindy over Simon, you have to be prepared to keep a low profile."

"So you think I should choose Simon?"

Roz took her face in her hands. "You're not listening. Alexandra, I'm your friend, not your mother, not your priest. If you want me to say what you did was right, I can't. I can't say I haven't done it, but even having done it, I can't say it's right. When you make a commitment to someone, you don't break it." She let go of her face and took her hand. "As your friend, I can tell you I understand. I can tell you your actions haven't discolored our friendship. I can even tell you you are not the first or the last to do what you've done. But, I can't tell you it's right. Which simply means the nuns did a real number on me."

"I know it's not right, but how am I going to fix it?"

"Be honest."

"You mean tell Simon?"

"I mean be honest with yourself—with Simon—with Mindy. If you follow your heart, the rest will fall into place. Maybe not today, maybe not even a year from now, but eventually you will realize you did the right thing. Whatever that might be."

She rose to her feet. "All right."

"Alex, don't drag this out. End it with whomever you're going to end it with now."

"But…"

Roz touched two fingers to her lips. "This much I know. The longer you take to make your decision, the more people will get hurt. And that is the last thing you want. I know you."

She nodded.

Roz kissed her on the cheek. "Call me in a couple of days and let me know how you're doing."

"Okay." She walked out of the office and toward the elevator. Roz did know what to do—choose. She knew that. Roz was right about one thing. Mindy was in her system. The question now was—how to get her out.

fourteen

Mindy was waiting on the stoop, leaning against the doorframe in faded jeans and a light pink sweater. She noted how Mindy's body caught the light in a way that outlined every feminine curve. Her breath caught remembering how often she had lost herself in those sensuous curves.

"How was your meeting?"

"Good." She opened the screen door and Mindy rose to her feet ready to follow.

"I missed you." Mindy was so close to her she felt Mindy's breath tickling her neck.

"I wasn't gone long."

"Long enough."

"Mindy—" She stopped in the kitchen doorway. The table had been set for two. A huge salad sat on the table and a bottle of wine was chilling. Alex's good silverware was out. Romance was always Mindy's strong suit.

"I thought you'd be hungry," she explained.

* * *

The dining room table was set with her parents' finest china and crystal. The candles were lit and a bottle of champagne sat by the table.
"What's the occasion?" Alex asked.

"My parents are away for the weekend and Willie gone..." Mindy smiled mischievously, "and I thought we could have a romantic dinner for two. I mean we can't go out so I thought we could have a real date."

"A real date?"

"Isn't that what people in love do? They go to dinner and the movies or dancing."

"But I'm all sweaty from basketball practice."

"You have time to shower and change. I laid out an outfit for you."

"You did, did you? You've just thought of everything, haven't you?"

Mindy touched her face. "I just want every moment with you to be special."

"Every moment with you is special."

* * *

None of this was going to be easy again. These feelings had to be stopped. Her marriage depended on it. "You shouldn't have gone to all this trouble. I'm really not hungry."

"Oh." She sank down into a kitchen chair. "I see."

"In fact, my stomach is feeling a bit queasy today. I think I'm going to change into sweats and take something to settle it." She had to get out of the room—the expression on Mindy's face was enough to bring her to her knees.

"How about some tea?"

She recognized the tenderness in Mindy's voice but she could not respond in kind. "No, thanks. I have some antacid upstairs. I'll just take two of those. If you'll excuse me."

The steps moved under her feet in pairs as she raced to her bedroom. Once in the bathroom, she closed the door and pulled the sweater and turtleneck off. Reaching for her tattered tee shirt, she noticed the red mark on her neck. Closer examination in the mirror brought to light a hickey the size of a quarter. Great, she told herself, now she didn't have to worry about telling Simon he could just see the evidence himself.

There was a knock at the door. "Alex?"

At least she knocked.

"Are you okay?"

She pulled the tee shirt on and opened the door. "I'm just fine, Mindy, why?"

"I forgot to tell you. Simon called. He said he'd be in at four. He said he'd take a cab and not to worry about picking him up."

"You didn't pick up the phone, did you?"

"No. I heard it on the machine. You can go play it for yourself if you want."

"Four o'clock. He'll be home at four o'clock and I have a fucking hickey."

"Where?"

She pulled back her shirt to expose the mark.

Mindy smiled sheepishly. "Guess I'm out of practice. I used to be good at not leaving a mark. Sorry."

"Sorry? Sorry doesn't really cut it, Mindy." She mimicked Mindy, "'Simon doesn't have to know. You don't have to tell him.'" She collapsed onto the bed. "What the fuck am I going to do now?"

"Try for a matching set?" she suggested sitting down next to her.

She rolled to the other side of the bed before Mindy could touch her. "I'm not amused."

"Aw, come on, Alex, lighten up."

"Lighten up? My husband is coming home in a few hours to find out I've been sleeping with someone else and you want me to lighten up? You got a lot of nerve, you know?"

She stood up. "Oh, I get it. Last night was a mistake."

"Well, yes."

"And we're certainly not going to let that happen again, are we?"

"I think you're getting the picture."

"Well, I'd have to be a fool not to. Don't worry; your secret is safe with me."

"Secret?"

"That's right. In the story I'll be the seducer and you'll be the seducee. I suppose that's a fairly accurate picture. Only, one does not allow oneself to be seduced if they don't want to. So what does that make you?"

"A fool."

"Well, just for the record, Alexandra, you left marks, too."

She looked at Mindy. She had no idea what she could be talking about. She purposely did not perform the one act that drove her wild because she could never master not leaving a mark and she always felt guilty leaving one. "I did not."

Mindy pulled her sweater off her shoulder and turned around. "Yes you did."

There on the back of her shoulder were tiny bruises she knew matched her fingertips. Without looking she knew the other shoulder looked the same.

"So, I guess I'll go back to the guest room."

"You're staying?"

"Alex, last night meant everything to me. Just to be able to touch you again." Her voice shook, "I can't just walk away. I'll be in the guest room if you change your mind." She pulled the door closed behind her.

She was alone. A feeling she told herself she might have to get used to.

fifteen

She spent the afternoon in the rocker in her bedroom, trying to think of what she would say when Simon came home. An eternity passed before Simon appeared in the bedroom doorway, hang-up bag slung over his shoulder, portfolio clutched in the other hand. "World traveler returns home: film at eleven." He smiled. "Hey, woman, how about a kiss for your man?"

She tried to mirror his mood. "Just one?"

He set his things down on the bed and put his arms around her. His shirt smelled of cologne and she settled into his familiar scent. "We'll start with one," he suggested, "and see how it goes from there."

His lips brushed against hers. She heard the voice in the back of her head, which she'd spent the afternoon trying to suppress, come alive again. *The last kiss—savor it while you can.*

His hands were on her shoulders, massaging gently. "Is something wrong?"

The smile was forced, but she hoped he buy it. "No. I'm sorry, my mind was somewhere else."

"I noticed we have company. It's been a while, but I know it's Mindy." He hung his bag up in the closet. "I didn't know she was coming to visit."

"Neither did I. I swear."

He turned to look at her.

"She showed up on the doorstep spur of the moment—took me completely by surprise."

"Are you trying to tell me she came all this way without calling first?"

"Why would I lie to you?"

"Well, we're on the edge, aren't we?" He put his overnight bag on the bed and unpacked. "It's not such an unusual question. What would she have done if you weren't home?"

"She said she would have visited some college friends." *And I'm just balancing on the edge*, she thought. *If only you knew how the two of us were balancing.* "How was the museum?"

"Well, you are looking at one of the up-and-coming artists to be displayed in the Steinhoff wing of the museum, which is under construction as we speak."

She threw her arms around him and kissed him. "That's wonderful, Simon! Who's Steinhoff?"

"Some rich guy who likes art."

"Thank God for rich people that like art."

"Yes, and they're going to take two of my works."

"Which ones?"

He picked up his shaving kit and put it back in the bathroom. "That's not really important."

"Sure it is." She helped him unpack.

He pulled his dirty clothes out and stuffed them in the hamper in the closet. "So what have you two been up to?"

"You're changing the subject, Simon." *And I don't want to change the subject. I want to focus on something else.* She unzipped the portfolio and pulled the sheet of slides out. "I can probably figure it out." She took them over to the window to look at them in the light.

He took the sheet out of her hand. "What if I want you to be surprised?" He zipped the sheet back in the portfolio case. "So, tell me what you've been up to?"

"What do you think we've been up to?" She tried to make it sound okay, but even she could hear the sarcasm in her voice.

He moved his portfolio and sat down on the bed. "Is there something you want to tell me, Alex?"

The knife in her back was turning now. She rolled her shoulders trying to ease the pain. Every muscle in her body constricted. "I love you." Even she heard how feeble it sounded.

"There something else?"

"What makes you think there's something else?"

"The way you're acting."

"There's nothing else." She forced a smile.

"How long has she been here?"

"Since yesterday."

"Oh." He took the empty bag and put it back in the closet. "What have you been doing?"

"What do you think we've been doing?"

"Hey, don't snap at me. I was just asking a simple question."

"We've been talking. That's all."

"Alex, you are sure nothing is wrong. You're acting strange."

She sat down on the bed. "My stomach's been a little upset. Something I ate maybe."

He sat down next to her. "Your stomach, huh?"

"Yeah."

"That usually means something's bothering you."

"I told you nothing's bothering me."

"I know and I don't believe you."

She stood up. She had to move. Her world was about to come crumbling down around her. She knew it. Being a writer, she searched for the words to make things all right. Words to patch things up. But there weren't any words.

"Talk to me, Alex."

"I am talking to you."

"No. We've been dancing around here. I want you to talk to me." He was trying to maintain his cool, but she could see the muscles in his neck tighten.

"Why? So, I can tell you what you don't want to hear?"

"So, I can hear it from you first."

She turned to look at him. "Who else would tell you?"

"No one."

Her eyes were floating in pools of water. All she needed was a cloudy picture of Simon to remember. Her tonsils were straining to touch the roof of her mouth, blocking the passage of words.

He sat, waiting, his hands placed carefully on the bed on either side of him.

"What do you want me to say?"

"Tell me what went on here that you won't talk about."

"What went on here? No, that's not what you want to hear, Simon. Trust me."

"I knew you were confused, but...in our house?"

Nothing needed to be said. He knew what happened. She could hear it in his voice. It was the ultimate betrayal. He had her there. "I guess," her voice cracked, "it wouldn't help if I told you I didn't mean to hurt you. Would it?"

There was no answer. Simon just looked through her. She couldn't bear to look at him, but she could feel his eyes on her.

He kept muttering over and over, "In our house."

She moved to touch him.

His hand shot out to stop her. "Don't touch me." His knees straightened and she looked up to see him standing. He'd found his voice. "I can't believe after all the shit she put you through you would even think about it, let alone…" He was shouting now. "I don't know you anymore, Alex."

"Simon."

"Don't say anything!" he screamed. "There isn't a goddamn thing you can say to me." He went to his dresser and picked up his keys. "I can't let this one just go by."

"Will you be back?"

"I don't know."

"But what about your things?"

"The hell with my things!" he shouted and swept his hand across the dresser so everything went flying. The mirror crashed to the floor and shattered. He didn't even notice it had broken; he just stepped over it and left.

She called after him and he stopped. "Simon, I'm sorry."

He disappeared down the steps, the thud of his sneakers against the wood echoing through the stillness. She heard him pick something up in the hallway and hurl it at the wall. Moving to the top of the steps, she saw it was the vase Willie had given them. From the top of the steps, she could see Mindy standing in the doorway to her study. She looked like a deer in headlights–eyes wide open, frozen in place. Simon stopped in front of her and for a moment she felt her heart stop at the thought of him hurting her.

"You." His voice was shaking as he tried to gain control.

Mindy bent her head and she stood very still as if she didn't dare move.

"I hope you're happy!" he said and stormed out, slamming the door behind him so loudly she thought it would come off the hinges.

The crash tore through her and then the tears came in torrents pouring through her fingers, which she had cupped over her face in a futile attempt to catch them. She sank to her knees and her mind went blank.

sixteen

Warm lips pressed lightly against her cheek drawing her back from the darkness somewhere between sleep and consciousness. She rolled onto her back, only to be greeted by Mindy's concerned look.

"Are you okay?"

"No. I'm not sure I'll ever be okay again." She struggled to sit up.

"You're still mad at me."

"Mad at you? Me? Please." She reached for the banister to pull herself up. "Why would I be mad at you? The only man I ever loved in my entire life just walked out of my life and am I upset?"

Mindy followed her down the stairs and into the kitchen.

"I am calm, cool, and in control. My life is crumbling around me, and yes, I'm reaching for a cold beer. Because when your life is destroyed, it's Amstel Light time." She opened the bottle and took a sip of the cool, frothy liquid, then started toward her study.

"Alex, your life doesn't have to be over."

"I know." She sank into her desk chair and set the beer down. "You and I could play house, right?"

"I wasn't going to use those exact words." Mindy moved closer.

She threw her arms up to stop her. "Don't come near me."

"Don't be silly."

"Do I look like I'm being silly here?"

Mindy retreated to the sofa. "Okay, I won't touch you."

"Thank you." She turned her computer on.

"What are you doing?"

"I'm going to write," she said as she opened her word processing program.

"Oh."

She opened a new file. "I think it's going to be my first adult fairy tale."

"What will it be about?"

"You figure it out, Mindy. I'm calling it THE SHATTERED KINGDOM."

"So you'd rather make up a story than talk to me?" Mindy stood up.

"And what is it we have to talk about?"

"Well, we could talk about us."

"Us." She clapped her hands together. "Mindy, there is no us."

Tears rolled down Mindy's cheeks and she wiped them on her sleeve.

"Oh, great. You're crying now. Please don't do that."

"You think I want to?"

She threw her arms up. "A part of me wants to kill you and yet I can't bare your tears."

"Kill me? For loving you?"

"For driving my husband out."

She handed Mindy a wad of tissues. "What is it about you? I can't seem to get you out of my system. You're like a disease without an antidote."

"Why don't you just face the fact you still love me?"

"But I love Simon."

"And you couldn't possibly love us both?"

"Mindy I need to be alone."

"Fine. I'll be in the guest room if you want me."

She sank back into her chair. *If I want you. What if I don't want you? Where will you be then?* She turned her attention to the computer and typed an outline. Channeling aggression was a specialty she had mastered.She typed:

> THE SHATTERED KINGDOM
>
> The tale and the history of the tale will be derived from the tales of Arthur. The story shall be told from Guinevere's point of view. It shall begin several hours before Guinevere is to be burned at the stake.

Well, perhaps that's my consolation prize, no public burnings, just a private singeing for the modern day woman.

> Guinevere is alone in one of the tower rooms where no one can reach her. Alone with her thoughts and her memories, which offer her little comfort when it's human contact she longs for.

Human contact is waiting for you upstairs. And it doesn't get any better than that. Concentrate.

> She longs for Arthur. She wishes to tell him all that is in her heart. She wishes she had Merlin's powers so she could right the wrongs she has done. Since she does not have those powers, she must simply pray Arthur knows the untold truths hidden in her heart.

What untold truths?

> Guinevere does not fear her burning. It is but little pain to endure for what she has caused her husband. She loves Arthur, not as she loves Lancelot, her love for Arthur is purer, a truer love. Arthur is her friend; no one will ever be a better friend. He is her lover, her husband. They have no children together, but not for lack of trying. Despite her feelings for Arthur she is drawn to Lancelot. Drawn in

a way she cannot fight, as if they had been destined to be together. Forbidden fruit is, after all, sweeter, they say.

She took a sip of her beer, thinking how silly it was to compare the love she and Mindy had to the love Lancelot and Guinevere shared. Theirs was a passion; they were like two combustible chemicals ready to explode when mixed together. She and Mindy were…well something did spark when they touched, but that wasn't…it couldn't be.

> Guinevere did not want to give herself to Lancelot. She fought their union with every fiber of her being, but something stronger, something deeper prevailed and they consummated their love. In their union they found a completion of each other…

She found completion. She had that with Simon, too. How could two totally different people be the missing piece in the puzzle? She had known from the beginning she did not want to lose Simon. The thought of losing Mindy again…

> Guinevere waited in her solitude, praying Arthur would understand and hoping Lancelot would save her from the stake.

That was it! She saved the beginning of the outline and turned the computer off. Then she finished her beer and started up the stairs.

She knocked on the guest room door.

"Come in."

Mindy was lying across the bottom of the bed staring at the tiny television set on the dresser.

"Anything worth watching?" She sat down beside her.

"Not really. Sitting a bit close, aren't you?"

"Feel like talking?"

"Does that mean you do now?"

"Yes."

Standing and stretching, Mindy turned the television off and settled into the rocking chair across from her. "Well, go ahead."

"Talking isn't my forte, you know?"

"But you make your living using words."

"Writing. It's different than talking. You're only talking to people you make up when you write. Not the people who make up your life."

"I suppose you're right about that."

"Anyway, I've been down there writing, and I think I have to stop hiding behind my computer and start dealing with the people in my life or I may find myself left alone with my make-believe world. So, I'm gonna give this a shot."

"I'm listening."

"I thought I had everything all figured out. Everything was all cut and dried in my world. I love my husband and my husband loves me. We have a good life, a nice house, money, friends...perhaps children someday. All of that is more than I ever dreamt of having."

"That's not true, Alex. We talked about all of those things."

"You're right, Mindy, we did talk about those things. But then you left and I thought none of those things would ever be mine again. I also know had I not known you and your family, I doubt I would have ever ended up here. No, I know I would not have ended up here. So, I was sitting downstairs and I was asking myself why I would mess up a good thing..."

"And?"

"There's something about you, Mindy, that pulls at me. I don't know what it is. I used to believe, when we were younger, we were soul mates. But then you left and I stopped believing in the whole concept of soul mates."

"So you don't think Simon is your soul mate?"

"I think Simon is the most wonderful man I've known and he's been good for me in so many ways."

"We were good for each other, Alex."

"I know we were, Mindy." She leaned forward to be closer to Mindy. "You don't know how much I wanted you back when you left. I tried to reach out to you, but you didn't respond. I mourned what you and I had for a very long time."

Mindy's face lit up. "So you admit you love me?"

"Something awful."

"Well, what are you going to do about it?"

"I don't know."

"Fair enough."

"I mean I had this picture in my mind…"

"I'm not in that picture, am I?"

"You have a picture of your own. You have children and a husband."

"Great."

"Mindy, you and I, maybe we could be happy together…"

"Alex, we could. You know we could."

"But who would know? I write children's stories. You don't think I could walk down the street with my love on my arm and be considered a wholesome role model?"

"There's nothing wrong with us, Alex."

"Tell the rest of the world that. Besides, what would you tell your kids? Mommy is leaving you for another woman? Better than that, what would you tell Mark? See, neither of us is prepared to deal with the hostility that exists toward a homosexual lifestyle. We weren't brave enough to come out when we were young. What makes you think we have the courage to come out now?"

"What makes you think we don't?"

"I know me. I have a lot of strength and I've lived through a lot. But, I don't know if I have that kind of strength. It's easy for me to say how I would have reacted to what happened to you, but honestly, I just don't know. And I don't think our love would survive that kind of test."

"We'll never know until we try, Alex."

"Mindy, you ended the relationship because your roommate found out about you. She threatened your world."

"I was eighteen for Christ's sake."

"You're not looking beyond your wants. You want me, so you think you can have me and everything will be just fine. Life doesn't work that way. Haven't you learned by now? My wanting you does not make having you any easier. It certainly makes it painful as hell to let go, but if we're realistic, not half as painful as holding on would be."

"Maybe you don't love me as much as I love you."

"I know I love you. I just don't know what life would be like with you. I know what it's like with Simon."

"That's no reason to stay with someone, Alex."

"I know. But I do love him."

"So we're just going to end it?"

"I told you yesterday I didn't want to begin anything."

"But then we made love and I thought things would be different."

"Why?"

The phone rang. Simon, she thought as she raced down the hall to the bedroom to grab it. "Hello."

"Alex?"

"Yes." She tried to place the voice on the other end of the phone.

"It's Paul."

Paul was Simon's brother, a larger version of Simon with a build more like a boxer. "Is Simon there?" she asked.

"What the fuck did you do to my brother?" There was anger in his voice she had never heard before.

"He didn't tell you?"

"He won't talk."

"Well, if he won't tell you…"

"Alex, he worships you. You're the whole fucking world to him. What happened?" He demanded.

"Paul, this is between Simon and…"

"Alexandra Russell, my brother is sitting in my living room in front of the television consuming more alcohol than I think he has in his entire life and weeping like a fucking girl. I keep telling him to call you, but he won't. And he'll kill me if he finds out I talked to you. So you tell me what we're going to do?"

"I need to see him, Paul."

"You better see him. He's scaring the shit out of my children."

"I'll be right over."

"No!" He lowered his voice, "He'll know I told you."

"Then bring him here."

"Listen carefully; I'm taking him to the Met the day after tomorrow for the O'Keefe exhibit. I'll have my friend Duane leave you a ticket. You can see him there."

"Are you sure he'll go?"

"I don't know, Alex. You tell me."

"Paul, can you tell him I love him?"

"No. I can't tell him I talked to you."

"What if I call there?"

"Don't. Just be at the museum at eleven a.m. And you make things right, God damn it!" He slammed the phone down.

She put the receiver back in the cradle and sat down on the bed. Two days from now at eleven o'clock...what would she tell him?

You just make things right, Paul had said in his all too direct way. Like she would snap her fingers and all would be resolved. And could she fix things? She wanted to see Simon. She wanted to talk...but what did she want to tell him? Did she want to tell him what she told Mindy just now, that she wanted him above her? Or did she want to admit she couldn't fight this attraction to Mindy? Their lovemaking had been more powerful than any experience Simon and she had had in years. But that was marriage, right? Sex was supposed to settle. It wasn't supposed to be explosive all the time—was it?

But had it settled with Mindy? There were nights, weeks even, when they would just hold each other, but on those nights they didn't make love there was still a connection.

There was more to life than just sex, she told herself. She had built a life with Simon; their careers were linked. If she left him would he still illustrate her books? What was she thinking? How could she leave him? It made no sense to go back to Mindy. No sense at all, if you thought about it, but if you let yourself feel...

* * *

"Alex," Coach Hamilton barked from the other side of the gym, "I'd like to see you in my office."

Practice was over and she had been working on her layup shot, but she could always work on it later. No one kept Coach Hamilton waiting.

Her office was not what you would have imagined a coach's office to look like with trophies and awards cluttering the walls. Instead there was very little on the walls, which were not the usual institutional white, but a light blue instead. The only thing hanging on the wall behind the coach's desk was a very large O'Keefe painting. She had brought in a Mexican rug from home to put under her desk and the overstuffed chair sat waiting for her guest.

She wiped the perspiration from her forehead with her towel and entered the room. "Have I done something wrong, Coach?"

"Have a seat, Alex," her manner softened, as it usually did when you went one-on-one with her in her office, "after you close the door."

She shut the door and sat in the overstuffed chair, waiting. She hadn't indicated one way or another whether or not she had done anything wrong.

"I wanted to talk to you about your game." She reached across the desk and moved a vase of flowers blocking their view of each other. "You can relax; I assure you it's nothing bad."

She let out the breath she had been holding and sank farther back into the chair.

"You're becoming an outstanding player, both on your own and as a team player. That's very rare, you know? I have begun to make some phone calls on your behalf. I think we can get you a scholarship if you'd like."

"A scholarship." She could hardly believe it.

"Yes. Your grades are exemplary and your game…well in the last year and a half you have grown."

"The last year and a half?" She thought just when she and Mindy fell in love.

"Oh, you were good before, but now there's an inner peace about you when you play that makes you very dangerous to play against … and a joy to watch."

"Thank you."

"Don't thank me. I just wish I knew your secret."

seventeen

"I heard the phone ring a little while ago. Was it Simon?" Mindy asked as she entered the bedroom carrying a tray with some soup and crackers on it.

"No."

She set the tray down on the nightstand. "I thought you might be hungry and this should sit pretty well."

"I'm not very hungry…"

"Well, just leave it there. You can always nuke it later if you change your mind." She turned to leave.

"Did you eat anything?"

"No. Can't. Look, I just remembered you get funny if you don't eat something, even when you're upset, so I thought I'd bring you something. Don't worry about me." She walked out.

"But I do."

Mindy walked back in and sat down. "Really?"

"Yeah."

Mindy put her arms around her. "Don't fight me. I just want to hold you. I like the way you feel against me."

And I like the way you feel against me. The warmth of her arms was overpowering. It always was. That hadn't changed; the physical hadn't changed. Why? Why couldn't it have cooled after all these years?

Mindy's fingers ran through her hair, over the temple above her ear gently stroking. "I want to talk to you. I don't want to fight. I don't want to upset you. I just need to tell you how I feel."

She tried to shift, but Mindy held her tightly.

"Please, just listen. I'm not trying to seduce you. I thought about what you said and I just want to talk. Okay?"

"Okay." She let herself relax into Mindy and tried to focus on what she was about to hear.

"You asked me what I would tell Mark? Well, I told Mark before I left I wanted a divorce."

"What?"

She touched Alex's lips with her fingertips. "Just listen. I'm not happy with him. I've never been happy with anyone but you. I'm not saying that to pressure you. I just know now I haven't been fair to Mark. I can't go on pretending someday everything is going to work out fine. You're happy with Simon. I envy you. Maybe it's just bad karma at work. I mean, I destroyed the only relationship worth anything in my life and now I'm destined to be miserable."

"That's not—"

"You don't have this listening thing down very well, do you?"

"I just want you to be happy, Mindy."

"I know."

"And I don't know—"

"Let me finish what I want to say, and then we can talk. Okay?"

"All right."

"I love you, Alex. I have always loved you. Since the first day I saw you in my Social Studies class…"

She watched Mindy's neck muscles tighten trying to fight back the emotion and remain calm. With her head cushioned against Mindy's breast, she could hear her heart race. She wanted to tell Mindy she had loved her from the first moment she laid eyes on her in class, too. That she had wanted her like she had wanted no one. Instead she listened.

"I know what I did to you was wrong and if I could undo anything in my life, it would be that night when I told you it was over. I thought I couldn't live my life as a lesbian. I didn't have the strength to take the criticism, to risk losing my family and my friends...but I was wrong. I would risk everything for you, Alex. I know that now. Only now it's too late."

"It's not too—" She saw the picture of Simon on the nightstand and stopped.

"What?"

"I don't know what I'm saying." She sat up, moving away from Mindy. "I haven't known since you walked through the door."

"You were going to say it's not too late."

"No. I don't know...I don't think we should talk anymore."

"Okay, then make love to me."

"What?"

"You heard me."

"Mindy, I can't..."

Mindy shifted so she was sitting on top of her. "I can't turn back time, Alex. All I can do is show you how much I love you now. I'm not going away. You choose who you have to choose, but it won't make me stop loving you." Mindy caressed her cheek. "This could be the last time you and I ever make love. If you choose Simon, and I'm almost certain you will, I'll walk away. I didn't come to destroy anything. I'm sorry if I did. I came here to reclaim the past, but I know now that's not possible."

She reached out to catch the tear running down Mindy's cheek on her fingertip.

"Please, be with me tonight."

This was the Mindy she knew all those years ago. The Mindy she loved. She reached up and wrapped her hand in Mindy's curls and drew her closer. And as their lips met, she knew she would not be able to let go of her again.

The night before they had consumed each other. But that night their lovemaking was slow and gentle. She lost herself in Mindy's tender kisses, savoring the sweetness of her mouth, feeling the warmth of her body pressed so tightly against hers. Mindy's fingers danced through her hair.

Mindy balanced on her lap and unbuttoned her sweater. She sat up and reached for the buttons. Normally the amount of buttons would have made her crazy, but she was in no hurry. She undid every button, kissing the bare flesh it exposed as she did. Reaching behind Mindy, she opened her bra with one hand.

Mindy chuckled, "You were always so proud when you could do that…like it made you more suave or something."

She kissed her and lifted her arms so Mindy could pull her shirt over her head. She kept her arms raised for Mindy to remove her bra.

As Mindy pushed her back onto the bed, she whispered, "It never ceased to amaze me how soft you were…are."

"Just for you," she whispered as Mindy buried her face in the tender part of her neck and kissed her.

"How can I still want you after all that's happened?"

Their skin melted together and Mindy wrapped her arms around her. Mindy's eyes were glowing. "Because we were never meant to be apart. You really are my soul mate."

All the talk of karma made her think Mindy was right. They had been lovers through the ages, destined to seek each other out at any cost.

eighteen

"Are you hungry?" Mindy asked, moving from her breast, where she'd been resting.

For a moment she didn't want Mindy to move. But she remembered she hadn't eaten all day.

"Are you?"

"Famished." Mindy kissed her breast and moved her arm from around her so she could sit up. "I could go get something…if you don't want to move."

It was so nice holding her. Why did she have to move? "It's not that I don't want to move."

Mindy lay next to her propped on her elbow, tracing the contours of her breast with her fingertip. "Did I wear you out?"

She grabbed her hand and licked the length of each finger slowly, kissing the tip of each finger. She smiled as each low moan escaped Mindy's lips. Then she held her hand tightly. "Don't tease me," she warned, "or I'll tease you right back."

"Point taken."

"There are robes behind the bathroom door, why don't you get them and we'll get something to eat."

Mindy disappeared into the bathroom for a few minutes and reemerged wearing her silk, teal robe. She carried Simon's black terry cloth robe in her arms, which she proceeded to hand to Alex. "This robe smells like Simon. I couldn't…" Her eyes filled with tears.

Alex drew her into her arms, feeling the silk against her skin, noting how even silk wasn't as soft as Mindy's skin. Cupping her face in her hand, she kissed her tears away. "Please, don't do this. I have another robe in the closet. I'll get it."

Mindy tightened her grip. "What are we doing?"

She didn't want to think about this now. She couldn't think rationally when Mindy was in her arms. Simon was from another lifetime. She let her eyes meet Mindy's. "I don't think either of us knows exactly what we're doing. But, we started it...let's not end it in tears, please."

Loosening her grip on Mindy, she reached for a tissue on the nightstand, and she moved to the closet to get a robe.

Mindy blew her nose and dried the rest of her tears. "You're right. I'm sorry." Mindy looked up at her. "Alex, do you think he'll do anything crazy?"

She pulled the soft terry cloth robe around her body. She didn't want to think about him right now. For the first time in the entire time Mindy had been here, she didn't want to think about him. Why? "He's pretty level-headed."

"Alex, I thought he was going to grab me or hit me when I was standing in the doorway..."

"He would never lay a hand..."

"I know. The thing is, I wouldn't have blamed him if he tried to kill me, if he thought he lost you."

She lifted Mindy's chin so their eyes met. "It's very fragile right now. Let's not—"

"I just fear I've broken your heart in more than one way."

"Let's not think about that now." She took her hand. "Let's go get something to eat."

Mindy sat down at the kitchen table. She opened the refrigerator, pulled out two Diet Cokes and set them on the table.

"What would you like?" She quickly took inventory of the contents of her fridge.

"You know what I like."

She did indeed. She reached for the bread, butter, and some cheese. "Grilled cheese."

"Sounds great."

The mood had changed. The robes were definitely not a good idea, but how could she be expected to remember Simon's cologne when she had just—? This wasn't fair. It couldn't unravel...not like this.

"Yesterday. Did you mean what you said during the survey?"

She was going to pursue it. "What part?" she asked as she sliced some butter and spread it on the bread.

"About your sex life."

She set the knife down and went to her. Wrapping her arms around Mindy, she kissed her on top of the head. "I don't want to do this. I just want to be with you now. Okay?"

"And I want to be with you. It just makes me crazy to think about him touching you."

She pulled Mindy's chair out from the table and knelt in front of her. "I was happy with him. Is it so crazy to think about me being happy?"

"No. I want you to be happy. No matter what. But you know what I mean."

"What makes it any different than you being with Mark?"

"I don't love him."

Letting go of Mindy's hands, she sat in the other kitchen chair and took a sip of her soda.

"Alex, say something."

"How could you marry him if you didn't love him?"

"Because that's what was expected..." she fought back tears building up, "and because I was pregnant."

"Mindy, I didn't realize. You know you could have—"

Her eyes darkened, "Don't say I could have had an abortion!"

"I wasn't going to say that." She moved closer and took her hand. "I was going to say you didn't have to marry him."

"After Willie? I was thinking of my mother. Why did you marry Simon?"

"Because I loved him." She recognized the pain in Mindy's eyes and reached up to touch her face. "As much as I could love anyone after you."

"Were there others?"

"Once."

"Who?"

Alex moved away. "I don't want to do this."

"I'll never ask again. But, I need to know."

"A teammate, okay?"

"You slept with another woman?"

"Only one time. And you'll be happy to know I called out your name…"

Her eyes lit up. "Really?"

"Oh, now you're happy."

Mindy moved over to the counter and finished the sandwiches. "What would make me happy is if you told me more about Simon."

"What do you want to know, Mindy?" She took the cheese out of her hand. "Look at me."

Mindy turned to face her but said nothing.

"You want to know if he's a better lover? If I love him more than you? What is it you want to know?"

"All of the above," she whispered.

"Why do you want to know?" Her hands were on Mindy's cheeks, forcing her to not look away. "You said we weren't going to do this. You said I should choose …"

"I'm not asking you to choose." Mindy moved her hands from her face and turned back to the sandwiches. "I just want to know how you feel."

Moving behind Mindy, she reached around and turned off the stove. Then she put her arms around Mindy. "You want to know how I feel ," she whispered into her ear as she slid her hand underneath the silk robe over Mindy's smooth skin. She wanted to make love to Mindy in every room of the house—a house she had bought, decorated, and lived in with Simon—and Mindy wanted to know how she felt. How could she even ask? Her lips were on the nape of Mindy's neck as she took a breast into her hand and gently squeezed it. As Mindy's nipple hardened against her palm, she untied the sash of the robe with her other hand. She could hear Mindy's breath quicken and she felt her own body awaken.

Mindy managed to breathe long enough to ask, "Shouldn't we go upstairs?"

"Not yet."

She wrapped her arms around Mindy, drawing her back against her until her breasts pressed into the silken skin. She rested her cheek against Mindy's curls. She could smell the herbal shampoo. When she held Mindy it was as if they had become one. She couldn't feel where she left off and where Mindy began…only the two of them melting together. "I think I've missed this more than anything," she managed to whisper, and then she kissed Mindy's shoulder blade.

"I've missed your arms. You'd turn me into jelly and then gather me into your strong arms, and then you would hold me all night."

"You remember?"

"I remember the first time we touched…"

"I thought I was dreaming." She stroked Mindy's hair.

"You were so scared."

"And you were so gentle." She moved the hair off of Mindy's neck and kissed it. She felt the warmth between them, the heat of their bodies against each other, but she still couldn't determine where she left off or where Mindy began. "I needed this when—" She stopped herself.

"When what?" Mindy tried to turn around, but she held her tightly.

"When I lost the baby."

"You miscarried?" Mindy whispered.

"About a year and half ago."

"Simon wasn't supportive?"

"He was supportive. He just couldn't understand why it happened."

"But women miscarry all the time, baby. It wasn't your fault."

"The doctor said it was."

"What kind of quack said that?"

"Said I was too scared to carry it to term. I don't think I'm supposed to have children."

"Baby, don't say that." Mindy tried to move out of her arms, but she wouldn't let go. "Alex, let go. I want to hold you."

She let Mindy turn in her arms.

"You would be an awesome mother." Mindy brushed the hair back off her forehead. "Just because your mother did those things to you doesn't mean you could ever do them."

"You saw what she did."

Mindy took her face in her hands and their eyes met. "I know you could never harm a child. Never." Mindy kissed her tenderly and then drew her closer. She let her head rest against Mindy's breast and breathed in her sweet scent. She loved when Mindy would hold her and stroke her back so gently, like she was doing now.

She closed her eyes and listened to Mindy's melodic voice.

"When my mother died, I went and changed the will. If anything ever happens to Mark and me at the same time…I want the children to come live with you."

"What?"

"There's no one I trust more."

"What about Willie?"

"Willie's not responsible enough. We both know that's why he never married Cindy's mother."

"But Mindy, what if we hadn't seen each other again after the funeral?"

"Are you trying to tell me you wouldn't raise my children if something happened to me?"

"No." She had to admit. "I would love your children like they were my own."

"And I know you would be a good mother. If you and Simon," she swallowed hard, "if that's who you choose, well you seem to love…"

"Love doesn't make a baby, Mindy," She pushed her back so she could see her face. "Biology makes a baby."

"All I was trying to say…"

She silenced her with a kiss. "If love made babies, you and I would have had one a long time ago." She swallowed the lump forming in her throat. "But, we can't. So don't tell me making a baby has anything to do with love. You and Mark had two and you don't love him. At least not…"

"Not like I love you. I have never stopped loving you, Alex."

nineteen

The lavender awning had the inscription "The Three Muses" painted across it in large white letters. She thought it was a clever title when Casey gave her the card, "The Three Muses" and then below it in the left hand corner "owner Cassiopeia" and the address and phone number. A stairwell led down to a large oak doorway with a stained glass picture of a Greek goddess. Leaning against the stairway in the corner by the street were two women locked in a passionate embrace. Suddenly feeling very brave, she took Mindy's hand in hers and smiled.

Mindy squeezed her hand and they started down the stairs.

She was expecting a smoke-filled room with a loud, noisy bar. What she found was completely different.

"This place is amazing," Mindy said as they walked in and looked around the room.

There was hardly any smoke, probably due to the incredibly high ceiling. The floor was a pattern of mosaic tiles in cream, hunter, lavender, and burgundy. In the corner to the left of the door was a four-tiered fountain. Its cascading tiers created soothing water music as you entered. Around the base of the fountain were flowerpots with a brilliant purple flower. The tables around the fountain were white wrought iron. Behind the fountain was a brick wall with vines covering it. Two women sat at one of the tables sipping from oversized cups. The instrumental music playing had a Celtic flavor to it.

In the other corner lay a large Persian rug with a large, overstuffed couch and four overstuffed chairs positioned around a coffee table. The coffee table was a thick piece of glass balancing on two Doric columns. Behind the couch was a large resin relief.

Mindy saw her looking at the piece and said, "That's the Three Graces. It's from First Century Greece, based on the mythological maidens who personified beauty, charm and grace."

She kissed Mindy on the cheek. "My little historian."

Adjacent to the relief was a large painting of two women lounging on a sofa. The painting had an airy quality to it. "Okay, how about the painting, show off?"

"British painter Albert Moore. The painting is called *Two Women on a Sofa*."

On the sofa itself was a heavyset woman with an equally large woman beside her. They were talking to another woman sitting next to them.

She looked around to see if she could spot Casey. In the corner opposite the sofa was a large bar carved out of what appeared to be oak. The sides were carved like two Doric columns and the piece was breathtaking. Behind the bar, the wall was no longer brick, but rather a deep hunter green, with a huge tapestry of a naked woman lying on a bed of flowers. The wall below the painting was lined with bottles of alcohol. Casey was behind the bar talking to several patrons while she mixed drinks.

Beside the bar were several wooden tables with Bentley chairs. Each table had a vase with fresh flowers. On the wall behind the tables was another painting of two women on a swing. The one woman wrapped in a green tunic was holding onto the ropes of the swing and the other in a cream tunic had her arms wrapped around the woman in green. Light seemed to radiate from the girls' faces. "What about that one?" she asked as she led Mindy toward the bar.

"It's breathtaking, but I really don't know. Is that your friend behind the bar?"

"Yes." She leaned over the end of the bar and waited until Casey noticed her.

"Alex!" Casey screamed and came around the bar to give her a hug. Casey picked her up off the ground and she saw Mindy laugh. "I didn't think you'd come, girlfriend."

"Well, I had to see what your aunt left you." She reached for Mindy's hand. "Casey I'd like you to meet Mindy. Mindy, Casey."

"Pleased to meet you." Casey shook Mindy's hand. "And any friend of Alex's is a friend of mine. What can I get you to drink?"

"What do you recommend?" Mindy asked.

"I have some interesting microbrews if you like beer."

"Beer is fine by me." Mindy smiled. "You decide."

"Okay, Alex?"
"Beer is good." She saw the other corner had a huge oriental rug and equally inviting chairs and sofa. "Why don't you grab a seat over there?" she told Mindy. "I'll bring the drinks over."

"Don't be long." Mindy dropped her hand and walked toward the sofa.

"I'll get Susan to cover the bar and I'll join you." Casey touched her arm. "Unless you'd rather be alone."

She followed Casey to the edge of the bar. "You can come sit with us. That would be nice."

Casey reached below the bar and pulled out two bottles. "Do you want glasses?" she asked.

"I think Mindy does," she told her as Casey opened the bottles.

"No problem." Casey grabbed a mug and emptied the contents of the bottle into it. "So, that's the love of your life?"

She looked across the room at Mindy. She was sitting toward the center of the sofa. Her indigo blouse was unbuttoned just low enough to reveal a bit of cleavage. She drew a deep breath, realizing she was thinking about unbuttoning the blouse and losing herself in those breasts. Even in faded old blue jeans she was sexy. "Yes," she turned to look at Casey, "she is."

"And Simon?" Casey asked.

"He stormed out. But his brother called. He's supposed to be arranging a meeting tomorrow."

"She is gorgeous." Casey handed her a beer.

"I'm crazy about her, Casey. I don't know why I am. Since the first day I saw her..."

"You look good together."

She pulled her wallet out and Casey looked at her.

"Now, you know your money is no good here."

"But—"

"But nothing." Casey poured herself a club soda and picked up Mindy's glass. "Come on, you don't want to keep a pretty woman waiting too long; it's bad form."

Casey handed Mindy her drink and sat down in a chair opposite them. Alex sat on the couch next to Mindy and Mindy took her hand."

"To friendship and love." Casey raised her glass. Alex and Mindy followed.

"Friendship and love."

"This place is absolutely gorgeous!" Mindy said, setting her drink down on the glass-top coffee table. "The tapestry behind us is part of the *Lady with the Unicorn* series?"

Casey smiled, "You know your art."

"When it pertains to history," Mindy admitted. "For instance that sword is a recreation of Excalibur."

"You're guessing," she said.

"No. It has the Pendragon inscription." She pointed at the sword. "And the sculpture in the corner there is a copy of Thorvaldsen's *Aphrodite*."

"Venus, you mean," Casey corrected her.

"Right." Mindy smiled. "I always gravitate toward the Greek names; I think they're so much prettier. But you are correct. It is Thorvaldsen's *Venus*."

"Thorvaldsen?" Alex looked at her. "There was an artist named Thorvaldsen?"

"Danish neoclassical, immensely popular in his time." Mindy took a sip of her beer.

For a moment she felt sad. She realized just how much Simon and Mindy would have really liked each other. How much Simon would have liked this place. She needed to think about other things. "This really isn't what I expected," she told Casey.

"You expected a smoky little dive with a bunch of dykes playing pool. Didn't you?"

"Well, I expected the smoke and then a sports theme going on. Is this how your aunt left it to you?"

Casey smiled. "Mostly. But, I love it this way. I wouldn't change it for the world. And you can't really tell tonight, because it's early in the week, but this place gets busy and the women really love it here."

"I can see why." Mindy snuggled into the crook of Alex's arm. "It's real cozy."

"On the weekends we play dance music and the center of the room here becomes a dance floor."

"That sounds great!" Mindy exclaimed. "You don't do that during the week, do you?"

"During the week it's a quiet place."

"That's too bad." Mindy squeezed Alex's arm. "You and I have never been out dancing."

She looked into Mindy's sea blue eyes. "We used to dance when your parents went away. Remember?"

"Yeah," Mindy told Casey, "we'd move the furniture in the living room around, close the curtains and turn on their sappy, old music and just cling to each other."

Casey leaned forward, resting her elbows on her knees. "And what sort of sappy old stuff does my pal Alex like?

"Oh, my parents had it all—Sinatra, Crosby, Peggy Lee. But Alex loved Nina Simone."

"Really?"

"She was so sad," Alex admitted. "I think I understood her."

"I know a part of you did." Casey stood up. "Well, if you'll excuse me I need to check on something. Would you like anything to eat? We have some light fare available."

"I'm not very hungry."

"Neither am I," Mindy added, "but thank you."

"You guys got it bad." She laughed, and then said, "I'll be back in a couple of minutes. I'm sure you won't miss me too much."

"She's very nice," Mindy commented. "She's the one, isn't she?"

Alex smiled at her. "You're the one."

"You know what I mean."

Alex silenced Mindy with her lips. She never dreamed she would ever kiss another woman in a bar, but it felt safe.

Mindy drank her in. Her arms drew her closer, and then they realized they were in a public place.

"I don't normally go for public displays of affection," Mindy smiled at her, eyes dancing with mischief, "but you seem to bring out the wild woman in me."

"Me?"

"Yes, you." Mindy rested her head on her shoulder. "I love you, Alex, and I don't care who knows."

"I love you, too."

"Today was incredible. Thank you."

She had taken Mindy on a carriage ride through Central Park, gone to Tavern on the Green for lunch, roamed around the Museum of Natural History, and then walked down to the Village where they ate a leisurely dinner in a quaint French bistro. They had spent the entire day talking, catching up on everything that had happened since they had parted.

"Alex, Casey said you were here." Anne set a small bowl of dip and a basket of crackers in front of them. "I know she said you weren't hungry, but I think you'll like this dip. It's my specialty."

"Anne this is my friend, Mindy; Mindy this is Anne, Casey's—" she stopped unsure of what word to use.

"Partner is okay." Anne shook Mindy's hand.

"What's in it?" Mindy asked leaning forward to examine the dip.

"Artichokes and the rest is a secret."

"Well, I love artichokes." Mindy smeared some dip on a cracker and handed it to her. "Alex does too."

"Thanks." She took a bite of the cracker and savored the artichoke and cheese flavor. "This is great, Anne, really."

"Yes," Mindy agreed.

"I didn't realize you worked here, too."

"Only once in a while."

"Who stays with your daughter?"

"My sister."

"You have a daughter?" Mindy asked, "How old?"

"Emma is seven."

"Do you have children?"

"Two boys. Alex and Jordan." Mindy spread dip on another cracker. "So, you were married before…"

"Yes."

"And when you split how did you get Emma?"

"I left because he used to beat me."

"Oh, I'm sorry. I didn't—"

"It's okay. I don't mind talking about it."

"So I guess it was easy to get custody."

"Piece of cake. Thank God. I don't know what I would have done if I had to choose between Emma and Casey."

Mindy sat back on the sofa. "I know what you mean," she said quietly.

She felt her heart sink. They both had a choice to make, she thought, only somehow losing your children seemed like a higher price to pay for happiness. "But there's a chance Mindy could get custody. Isn't there?"

Anne drew a card from her back pocket. "Call me at the office tomorrow. I'll give you the name of a good attorney."

She tucked the card in her pocket. "Thanks."

Anne picked up the empty beer bottle and glass. "Let me get you a refill."

"Mindy, I don't want you to—"

"What if I can't get them?" Mindy asked before she finished.

"Does Mark want them full time?"

"He loves them. But he's never been with them for more than a day or two on a camping trip, and that's usually with other dads."

She reached for her. "You told me you wanted to leave Mark; you didn't want to lie anymore. Would you go back to him if you didn't think you had a chance with me?"

Mindy's eyes filled with tears as she turned to face her, "Are you saying I don't?"

"No. I'm saying what if, like hypothetically; would you go back to Mark?"

"No."

"And when you asked for a divorce, did you think about the kids?"

"I just assumed they'd be with me."

"So you think he might do something spiteful?"

"I don't know, Alex. I just don't know."

Anne returned with two more beers and set them down. "Sorry, I got sidetracked for a moment. Alex, Casey can't leave the bar right now, she asked if you could go over and talk to her for a moment."

Mindy stood up but Anne motioned for her to sit back down. "I'd like to see pictures of your boys if you have them."

"Of course, I do." She opened her purse and pulled out a billfold with pictures.

Alex walked over to the bar where Casey was busy telling a joke. She waited until Casey was finished and everyone was laughing, and then she walked over to the corner of the bar. "Anne said you wanted to talk to me."

"Actually, Anne wanted to talk to Mindy."

"About what?"

"Children. Do you want a shot of something?"

"I haven't done a shot since I went out with the team."

"Then it's about time. Lemon drop?"

"Sure."

Casey pulled out two shot glasses and the bottle of Absolut. "So, Alex, do you know what you're doing?"

She watched as Casey sliced the lemon. "I'd be lying if I said I did."

She took two napkins out and put a wedge of lemon on each along with a packet of sugar, and then she filled the shot glasses. "You ready for kids?" Casey asked as she poured the shots.

She opened the packet of sugar, dumped the contents onto the napkin and dipped the lemon in it. "You assume I'm leaving Simon?"

"No." Casey raised her glass. "To Friendship."

"Friendship." She downed the shot and sucked on the lemon wedge. "Those are good."

"Come back some other night and we'll do a bunch of them. Tonight I think you need your wits about you." Casey took her hand and their eyes met. "So, what are you going to do?"
"As much as I love Simon," she put her other hand on top of Casey's, noting how strong and dark it was, "I just want her something awful."

Casey lifted her chin with her free hand so they were looking into each other's eyes again. "But are you ready for this?"

"It's not like I haven't done it before."

Casey just smiled.

"Casey, I don't know what to tell you. I keep thinking all this time with Simon was…"

"Good for you. Simon was good for you, Alex." Casey patted her hand. "He is a good man, Alex, and he's been good to you."

"You think I don't know? That's what makes all of this so hard. Every logical bone in my body says don't do it, but my heart, Casey…my heart…"

"Well, just be careful." Casey let go of her hands.

"Casey, I know I've been bad about keeping in touch, but I'm really glad I called you again."

"I'm glad Anne and I could be here for you. Just don't be strangers anymore."

Anne leaned over the bar next to her. "I think Mindy's getting lonely for you."

"I better get back then."

Anne touched her arm. "Alex, if you want to be with her, there will be some compromises. But if it's worth it to you…she really loves you and she wants to be with you more than anything."

"I know."

Anne kept hold of her arm. "But, Alex, there are children involved."

"She's going to leave me again, isn't she?" She searched Anne's eyes for an answer.

"She won't be the same if she has to choose. But, I have a feeling she's already made her choice."

"Thank you. I think I should go back to her now."

Mindy reached out and took her hands pulling her down beside her on the sofa. "I missed you."

She kissed Mindy passionately. When she stopped to catch her breath, she realized Mindy was crying. "What's wrong?"

"I just can't believe I'm in your arms after all this time. It's like a dream."

"I don't want to let go."

"I don't want you to. Can we go home?"

"Absolutely." She stood up and offered her hand. "Let's just say our goodbyes."

Once they hit the street, Mindy said, "Boy, your friends really care about you a lot."

"What makes you say that?" She asked walking toward the avenue where it would be easier to catch a cab.

"Because Casey told me if I hurt you I'd be sorry."

She laughed. "That's Casey."

Mindy touched her shoulder. "She's the teammate, isn't she?"

"Mindy, I'm not in love with her and she's not in love with me. Okay?"

Mindy snuggled into her arms. "Yeah."

"Maybe we should just stand here," she suggested as she stuck her hand out to catch a cab.

"I keep forgetting we're not alone," Mindy apologized.

"I do, too."

The cab zipped across two lanes and stopped. She opened the door and motioned for Mindy to climb in. She followed and closed the door. She told the cabby her destination.

He repeated the destination and flipped on the meter. Mindy lifted her arm and put it around her to snuggle closer. "Did you ever do it in a cab?" Mindy whispered in her ear.

"No." She saw the mischievous look in Mindy's eyes. "And don't get any ideas."

"Okay." She leaned in closer. "There's no harm in kissing, is there?"

Alex could feel the heat rising between them, and she moved over so she was closer to the door.

Mindy moved with her. "Why are you running away from me?"

"I'm not running. I just think we should be careful."

Mindy took her hand and began stroking the palm with her finger. She knew exactly what she was doing. She tried to pull her hand away, but Mindy held on. "Don't be such a stick in the mud."

"I'm not a stick in the mud."

"Prove it." She leaned closer so her breasts brushed against her arm.

She glanced at the cabdriver. He seemed to be focusing on the traffic, so she put her arms around Mindy and kissed her.

twenty

She awoke before Mindy, as she usually did. Mindy always looked so angelic when she slept. Her arm was covering her eyes and her hands looked so small and delicate. It was hard to imagine those were the same hands that could set every nerve in her body on fire. Carefully, she withdrew her arm from under Mindy and crawled out of bed. She needed to get dressed and get ready to see Simon.

She went into the bathroom to get dressed. A time check let her know she had some time, which was good since she needed a shower. She knew the smell of lovemaking lingered on her body. She showered slowly, trying to think of what she was going to say to Simon. He hadn't called at all. That was so unlike him. Since they'd been together they hadn't gone a day without talking. Even when he was away on business he would phone at least once a day. She missed him. Or at least a part of her missed him. Perhaps a part of her always would. She hoped someday they could be friends, since that was the strongest part of their relationship. She knew that would take time. She had betrayed him and the knowledge tugged at her insides. Simon didn't talk when he was hurt. She knew that. But he had always been around; she could always try and draw it out of him. In all these years Simon had never done anything to break her heart and she had gone and broken his. She never wanted to break his heart. She let the water beat down over her face to wash the tears away. She broke Simon's heart. How would she ever get beyond that?

Mindy was awake when she emerged from the bathroom. "Good morning."

"It is, isn't it?" She smiled and went to the dresser to get some clothes.

"You're going to see Simon?" Mindy asked.

"You understand I have to go." She tucked the button-down denim shirt into her jeans.

"Yes." Mindy sat up, letting the sheet fall around her waist, and put her arms around her.

She wanted to bury herself in Mindy's breast and spend the rest of the day there. Why did she have to look so good after all these years? She was the most desirable woman Alex had ever known.

"I can't believe you're going to leave him, Alex." Mindy starred into her eyes. "I feel like the luckiest woman on earth. And I feel awful about Simon. You know I'll go if you think it's best. You did say Simon was everything to you."

Putting her arms around her, she pulled Mindy toward her and whispered, "I was wrong." She kissed Mindy. "You're not really thinking about walking away from me again."

"I don't want to. I just thought…"

She put her finger to Mindy's lips. "Don't think. If you think too much, we won't do this."

"Do what?"

"What we should have done a long time ago. Just like we planned."

"Get married on the beach?"

"As soon as the divorces come through."

"You're asking me to marry you?"

"According to Simon, I've always wanted to be with you. I just didn't know it. So, yes, I guess that's what I'm doing. I'm sorry it's not more romantic. But, Mindy, before I go and annihilate my life with Simon I have to know you're in this for the long haul."

"What about your books?"

"What about your family, Mindy?"

"I think Mark will try and keep the boys. Especially when he finds out about…"

"We can fight him."

"But will we be able to win?"

"Anne said she had the name of a good lawyer, Mindy. Mark's not going to take your children."

"Alex, I'm scared."

"Don't be scared. I'm going to take care of you."

Mindy jerked away from her. "I don't want you to take care of me. Mark took care of me. I just want you to love me."

"Mark loves you, Mindy."

"Not like you do."

"You just don't love him like you love me," she reminded her as she pulled Mindy back into her arms.

"What about your reputation?"

"I don't care about that."

"The other day…"

"The other day I thought I wanted you out of my life. I thought it was just bad karma, as you so eloquently put it, that I still wanted you physically. I thought I should be loyal to Simon. I thought I owed him something. But if I owe him anything it's honesty."

Mindy took her face in her hands. "I don't ever want to hurt you again."

"I know."

"I just want to love you forever. I don't want us to be apart again."

She held her tightly. "So, are we really making a commitment here?"

"Alex, I lived without you for five years and it was hell. I don't ever want to feel that again."

She pushed her back on the bed. "I want you to promise me."

"You're really frightened."

"I lost you once and I almost lost my mind…"

Mindy touched her lips. "Sh. I will marry you on a beach, on a street corner, in a church, in your friend's bar…wherever you want to stand before God and say we'll be together forever I will be there. I promise." She kissed her. "But…"

But? Alex thought. *But what?*

"I don't want to live in Simon's house."

"We'll move."

"And I don't want to raise my babies in New York City."

"You could give it a chance."

"I'm serious."

"I can write anywhere. As long as you know you don't have to stay home anymore if you don't want to. Willie said you might want to teach."

"I did." Mindy reached around to undo her bra. "Maybe we can talk about it later."

Catching her hands, she said, "We can't do this now. Simon, remember?"

Mindy moved away. "I almost forgot."

Alex kissed her softly. "I'm sorry." She opened her wallet and pulled out the card Anne had given her. "I don't know how long I'll be. If you want to call and talk to Anne, here's the number."

"That's a good idea."

She took a deep breath and let it out slowly. "I'm so scared, Mindy." She buttoned her blouse.

"Just go, Alex. Whatever happens happens."

Shoving money into her pocket, she left Mindy in her bed. She would have to take a taxi across to the Met to make it in time to bump into Simon. She had to be there early to catch him. She had to talk to him. Only she had no idea what to say. Roz was right; you could love two people at the same time.

She put her arm out to hail a cab and got one immediately. *Must be my lucky day.* She slid into the leather seat, closed the door, and told the driver her destination. Then she settled back into the seat and thought about last night. Nothing like last night had ever happened to her before. She remembered looking up at one point and seeing the cab driver looking in his rearview mirror at them. She told Mindy he was looking and without missing a beat Mindy replied, "That's because he wishes he could feel how wet you are right now."

The exhibit was on the third floor of the museum. O'Keefe was one of her favorite painters. At least they would be surrounded by beauty when they broke up, she told herself. She took the ticket Paul had left for her, asked if Simon had picked up his ticket yet, and went to wait for him when the young woman said he hadn't.

She knew it would be an eternity until he came, if only in her mind. She had so much to sort through…so much to think about before she could even talk to him. Yesterday had been so perfect she didn't want it to end. She didn't even think of Simon except once when they were in the bar and then again that morning when the alarm went off.

She stood in front of a flaming red flower, its red petals shooting up from a yellow and orange center like flames consuming the air. The passion was like the passion she and Mindy shared. She had thought she had passion with Simon. How could these past few days change everything?

She saw Simon take his ticket from the young woman at the desk and waited for him at the door to the exhibit. His beard was unkempt, his eyes sunken from lack of sleep. Paul was right behind him. *He looks horrible all because of me*, she thought as she moved toward him. "I thought you might be here."

He stopped, crumpled his ticket in his hand, and stared at her. "How did you find me?"

"I have to talk to you."

"Not here." His tone indicated he would not tolerate this now.

"Then where?"

"I don't know." He pushed past her into the first exhibit room.

She followed him. "Because we can go anywhere you want to talk."

"I don't want to talk to you." He mumbled and moved away from her. His hand shot out and he caught Paul's collar in his hand. "You did this. Didn't you?"

"Simon, she's here. Just talk to her."

"I told you. I don't want to."

"That's right, Simon. Torture yourself." Paul reached up and removed Simon's hand from his shirt. "What's that, like, an artist thing? She's your wife, God damn it. Talk to her!" He walked away leaving the two of them standing there.

"Simon," she grabbed the sleeve of his jacket, "I'll buy you another ticket. Let's just go somewhere and talk."

"I called my lawyer. I'm sure your lawyer will be hearing from him shortly. Why don't we just let them handle it?"

"Handle what?"

"The divorce. That's what you want isn't it?"

"You haven't even talked to me, Simon."

"I don't need to talk to you," he said, between clenched teeth.

"Well, I need to talk to you," she shouted, knowing a scene would get his undivided attention.

"Lower your voice! Please!"

She dropped her voice down to a whisper. "Fine. But if you don't walk out of here with me and talk to me, I will make a scene to end all scenes right here and right now."

"Fine. You win. Let's go." He grabbed her by the arm and pulled her out of the exhibit room.

"Simon, you're hurting my arm."

"Oh." He let go without an apology. "Where do you want to go?"

"Somewhere we can talk."

"Fine. Let's go back to the house."

"Well…"

His face turned crimson. "We can't go back there because she's there, right?"

"I'm sorry."

"That's rich. You're sorry." He started down the staircase and she followed him until they were safely outside and away from the crowds.

"I am sorry." She called out after him.

He sat down on the large stone steps. "This isn't a situation rectified by an apology, Alex."

"So, my apology means nothing to you?"

Staring at the ground he said, "It doesn't change anything and I don't see there's any reason to prolong this."

"Simon, I love you, too."

"It's not the same, Alex." He let his eyes meet hers. "It's never been the same. I think its time we stopped lying to ourselves."

"Are you trying to tell me these past five years have been a lie?"

"No. I'm trying to tell you you're in love with Mindy. You have always been in love with Mindy. I'm going to step aside so you can be with her. So let's just let it go, Alex."

"You don't even know how I feel!" she screamed.

He slammed his hand over her mouth. "Calm down."

"Don't tell me to calm down," she said, pushing his hand away. "I have, as far as I knew, loved you and only you…and now you're telling me how I feel…"

"Well if you're not going to be honest, one of us has to be!"

"You think I knew this?"

"Don't you fucking get it, Alex? It doesn't matter. I knew when the phone rang you would go. And I knew you would come back changed. I just didn't know how changed."

"This is not what I wanted to happen." She knelt in front of him. "I love you, and I thought…well, I was going to come here and tell you not to leave me. That I couldn't live without you…"

"But you can't say it."

"I want to." She grabbed his hands. "I owe you so much…"

"You don't owe me anything, Alex." He pushed her hands away. "This isn't doing either of us any good." He stood up.

She stood to block his path so he couldn't leave. "You just want to let in unravel?"

"Jesus Christ, Alex, it has unraveled. You fucked her in our house! In our bed, for Christ's sake. How am I supposed to forget?"

"I'm not asking you to forget."

"Yes you are. You're trying to apologize like that's going to make everything better. Is that what Mindy did? Did she apologize for smashing your heart into a million fucking pieces? Did she Alex?" he shouted.

"Its not that simple, and you know it."

"I have done nothing but love you through all of the bullshit she put you through…and this is the thanks I get? You fuck her in our house."

"Quit saying that."

"Why? It's the truth, isn't it?"

"And to think I was just wondering how fair I've been to you."

"Hey, I'm the one that's lost everything here. Let's just keep that in perspective." He sank down onto the steps again and buried his face in his hands. He was shaking, struggling not to cry.

"I kept telling myself I wasn't gay…my mother abused me and I needed Mindy's warmth…that was all it was, nothing more…a phase. Because I found you and I wanted you." She knelt again, taking his face in her hands. The pain in his eyes stabbed at her heart. "I'm so sorry, Simon. It's not like I haven't been happy with you. You've been nothing but faithful and loving. I know I have no guarantees with her. I feel like all this has been a dream. I know it's not a lie. I never would have lied to you like this. You have got to believe me when I tell you I didn't know."

"What do you want from me, Alex? I told you I filled out the papers."

"I loved you, Simon, I thought…"

"What?" he screamed. He pushed her back and she landed on her butt. "You thought what? I would fight for you? It's pointless and we both know it. Besides, I already fought for you and look where it's gotten me."

She pulled herself to her feet. "I don't know what I thought…"

"Yes, you do. You wanted me to make it all better for you. You wanted me to tell you we could be friends."

"Simon, you'll always be in my heart." She touched his cheek.

He removed her hand from his cheek. "Just go, Alex. I can't give you what you want. Not this time."

"You don't know what I want."

"You want absolution. You want me to forgive you for fucking…" He clenched his fists and stopped himself. "Well, I can't. I can't forgive you. Not now."

He was right, she thought. She did want his forgiveness. She wanted him to understand. She knew it wasn't right or even fair of her to ask, but she did want him to understand. "I can't imagine never seeing you again."

"I guess you should have thought about that before." Tears were building up in his eyes and he tried to blink them back.

"This is not at all what I thought was going to happen," she whispered, fighting back tears of her own.

"I'm begging you. Just go."

She couldn't move. She couldn't leave. Not like this. "Simon…"

"What are you trying to do to me, Alex? Isn't it bad enough you ripped my fucking heart out? What do you want to do, watch me twist on the knife? I don't want apologies from you. I don't want explanations. I don't want anything!" he screamed. "Go!"

There wasn't anything she could do. Her insides felt like they had been shredded. She turned and walked away.

twenty-one

"Alex," Mindy called out from the other room, "where are you?"

Alex wanted to let Mindy know she was in the bathroom, but she was too busy clutching the toilet bowl and trying not to throw up again. She had no idea where she could have gotten this stomach flu, but it was holding on.

"Alex," Mindy opened the door and bent down next to her. She wrapped one arm around Alex's waist gently and placed a hand against her forehead. "Why didn't you tell me you were in here?"

"I've been a bit busy," Alex said. She'd forgotten how gentle and nurturing Mindy could be. She had gotten used to getting up on her own and cleaning up after herself, as Simon slept like a log.

"Do you need to throw up again?"

"I don't know. Maybe not."

"Well, why don't we get you cleaned up, then?" Mindy helped her to her feet, flushed the toilet, and wet a washcloth. "Do you have that icky taste in your mouth?" Mindy asked as she dabbed her face with the cool cloth.

Alex nodded and Mindy squeezed some toothpaste on her toothbrush, "Here."

Alex brushed her teeth and watched as Mindy rinsed the washcloth and wrung it out. Mindy led her over to the bed and helped her sit down. Mindy leaned her cheek against Alex's forehead.

"You shouldn't be so close. I could be contagious."

"Like it makes a difference."

"There's no reason for both of us to be sick."

"You're not running a fever. But you haven't been able to keep anything down have you?"

"Doesn't want to stay there."

"Let me get you some crackers and ginger ale. Maybe you'll be able to keep them down." Mindy kissed her lightly on the cheek. "Close your eyes for a couple of minutes. I won't be long."

Alex looked up at the canopy of white eyelet above Mindy's bed. They had only been in her parents' house for weeks and they still couldn't decide what room to settle in. The master bedroom belonged to Mindy's parents and settling in that room was probably inevitable, but they both felt weird about it. Mindy's room shared a bathroom with Willie's room, which made those rooms perfect for the boys. The guest room was entirely too small. Alex suggested moving the waterbed into Mindy's parents' room and getting all new furniture.

Alex was particularly excited about Mr. Martineli's study. She had always loved that room of the house. Not only because it had a working fireplace where she and Mindy used to cuddle when Mindy's parents were away, but also because she spent hours curled up in the oversized rocker reading. That's where she discovered the *Chronicles of Narnia* and found escape in the pages of a book. Where she learned of honor and courage from Dickens's *A Tale of Two Cities*, redemption from Hugo's *Les Miserables*, and met and fell in love with William Shakespeare. She and Mindy would spend hours reading Shakespeare aloud together, dividing the parts up and trying to make sense of the language and meter.

The queasy feeling crept up on her again. She closed her eyes. The last thing she needed right now was to be sick. The judge had granted temporary custody to Mindy until the actual trial date. Willie left that morning to pick the boys up and would be back in two days. Finally, she would get to meet her namesake.

She tried the deep breathing exercise the coach had taught them in practice to focus, to take her mind off her stomach. She thought about Mark. He had put in for joint custody, which would mean they would either have to move five hours to where he transferred to or vice-versa. Since Alex had a job she could do anywhere—the likelihood of having to sell the house seemed a distinct possibility. The sale would more than pay for another house, not to mention her cut from the sale of her home with Simon, but they had been so excited about the prospect of living in the house they had fallen in love in together. Their hearts were in this house. For that reason alone, Mindy believed, Mark had filed for joint custody. He was hurt and he was striking back any way he knew how. Alex didn't blame him. She might have done the same thing in his shoes, though probably not.

Simon, on the other hand, was letting go. Alex hadn't seen him since the day at the museum. Their lawyers did all the talking and they did all the signing. She let Simon have the first pick of whatever he wanted in the house. There would never be a way to make up for breaking his heart, so she didn't want to add insult to injury.

She wondered what was taking Mindy so long. This better be over soon, she thought. She'd felt this way for about a week now and with the boys coming she couldn't be sick. She was looking forward to being a family and she was praying the boys wouldn't hate her for taking their mother away from their father. Her understanding was they were close to Mark and they would spend hours together on the weekends. That probably wouldn't change too drastically. But, if Mindy went back to school full time, she would be home with the boys all day, which would be an adjustment for everyone. Willie assured her the boys would love her, and they couldn't get a better basketball coach. Roz told her she would handle any book idea Alex brought her, but she wouldn't negotiate an advance until she got a solid outline. Roz was convinced Alex's writing would suffer until her life balanced itself again. Roz was also convinced a hiatus from children's books would not harm her career. Mindy didn't want Alex to stop writing and Alex assured Mindy she could write any time. She wanted Mindy to go to grad school and she had the money to make it possible.

"Sorry it took so long. I had to run around the corner to the store. We didn't have any ginger ale." Mindy set a plate of crackers and a glass of ginger ale chock-full of ice on the nightstand.
Alex noticed the brown paper bag under her arm. "What else did you get me?"
Mindy set the bag on the floor. "Let's try and get some fluids in you." Mindy helped Alex sit up. "Just take small sips."

Obediently, Alex did and then let Mindy ease her head back onto the pillow. It wasn't like Mindy to avoid questions and she really wanted to know what was in the bag, so she asked again.

Mindy pushed the hair back off her forehead gently. "Alex, it's been almost eight weeks. When do you think you'll be getting your period?"

"Why?"

"Just wondering."

"I'm not very good at keeping track."

"Why, has it gotten irregular?"

"No."

Mindy was playing with Alex's hair now, sifting her hand through it and watching it fall. "When was your last one?"

"Not since Simon left...no, before that." Alex tried to remember, but she really couldn't remember having one since right after the funeral. *But that couldn't be right.* "I don't remember."

"Take a little longer and think about it."

Alex hated when people said that. You either remembered something or you didn't. "I really don't remember. Why?"
"Honey, I don't think you have the stomach flu."

"Tell that to my stomach."

Mindy touched her cheek. "Alex, I think you might be pregnant."

"Pregnant! What are you crazy?" (*I had my period, didn't I? I came back from the funeral, and then...no I didn't. It was about a week before the funeral, and then I came back and tried to keep proving I loved Simon.*) Alex sat up. "Oh, my God!"

"It is possible, isn't it?"

Alex was speechless. This couldn't be happening.

Mindy reached for the paper bag and handed it to her. "There's one way to know for sure."

Alex pulled a home pregnancy kit out of the paper bag. "Mindy, what if I am?"

"Let's find out before we get all worked up. Okay?"

"How accurate are these things?"

"They're pretty good." Mindy laid the contents on the bathroom counter. "Do you know what to do?"

"What's to know? You pee on the strip and it changes color."

"This one turns blue if you are." Mindy put her arms around Alex. "Either way, Alex, it will be okay."

(*How could she say that? What if I am pregnant? What will happen to us?*)

"I'll wait outside." Mindy pulled the door shut. Alex picked up the instruction sheet and read. After all the time she and Simon had spent trying to have a baby what would the chances be? She took her watch off and set it on the counter. The box said ten minutes. She noted the time before doing the deed. She had stopped using birth control pills over a year and a half ago. But nothing had happened since the miscarriage. They had sex a lot, but when she got back from Mindy's it was easier to make love than to talk. And she kept trying to convince herself she wanted Simon more than Mindy. Mindy had told her with Mark it wouldn't have mattered if she was there at all or not, but with Alex every minute counted. Part of her understood exactly what Mindy meant, but she couldn't deny Simon had been a decent enough lover. With Mindy it was different…they understood each other's bodies almost better than their own. Even now, if she were pregnant Mindy would get her through it differently than Simon would have.

"Mindy, come wait with me."

Mindy opened the door. "How much longer?"

"Eight minutes." Alex held out her hand and Mindy took it. "Talk to me."

Mindy put her arms around her and held her close. "I know you're scared, Alex, but a baby is a very wonderful thing."

"Do you want another child?"

"Your child? Yes."

"But we have your boys."

"We don't know that for sure."

Alex heard the fear in Mindy's voice and tried to comfort her. "Mindy, we're going to get them. I promise you we'll do everything in our power."

"What about Simon?"

"I would have to tell him." Alex knew that much.

"He's going to want you back, Alex. You know that don't you?"

"No. I don't know that. You didn't see his face, Mindy."

"Alex, it's his baby. A baby changes everything. He's not the kind of guy that's going to back away from this."

"I don't want him back." Alex reached for the strip and handed it to her. "Maybe it won't be an issue. You look."

Mindy took the strip and looked at Alex's watch. "It's not time yet. So, Alex, what do you want it to be?"

"I don't know."

"You've said that a lot today. But seriously, do you want to be pregnant? Or not?"

Alex took a deep breath. "It terrifies me you know how much it scares me."

"Being pregnant?"

Alex put her arms around Mindy. "I'm so scared I won't be a good mother."

"Which is silly."

"It's not silly if you think about it. Besides, I'm also scared I'll never be a mother. So you figure it out."

"You would be a great mother, Alex." Mindy assured her. "If I go back to school, you'll be with the boys all day long. Do you think I would leave my boys with you if I had any doubts?"

"You love me, Mindy. And you know love is blind."

Mindy moved behind Alex and put her hands on either side of Alex's face so they were both staring into the mirror. Mindy lifted the hair off Alex temple and pointed to the scar there. "Are you going to tell me you could do this to a child? With a coat hanger no less?"

Before Alex could answer Mindy pulled her shirt off her shoulder to reveal another scar, "Or this with a belt?"

(*No. I couldn't understand how anyone could do it to me. How could I do it to someone else?*)
Mindy kissed her cheek. "It'll be all right either way. So, which is it? What do you want, Alex?"

"I'd like a little girl as beautiful as you are."

"Only if there is a star in the East, but thank you." Mindy picked up the strip and looked at it.

"Is it time yet?"

Mindy smiled. "Would you settle for a child as beautiful as you are?"

"Are you sure?"

"We should confirm it with my GYN, but yes." Mindy held the strip out for her to see the blue dot.

"Oh, my God!" Alex leaned and grabbed hold of the sink. She felt dizzy. "I really am?"

Mindy's eyes sparkled. "Yes." Mindy kissed her and Alex knew the excitement was genuine.

"I have to tell Simon. This isn't something he should hear from a lawyer."

"No." Mindy set the strip down on the sink and walked back into the bedroom.

Mindy's back was to her, but Alex could see Mindy rubbing her forehead and she knew without looking Mindy's eyes were closed. Mindy was trying not to cry. It was an old trick. But Alex knew her too well not to know what she was doing. She sat on the corner of the bed. "This changes everything. Doesn't it?"

"Only if you want it to."

She had to tell Simon. She couldn't not tell him—could she? No! It was just easier to sign the papers than talk. Simon didn't want to talk. He wouldn't even go to the house and pick up his things while she was there. But he was excited the last time and he would be a good father; Alex knew that. In fact, she often thought he would make up for any shortcoming she might have.

"If you want to go back to him, I would understand."

"You say that Mindy, but you don't really mean it."

"Alex—" Mindy choked. She was crying.

Alex touched Mindy's shoulder. "I'm not saying that to upset you or be mean. It's just the truth. You practically risked everything for me."

"It's different." Mindy wiped her tears away with her hand. "I knew what I wanted from the beginning."

Alex moved beside her. "Is that what you think?" She reached for Mindy's face. "You think I don't want you?"

Mindy threw her arms around her and hugged her so tightly she could begin to feel her fingers tingle. "I don't want to lose you, Alex."

"I don't want to lose you, either." Alex tried to soothe Mindy with her voice. "I just have to at least tell him. I mean, it is his child, too."

"But what if he tried to take the baby?"

She wiped Mindy's tears away with her thumb. "He's not going to."

"How do you know?"

Alex laughed. "You watch too many movies."

"Alex, you hurt him pretty bad."

She was treading on thin ice here; she knew it. And Alex wanted to make sure in light of what had happened with Mark she didn't say the wrong thing. "Mindy, Simon isn't spiteful."

"You mean like Mark?"

"Mindy, I can't go back to Simon. He's never going to take me back, not after I betrayed him. I know him. If he did take me back it would only be for the baby, and what kind of life would that be?"

"But, Alex, you took me back."

How could Alex possibly explain this to her? She could barely explain it to herself. "I just know. The damage is done."

"So, you and I will raise the baby?"

"We were going to raise your boys together. I guess baby makes three."

"Alex, you're going to love motherhood."

"Not if these past couple of days are any indication."

"That only lasts for a little while."

"Mindy, I'm not going to exclude Simon from the baby's life if that's what he wants. You should know that."

Mindy kissed her lightly on the lips. "Whatever you want." Standing up, she said, "I think you should call and talk to him. I'll leave you alone."

She reached for Mindy's hand. "Thank you. But, I don't think I want to be alone."

"Okay."

"And I want to make sure before I call him."

"That's probably a good idea." She sat back down. "I'll make an appointment with my GYN. You'll like her."

"Good."

Mindy rested her head on her shoulder. "This is a rather pleasant turn of events."

"I'm glad you see it my way."

"Maybe you're right, Alex. Maybe love does make a baby. Maybe it's ours."

Alex kissed the top of Mindy's head. "I'm still going to want to name the baby Simon."

"Even if it's a girl?"

"Then Simone."

"That's pretty, too."

epilogue

23 November 1992

Dear Simon,

Plans for Christmas seem to be firming up. We're trying to get everyone to come here. Mindy, Simone, and I hope you and Kate will come. Simone hasn't seen you since her third birthday and she misses you. Willie will be here with his new girlfriend.

I hope your show in Milan went well. Kate sent me the review...never had any doubt they would love your stuff. Also, just got the illustrations for the new book and as always they're perfect. Sorry I missed you when you were in town. Roz said you looked great.

Mindy is busy with her classes. She's supposed to attend a conference on the west coast in May where she'll be speaking. I was thinking we could all make the trip since only Simone has seen sunny California. Alex and Jordan should enjoy the beach and all the sights. The conference is in San Francisco, but we thought we could take a side trip and see you. Hope you're in the country then.

Look forward to hearing from you all about your latest exploits.

Love, Alexandra

ABOUT THE AUTHOR

Novelist and playwright, EA Kafkalas is the author of the novels *The Second Heart, Soul Mistakes,* and *Frankie & Petra*, and the plays *Lopsided* and *Pandora's Golden Box*. A true Renaissance woman, she has worked in the theatre as an actor, director and a producer. In addition, EA is a mixed media artist working with clay and acrylics.

She lives alone with her vast library of books, movies, and art supplies. EA is never alone—when she's not writing about the characters living inside her head, she can be found with her circle of actual friends, who have become her family and greatest support network.

For more visit eakafkalas.com

Other publications by E.A. Kafkalas

THE SECOND HEART
Is love truly universal?

Major Kate Winston is a decorated officer with a promising career until she wakes up naked in the arms a strange woman with no memory of how she got there.

Alexia is from another planet sent by the elders to kill Major Winston to put off the foreseen destruction of their planet by Earth's mistakes.

From the backwoods of Pennsylvania to New York City to Alexia's home world, the novel weaves a tale of emotional intrigue as two women from different words struggle with their desires, and life and death decisions.

FRANKIE & PETRA
Is chemistry enough?

Homicide detective Petra Theopholis is good at her job. She closes cases, but her world is turned upside down one morning when she meets a young grad student.

Painter Frankie Martineli has lost everyone she's ever loved in this world, so she wants nothing to do with someone that puts their life on the line every day.

After a one night stand they go their separate ways. When a case draws them together, they find that their passions can't be contained. But when fate throws them both into the face of danger, will their love survive?

Visit Eakafkalas.com